THE COLOR OF
DEATH

THE COLOR OF
DEATH

A Novel

TREY GOWDY

with Christopher Greyson

FOX
NEWS
books

THE COLOR OF DEATH. Copyright © 2025 by Fox News Network LLC. All rights reserved. Printed in the United States of America. No part of this book may be used or reproduced in any manner whatsoever without written permission except in the case of brief quotations embodied in critical articles and reviews. For information, address HarperCollins Publishers, 195 Broadway, New York, NY 10007. In Europe, HarperCollins Publishers, Macken House, 39/40 Mayor Street Upper, Dublin 1, D01 C9W8, Ireland.

HarperCollins books may be purchased for educational, business, or sales promotional use. For information, please email the Special Markets Department at SPsales@harpercollins.com.

hc.com

Fox News Books imprint and logo are trademarks of Fox News Network, LLC.

FIRST EDITION

Library of Congress Cataloging-in-Publication Data has been applied for.

ISBN 978-0-06-345191-9

25 26 27 28 29 LBC 5 4 3 2 1

To the women who inspired Belle, mainly my wife, Terri.

To the victims of crime who give prosecutors and cops a reason to wrestle the demons and pursue justice.

To the prosecutors who speak up for those too scared, too injured, or too dead to speak up for themselves.

THE COLOR OF
DEATH

CHAPTER 1

"WHY DON'T WE JUST kill him?"

"Not yet, Knox. Not yet."

Footsteps moved away from him, and a door closed.

Frank Hastings slowly regained consciousness. His hands, legs, and chest were tightly bound to a high-back wooden chair, like a prisoner strapped in for execution. The gag in his mouth made it hard to breathe.

The last thing he remembered was turning off a paved road and heading toward a cabin near the river. A potential client with a significant personal injury claim wanted to meet, and he, a lawyer with significant financial issues, was more than willing to make the drive and pitch his services.

He knocked on the door, it swung open, and everything went black.

Frank blinked and shook his head like a patient emerging from a coma. The room came into focus. In front of him sat a small, round table with a notepad and pen, an old TV, and a video player. The place seemed familiar—like many of the cabins where people come to fish the North Pacolet River.

A door opened behind him, followed by the sound of two sets of footsteps entering the room. Judging by the trembling floor beneath his feet, one of them was massive. They stopped directly behind Frank's chair.

Frank attempted to speak, but the gag made it impossible. He tried to twist around and see who they were, but the restraints and the high-back chair prevented that.

"He's awake, JD," Knox said.

"Let's hear what he has to say."

Knox wrenched the gag out from between Frank's teeth.

"If you want money . . ."

"This isn't about money," JD cut him off. "It's about seeking justice for Larry Stafford and our mom."

Frank remembered the case well. "No one could have won that case."

"That's not true, Frank. Someone did win—it just wasn't you. But now it's time for you to stop asking questions and start answering them. Your trial is about to begin. I even brought my own .38-caliber gavel."

The cold metal of a gun pressed against the skin on Frank's neck.

JD mockingly imitated a bailiff: "The first item on the docket is a malpractice case—*The People v. Frank Hastings*. Mr. Hastings, you have the right to remain silent. Anything you say . . . well we can skip the rest. It won't matter."

"We don't need to do this. I want to find a way to make it right."

"Oh, we're going to make it right, Frank. Exhibit one is a video. Let's watch."

The TV on the table flashed to life.

Frank attempted to turn his head to the right to plead with JD, only to find himself staring down the dark barrel of the revolver.

"Watch the TV, Frank."

Frank gulped and stared at the screen.

"This was one of the first cases featured on *Trial TV*. It didn't receive the same attention as OJ or Scott Peterson did, but they show it in law schools now. Not your part, of course. Who wants to watch a fat, bald lawyer sweating his way through a trial? They want to see the prosecutor, Colm Truesdale. What did the paper call him?"

"The Artist," Knox said.

Frank glanced down and to the left. He could see only the man's boots, which were twice the size of his own shoes.

"That's right, 'The Artist,'" JD continued. "But that's a lie as well. Artists create. Colm destroys."

On the TV, Assistant District Attorney Colm Truesdale rose from behind the prosecutor's table. Tall and broad-shouldered, the fit young prosecutor exuded Southern charm wrapped in a disarming smile. He gazed at the jury box, not saying a word but already working his magic.

"See how he's connecting with each jury member, making each one believe they're the most important person in the room. Those dumb jurors—the ones you handpicked—are playing right along."

"I'll start by simply saying thank you"—Colm broke the silence, and a few jurors nodded politely—"for your willingness to do such a difficult, challenging, even excruciating job, but one without which we would have no justice system. During these past two weeks, you had to hear and see things you won't . . . you can't forget. If there had been any way to spare you from having to bear witness to this depravity, this perversion, we would have. But I would respectfully remind you, as hard as it was to watch and listen, imagine having to live through it. Imagine the pain, the fear, the isolation this child endured."

"What hypocrisy!" JD screamed. "Truesdale used that child to garner sympathy while you sat there and said nothing. You did nothing."

Frank sobbed and lowered his gaze.

"Pay attention!" JD shouted.

Knox's huge hand seized Frank's head and jerked it back, forcing Frank to stare at the TV.

Colm continued. "Now, you get to give that child a chance to be heard, listened to, and believed. This is where the power changes. This is where you give the powerless a voice. The defendant is no longer in control. You are." Colm paused and met the eyes of each juror in turn.

"Listen to the silence, Frank. His silence was more powerful than anything you said."

"I know it was hard to hear the things done to that child and not be moved. The pictures made us turn away in disbelief and disgust. But we had to show you what was done."

"Do you see what's happening? Colm's practically climbed into the jury box with them by saying 'us.' Look at juror seven! She's in love with him. She can't take her eyes off him. Why didn't you move for a mistrial? Why didn't you object or try to switch her out for an alternate juror?"

Tears rolled down Frank's cheeks.

"Stop crying, Frank. You should have shed those crocodile tears during the real trial."

"My work here is finished," Colm said. "I feel powerless to adequately convey what she endured—it was nothing short of murder, the murder of a child's innocence." His voice rose to a crescendo at the words *murder* and *innocence*.

"Here it comes! The nail in the coffin, Frank."

"In just a moment, when the defense attorney is through, you will retire to the jury room, and then the judge will send all the exhibits back to you. One of those exhibits will be State's Exhibit Number Forty-Two. A simple ink pen. You may be wondering why we, the prosecution, introduced this simple ink pen from her bedroom into evidence. Amid the teddy bears, the stuffed animals, and all the pictures of Cinderella and Snow White, was this little pen. It's the pen she used to write in her journal, asking, 'Why? Why is he doing this, God? Jesus, please make him stop.' I want you to use this same pen to write your verdict. As you each sign your name to the verdict form, honor her courage, honor her innocence, and give her the power she didn't have . . . use this same pen. Give her what she begged for—peace, mercy, protection; but most of all, justice. Give her justice by writing your name under the word *guilty*."

JD slowly clapped. "Masterful. Now it's your turn. Let's see how you did."

Frank shook his head and closed his eyes.

"No, Frank. You're going to watch." JD shoved the barrel of the gun under Frank's chin and pushed up. "Let's see what our mother's life savings got her."

On the screen, dressed in a suit straining at the seams, Frank Hastings mopped his sweaty forehead as he strode uncomfortably back and forth in front of the jury box.

"What are you doing?" JD asked. "You look like a lazy gym teacher lecturing the kids in detention. Look at the jurors' faces. Number four has his arms crossed. Number nine is leaning back in her chair. And seven? That green-eyed devil loves Colm but can't stand you. She'd been taking notes all trial, but she put her pen away. Not just down, Frank, *away*—cap on and laid off to the side."

On the TV, Frank began his closing argument. "Members of the jury, let me explain a simple term—*circumstantial*. While you did hear a number of so-called facts, you have to ask yourself one question: Do they add up?"

A gunshot rang out as a round struck the TV.

Frank shook uncontrollably and his ears stung.

Smoke poured out of the large hole in the screen.

"Apparently, they added up pretty quickly. How long was the jury out? Less than thirty minutes. That's not even long enough for a smoke break."

"I'll give you the fees back! I'll do an appeal. I'll petition the court that I was unprepared. I'll do anything you want!"

"You're worse at defending your case than when you defended Larry. But if you're serious about helping, there is something you can do. Left- or right-handed?"

"Right-handed," Frank replied, terrified.

JD cut the rope that bound Frank's right hand to the chair. "You're going to write down everything you just said. You're going to write that you didn't adequately prepare for the trial, that you and other attorneys conspired to defraud clients of their money . . ."

Frank chewed his lip. If he didn't do it, they'd kill him. He still hadn't seen their faces, so they may let him go. Frank's hand shook as he hurriedly transcribed what JD had said.

"Okay, it's done now."

"Not yet. Write 'I'm sorry' and sign it."

Frank wrote the words and signed his name.

The giant Knox grabbed Frank's arm and tied it back to the chair.

"Open your right hand," JD said.

"I did everything you said. Let me go," Frank sobbed.

Enormous fingers tightened on Frank's neck, and Knox clutched Frank's right wrist.

Frank opened his fingers, and to his amazement, with a gloved hand, JD placed the revolver in his grasp.

"Pull the trigger," JD said.

With Knox pinning his wrist to the arm of the chair, Frank could only point the gun straight ahead at the wall.

Frank whimpered and pulled the trigger.

The gun fired. Smoke burned Frank's nose, and his ears rang.

JD reached out and removed the gun from Frank's grasp.

"Please don't do this. Imagine the trouble . . ."

"Why would we get in trouble because a crooked lawyer decided to blow his brains out?"

"No, please."

"If it makes you feel any better, you'll soon have company. Your law partner, the judge, even Colm Truesdale, will be joining you. Any last words?"

Frank Hastings sobbed one last time.

CHAPTER 2

I PULL MY RINGING PHONE from my pocket but choose not to answer it. Instead, I wait and listen to the voicemail.

"Hey, Colm. It's Mae. I wanted to check up on you and see how you're doing. Please give me a call when you can. Love you."

Like the good therapist she is, she knows it's time to talk. But while I love her, I'm not in the mood to talk—even to my sister-in-law. Not now, and especially not here.

Located on the edge of Spartanburg, on a clear day you can see the Appalachian Mountains straining above the horizon. Quite a view for a cemetery. Today, I know something beautiful is out there, but I can't see it. It's a gray, cold, rainy November afternoon. Aside from the weather, it's a serene place. Right beside an old church surrounded by hardwoods born before any of the people lying here. I'm sitting in my car debating whether to get out or not. Maybe the rain will let up. In the meantime, I note the cruelty of nature—especially in autumn. It used to be my favorite time of the year. Beautiful days with crisp mornings and chilly evenings as bookends. Everything conspires to remind you of life. The temperature, the colors, the holidays, how can you not be hopeful in autumn? But it's a façade. Autumn is death masquerading as beauty.

The rain lets up enough to convince me to at least try. I make my way along a curvy path weaving between the graves as a gust of wind catches my umbrella. We are so careful to honor the dead by not walking over graves. We don't mind walking over people when they are alive, but death changes all of that, I guess. There's another car parked in the distance. Must be the groundskeeper. Who else would be here on such a bleak day?

I don't want to be here, but I need to tell her I've made my decision, and it's final. My resolve hardens as my fingers tighten around the two bouquets of orchids in my hands.

At the end of the high row of bright green boxwoods, I freeze. It wasn't the groundskeeper's car I saw—it was Bethany Barnett's. The elderly woman standing at the end of the path appears even smaller beneath the large umbrella she carries. Her thin back is hunched, and she grips her jacket tightly together with her free hand to ward off the chill. Facing away from me, she bends over and brushes some leaves off the granite tombstone before her.

It's been five years since the trial. I'm a little ashamed I have not kept in better contact with her, but there's always another file, another family, another loss. I try to slip back toward my car, but her shoulders shake and the sound, it's the sound that draws you in. The sound of unabated grief. For me, it was a weak murder case assigned to me early in my career. To her, it's the only case that matters . . . and the sound of grief pulls me toward her. Time doesn't change anything. Closure is a myth created by those who haven't suffered loss.

So, I march forward.

"Oh." She steps back. "I didn't know anyone was here." Mrs. Barnett's umbrella rocks back and forth as she dabs at her eyes. "Colm? You're so thin I hardly recognized you."

I nod and smile.

She looks at the grave. "I think we're the only ones who remember them."

I nod because there are no words worth saying. Presence is usually enough. I glance down at the solitary vase at the base of the tombstone and hand her one of the bouquets of flowers.

Fresh tears rim her eyes.

I take a deep breath as we stand in silence for a moment.

"I slept last night," Mrs. Barnett whispers. "Do you remember? Do you remember how bad I was?"

She reaches out a hand twisted by time and toil, takes mine, and squeezes it.

"Yes, ma'am, I remember you were having a little trouble sleeping."

"Little trouble?" She sighs and strokes the back of my hand with her thumb. "I was dying. You saved me."

Overwhelmed by emotion, I want to pull my hand away but don't. She's probably right. When I first met her, she looked like she hadn't slept in weeks, because she hadn't. It was over a month since her husband and grandson went missing. We knew they were gone, but you don't step on people's hope—not until you have to.

"I don't think their bodies would have ever been found, and I know it never would have gone to trial if it hadn't been for you, Colm." Mrs. Barnett squeezes my hand tighter. "I would be wondering what happened for the rest of my life."

"Mrs. Barnett—"

"It's the truth . . ." Her lip trembles, and her voice trails off.

I angle my umbrella to the side and drape my arm over her shoulders. Rain dampens my hair and drips down the lapels of my suit. Even if I hadn't met Mrs. Barnett, I would have pressed forward with the case. Henry Barnett was a seventy-five-year-old man still working his farm. He took his young grandson with him to sell some tools to someone they met online. They never came home.

I've felt what she's gone through. Death is constant, but it is not equal. There's a difference between death strolling up to the front door of your life, knocking gently, and saying, "Take your time, say your goodbyes, and safeguard your soul," and death kicking in the front door of your life—with no warning, no time to prepare, no time to make amends with those you love, no time to whisper a prayer of forgiveness or say your goodbyes. Like a thief in the night.

"Thank you," Mrs. Barnett says, breaking my train of thought as she stares up at me. "I pray every night God will continue to use you mightily."

I swallow my cynicism long enough to say, "Your courage inspired me to work harder. Would you like me to walk you back to your car, Mrs. Barnett?"

"No. I think I'll stay a few more minutes."

Making my way back down the path, the rain let up a bit. When I reach the fork in the path, I stop. They trimmed back the bushes, and I can see the tombstones in the distance. They look small from here.

My wounds haven't healed. I can't do this today. I should have known. This is as close as I can come. I place the bouquet of orchids on the nearest tombstone and walk back to my car. I rationalize it's better this way, but it's not rationalizing so much as running away.

I look out through the rain-covered windshield. If it weren't for me, they wouldn't be here. No flowers or apologies can absolve me of my guilt. They're here because of me.

CHAPTER 3

PICK UP YOUR PHONE!" Judge Martin Weber shouted at his dashboard as he sped down a winding stretch of back roads bordered by barren fields on either side. Well past the peak of foliage season in the high country of South Carolina, the towering oak trees cast dappled sunlight onto the asphalt.

"Thank you for calling Cutz for All," Rachel's voicemail answered. "Sorry I missed your call."

Martin angrily jabbed the disconnect button and stomped on the gas. His Audi's V6 engine thrummed as he passed an old, rusted Ford F-150 truck. The farmer behind the wheel flipped him off.

Judge Weber returned the gesture, but with his car's tinted windows, what was the point? He exhaled loudly and eased his foot off the gas, trying to calm down. Why was Rachel ghosting him? Maybe she was busy. She did have a kid, after all, and was dealing with that jackass of an ex-husband.

Martin ran his fingers through his peppered gray hair. He stared at his plugs in the rearview mirror. He was self-conscious and thought it looked like "planted corn," but Rachel was a hairdresser and swore she could barely tell.

Martin jammed on the brakes and pulled into the gravel parking lot. He almost drove past it—the CUTZ FOR ALL sign was hung on the side of the house, so you didn't notice it until you were right on top of it.

The parking lot was empty, but he pulled in sideways, taking two spaces. Rachel had converted this simple mobile home she once shared with her ex into a hair salon, although she still lived here, too. Her bedroom was in the back, but it had been a while since he'd gotten either the haircut or the post-haircut rendezvous.

The bell above the door chimed as he slipped inside. The salon's interior was surprisingly spacious. The walls were lined with mirrors, reflecting the bright fluorescent lighting. A new salon chair, still wrapped in plastic, sat beside a worn brown leather one.

The door to her small office on the left was partially open. "One sec!" Rachel called out. "Be right with you."

"Take your time." Martin shut the front door and stood there.

Rachel's high heels clicked off the linoleum.

Martin rubbed the back of his neck. How could he tell a woman was upset just by the way she walked?

Rachel marched into the room, stopped with her hands on her slender hips, and stared at him like a gunslinger about to draw down. Her gorgeous long blond hair draped across her shoulder and flowed down her apron and over her breasts until it reached her thin waist. Twenty-six, she looked like a runway model.

"We're closed, Martin." Rachel's red lips frowned. "Get out."

Martin worked up his best good ol' boy grin and turned his palms up like a beggar asking for a handout. "Talk to me, darling. What is it you think I did?"

"Are you serious? Where do you want me to start?"

"If it's about the implants, I was only kidding. You're perfect . . ."

"No, Martin, it's not about what you think I should or should not do to make your sex life more enjoyable. You lied to me, and it's over."

Frankly, Martin didn't remember much about Friday, their last night together, but he wouldn't let that stop him from winning the argument. Before he became a judge, Martin was one of the best trial lawyers in the area. "I can explain. It's a marriage in name only."

"You lied about it."

"That's why I am here, baby. To apologize."

"You don't even remember what you did."

"No, no, you have it all wrong."

"You made a fool out of yourself because you were drunk and acting like an idiot."

"Okay, I drank too much. I will . . ."

"It wasn't just drinking, Martin." Rachel's manicured eyebrows knit together. "When we were at the club and you came back downstairs, you were a different person, and not in a good way. I told you I don't do drugs, and I certainly don't date married men who do."

"I don't do drugs, Rachel, and I object to your accusation."

"This isn't a courtroom, Martin. You aren't the judge," Rachel spit back. "Who do you want me to believe, you or my own eyes?"

"Give me another chance—"

"I went through all this crap with my ex. Do you even remember the bouncers carrying you out? I had to drive you home, and then you started whining about what your wife was going to think. That's when I realized you're not divorced."

"It's just not official yet."

"Have you filed?"

"Well, no but . . ."

"So, it's not final because it hasn't even begun, Counselor!"

"It's Judge! And that's something you would be wise to remember."

"Yes, mainly because you brag about it all the time."

"I'm sorry I acted that way. I'm sober now. And I really care about you, Rachel. I do."

"You care so much that you had me walk three and a half miles back to the club to get my car?"

"Why didn't you call a car service?"

"Because you thought your wife would figure out I drove you home. You didn't want a record of me calling an Uber."

"I am so sorry. Let me make it up to you. Let me take you somewhere nice. How does a week in Paris sound?"

Rachel shook her head and slowly walked forward. "Look, I liked you when we first met. But you're married. You're inconsiderate. You're condescending. And I don't need that in my life again. I have lived it once, and I will not live it again."

"One more chance. Let's take this trip—just you and me for seven days in 'The City of Light.' I already booked the flights. We'll be back by Thanksgiving. You fly out on the seventh and—"

Rachel crossed her arms. "Why would you book different departure dates for us?"

"I'm leaving first to ensure everything's ready for your arrival."

"What a load of crap. You're worried your wife will drive you to the airport and find out about us. Martin, I'm done with this. It's over. Go home to your wife. Go to France. I don't care. Just leave here and don't come back."

The muscles in Martin's jaw tightened. "You might want to rethink that. Remember, you need me, sweetheart."

Rachel scoffed.

"I have friends in the family court."

"I never asked you for anything, Martin."

"Now, who's lying?" Martin stomped forward.

Rachel stepped back and slid a rollout cart between them. "I don't want this to get nasty."

"Give me another chance. You owe me that."

"I don't owe you anything."

"You're still fighting your ex for sole custody, aren't you?" Martin grinned. "I could help you with that. Or not."

"Are you threatening me, Martin?"

"I wouldn't call it a threat, Rachel, I would call it sound legal advice."

"Call it whatever you want." Rachel lifted her chin. "But could you say that again—a little louder, please?"

"Say what?"

"The part about a judge either helping or hurting—say it clearly, too!"

Martin lifted an eyebrow. "Are you recording me?"

Rachel's glare softened. "Listen, Martin. I don't want to hurt you, but I'm not going to let you use me or my child as leverage."

Martin tried to swallow, but his mouth was so dry he couldn't. His gaze darted around the room like a bird caught in a cage. What if she had recorded everything? If Tiffany heard it, she'd take him for all he had. Or leak it to the press. What if she gave it to the Commission on Judicial Standards? His large hands balled into fists.

Gravel crunched outside as a red sedan pulled into the parking lot. He recognized Shauna Phillips, from the business consortium, behind the wheel. She was talking on the phone and parked facing the street.

"I have no idea what you're talking about. You're clearly a disturbed woman who needs help." Martin marched to the door, shoved it open, and thundered down the steps.

He got into his car and sped away. His hand shook as he opened the center console and fished around for a belt of brandy. The metal cap snapped as he opened it, and he drained the nip in one go. The liquid burned like the rage building inside him.

"This is blackmail. She can't . . ." Martin threw the empty bottle into the back seat. "Oh, but she can."

The truth slammed him between the eyes. South Carolina is a one-party consent state. Legally, she could record him, and he could do nothing about it. Regardless, the Commission and the Disciplinary Board would not be applying recording consent laws to his judicial standing.

Over and over, he smashed his hand against the steering wheel.

That recording could never see the light of day.

As he drove, Martin panicked his way into a plan. He'd talk to Bob Hughes in family court and get Rachel full custody, but before Bob signed off on any deal, he'd get Rachel to give him the recording.

He pulled into his driveway, opened the last door of his four-car garage, and eased into the bay. Entering the house, he tossed his keys on the counter and headed for his office. He grabbed a tumbler, uncorked the whiskey decanter, and poured himself a double, neat.

Footsteps sounded in the hallway.

Tiffany's smile disappeared when she saw the drink in his hand. "You're starting early."

Martin took three giant strides and slammed the office door. He had enough problems to contend with. The last thing he needed was to deal with her incessant questions and accusations. He had to focus on getting his hands on that recording. He could play hardball, too, and there was no way he'd let some trailer trash bring him down.

CHAPTER 4

I N THE MIDDLE OF my fourth set of wide-grip pull-ups, which get harder with each birthday, my phone vibrates on the workout bench. I drop down on the concrete floor, walk over, and read the incoming text.

SHERIFF'S DEPARTMENT REQUESTING ASSISTANCE. POSSIBLE HOMICIDE AT 151 ENDER ROAD.

I wipe my phone screen with my shirt and set it back on the bench. I was the "on-call" prosecutor tonight. You shouldn't need a prosecutor if you have the right detective at a crime scene—not for a garden-variety homicide.

I catch myself at the mere thought of the phrase "garden-variety homicide." There's nothing commonplace about working these cases. Even thinking that way confirms I'm right to resign tomorrow.

I should have done it before while I was out on leave, but as assistant district attorney, I owe it to Cindy Porter, the DA, to give my notice face-to-face. She'd been a great boss and was more than accommodating with my extended leave. And Cindy was more than my supervisor—she was a friend.

Welcoming the excuse to get out of this house, I jog up the stairs to the bedroom, towel off, and pull on a fresh shirt and pants. I'm out the door and punch the address into the GPS on my phone, and it comes up with a listing for a beauty salon. The map says twenty-one minutes. I'll see if I can do it in fifteen. Regardless of how fast I get there, the victim will be dead, and nothing can change that. Homicide prosecutors can't save anyone.

As I drive around the corner, I glance at my house in the rearview mirror, and the pain slices through me again. As I see my reflection, I don't even recognize the person staring back at me anymore. I pity what he has become.

I turn out of the neighborhood onto the main road and speed up, heading for the outskirts of town. The winding back roads of Spartanburg at night paint a haunting image. The dim streetlights cast an eerie glow on the bare, twisted tree branches, like skeletal fingers clawing at the black sky.

I shudder as I take Route 29 and pass Oakwood Cemetery. As a kid, we all knew it as Hell's Gate—the most haunted place in all of South Carolina. Now that I'm grown, the place still scares me. But tonight, I'm not running away from the imaginary ghosts of my boyhood, I'm heading toward real evil.

Of course, I shouldn't be going to any crime scene. I should have left. I should have turned in my notice weeks ago when I made up my mind. But that's a different kind of death—professional death. My job, my calling, being a prosecutor. Of all the people who should be able to bounce back quickly from a death, it should be someone who has been surrounded by it. The best prosecutors can put themselves in the shoes of the victim. They take on the fear, the pain, and the grief because it makes you a better advocate. Now that I have the best empathy of all, I lost all desire to use it.

I'm still a quarter of a mile away, but I don't need GPS anymore. The blue and white emergency lights of a half dozen vehicles are up ahead. There's an ambulance, too, but the lights are off, another reminder that there's no use hurrying.

My throat tightens as I slow down. I really didn't want to do this anymore. I don't even know if I *can* do it anymore. I put my hazard lights on and power down the window. *This is your job, Colm,* I tell myself—at least for one more night. You owe whatever or whoever is inside that mobile home your best tonight.

A deputy nods as I pull into the parking lot and park behind Sheriff Lloyd Fuller's cruiser. It's easy to pick out the sheriff's car because everything is bigger. Sheriffs want you to know who the boss is before you even have to ask. The emergency lights are taller, wider, and brighter. The front grill has been painted gold to match the color of the star on the hood, not the traditional black of a mere deputy. All the trappings for the one person least likely to ever need them. And of course, there is the SHERIFF LLOYD FULLER printed so large along the side it looks like a campaign sign. In essence, it really is. A lawful form of an in-kind campaign contribution.

The EMT crew is speaking to an older woman sitting on the bumper of the ambulance. She's cradling a bottle of water in her shaking hands.

I cross to the stairs and notice the open box of booties and gloves on the steps. I slip on the shoe protectors and a pair of latex gloves. While I'm trying to pull on the second set of gloves, a tall man in his late twenties appears in the doorway and stares down at me.

"What are you doing?" he asks.

"Double-gloving."

"Why?"

I glance at the gold detective shield on his belt. "To avoid cross-contamination, DNA transfer, and so I can remove and replace the outer set if I need to." I rattle off the textbook answer, wondering if he's testing me or if he really doesn't know.

Sheriff Lloyd Fuller's wide frame fills the doorway behind the man. Lloyd is five foot five but wears cowboy boots with two-inch heels and lifts. "Colm? I'm surprised to see you. What brings you out?" Lloyd nudges the young detective aside.

"You texted me, Sheriff." I climb the steps and shake his hand.

Lloyd's face barely conceals his mixture of surprise and displeasure. The sheriff tolerates me because I make his office look better than it is, but he doesn't like me because I remind him how his office really operates.

"Actually, Sheriff, I contacted the DA's office, and Mr. Truesdale is on call." The young detective nods. "Travis Hendrick, sir. I'm lead detective on this."

Lloyd's lips purse together, and his cheeks redden. He looks like he's either going to start cussing, or lay into Travis, or both.

"Well, for better or worse, Detective Hendrick, you got me," I say as I wink at Sheriff Fuller. "Happy to help if I can. Tell me what you got."

Lloyd's phone rings. "I've got to get this. I'll let Hendrick take it from here." He shoots Travis a look that says, "We're going to have a conversation about this later," and passes me on the stairs as he puts the phone to his ear and walks away toward his cruiser.

I turn back to Travis. "Where is Detective Denton? I thought he ran point on new homicides?" I ask, trying to sound naïve, but actually a little defensive for my old friend and frequent collaborator, Rick "Bones" Denton.

Travis gives a one-shouldered shrug. "I asked the same thing. The sheriff said Captain Denton was full up on casework. I've heard a lot about you, Mr. Truesdale."

"Colm is fine. So, tell me what we have?"

Travis reaches into his jacket and takes out his phone. He pulls up his notes app. "The victim is Rachel Simone. Age twenty-six. Mother of a two-year-old boy. She lives and works here. There's a bedroom in back."

Memories crash into my heart, and panic rips through me. "Where is her child?"

"He's all right. He's not here."

I stuff my hands into my pockets to hide the fact they're shaking, trying, without much success, to drive the memory of finding my little Jaci out of my mind.

"Rachel's ex-mother-in-law was watching him today. Helen Greer. She's the one over with the paramedics. She's having chest pains, so they're checking her out. She was babysitting, but when Rachel failed to pick up the baby, she took the boy to the neighbors, came out here, and found the body." Travis backs up and points at the end of the room.

I step into the room and freeze. Two crime techs in full white suits are processing the scene. A camera flash gleams off the mirrors around the room, setting off stars in my eyes. A lifeless, beautiful young woman lies on the floor outside an open door that appears to lead into an office. I walk forward, careful to step well outside the pool of drying blood surrounding her body.

"The register was closed, and there's still cash in it," Travis says. "It's not looking like a robbery."

"Maybe," I say. "I wouldn't rule anything out yet. Sometimes people take other things of value, aside from the victim's life."

"No one has touched the body. Her ex-mother-in-law said she only opened the door and ran back out."

The victim is on her side. A wide gash is visible on the left side of her neck. From the amount of blood, I suspect the wound severed the carotid artery. I'm not a doctor, but I've seen enough bodies to be a half-way decent forensic pathologist.

Long, thick strands of blond hair have been cut from her head and tossed around the room—some clumped in the blood. A partial, large, bloody shoeprint is visible on the side of her face.

"The killer stomped on her head," Travis states the obvious. "From the size of the print, it's a man's shoe. Look at her chest."

A pair of scissors is embedded in Rachel's chest. I crouch down and scan the floor around her. Travis continues to speak, but I'm only half listening. The person I want to talk to isn't available, but I ask her anyway.

Who did this to you, Rachel?

Why here?

Why that weapon?

Why so many stab wounds?

Why did he step on your face?

Why cut your hair?

A strand of her bloodied hair is matted to her forehead. Beauty is no defense against death.

Travis points at the scissors jutting out of Rachel's chest. "The killer had to use a lot of force to do that."

While Travis states the obvious, I'm looking for what is hidden. What would she tell me if she could? Her body can still testify, even if her voice has been vanquished. What did those brilliant blue eyes see while they still had life? Even a few hours after she stopped breathing, those eyes are already turning opaque—the color of death.

The camera flash gleams off the blood, but nothing bounces off her eyes anymore. It flashes again, and a tiny circle of gold sparkles in the pool of blood on the floor.

"Come here, quick. Get this shot. I see something." I snap to get the tech's attention, focusing on the spot on the floor and pointing.

The two techs move in unison. One keeps taking pictures while the other finds what I am pointing to and uses long, sterile tweezers to lift a broken gold clasp.

Travis chews his lip.

Rachel wears a necklace and a few rings on her fingers. Her left arm is bent at an odd angle, and the blood near her hand is smeared on the floor.

The tech must notice it, too, because he's focused his lens on Rachel's left wrist and clicking away with his camera.

"Is someone from Ardell's team on the way?" I ask Travis.

"Who?"

"Ardell Sharp."

"Dr. Sharp? The medical examiner? Yes, sir. They should be here soon."

An EMT knocks on the door and calls in. "Travis? Hey, Travis?"

Travis hurries over, and I hear him whisper, "It's 'Detective' in the field. What do you need?"

The EMT rolls his eyes as I roll mine. "Sorry, Detective," he says, drawing out each syllable for an uncomfortable length of time, "Mrs. Greer is ready to give a statement."

I glance at the bloody shoeprints heading away from the body and toward the back room. I should follow them, but you only get one chance to listen to the raw recounting of eyewitness testimony, so I follow Travis.

As I pass the sink, I notice an appointment book lying flat on the counter. The name "Shauna Phillips" is written in black and circled in red, with a heart next to it. Shauna's name is the only one on it. At 3:30

p.m., she had an appointment with Rachel for a complete hair treatment. I pull out my pen and lift the corner of the page up. Shauna was the last person listed—the last customer ever.

After following Travis outside, I remove my gloves and booties and head to the ambulance. Helen Greer stares at her feet as she speaks with Travis.

"I knew something was wrong, but I thought maybe her car battery died again. I called, and she didn't answer. I tried Macon, but he didn't pick up either."

"Who is Macon?" Travis asks, his thumbs hovering over his phone.

"My son. He's the father of Rachel's baby. They're in a custody fight so . . ." Her lips press together, and her words trail off.

I place my hand on her shoulder. "It's okay, ma'am. Take your time."

"I couldn't get hold of Macon, so I took Henry to my cousin Liddy next door and headed straight here." Helen covers her mouth with her hand. "What am I gonna tell that little boy?"

I expect Travis to write something down, but he doesn't.

"When was the last time you spoke with Rachel?"

"When she dropped off Henry this morning. About seven o'clock. You don't think she was laying there all day, do you?" Fresh tears wet her lashes and roll down her cheeks.

Headlights sweep across the parking lot as a pickup truck races in, sending gravel flying like shrapnel.

A bear of a man drops down from the truck and hikes up his pants. "Where's Rachel?" he bellows as he heads toward the house and not his crying mother.

Helen stands up, knocking her bottle of water off the ambulance bumper. "Don't you go making things worse than they are, Macon!"

I jog over to cut him off, with Travis coming up behind me. I'm six foot two, but Macon is at least three inches taller and looks to outweigh me by fifty pounds. I sure wish Bones had caught this case and had my back right now.

"You can't go inside." Travis steps in front of Macon with his hand raised like a school crossing guard.

Macon stops, but he doesn't even glance at Travis. He's staring daggers at me. "Truesdale." His deep voice drops to a low growl. "Try telling me I can't go in my own home."

"You can't right now," Travis said. "Why don't you come over to your mother so we can talk."

Macon steps forward so we're nose to nose. He reeks of beer and tobacco.

I recognize him now. He didn't have the beard when I prosecuted him for assault a few years back.

"Will you stop acting the fool!" Helen hollers as she runs up behind me.

I turn to motion for her to stay back, knowing there's no reasoning with a drunk.

Helen's eyes widen, and I realize my mistake a split second before Macon's right fist slams into my jaw.

The parking lot lights sparkle brightly as I stagger backward. It's a nice right cross, but I stay on my feet.

Travis, another deputy, and one of the EMTs wrestle Macon to the ground. Helen starts wailing, more police come running, and everyone is shouting as I lean against the pickup and try to regain my focus and check for loose teeth.

Above all the noise, I hear Macon crying. He tries to scream, but the anguish inside him has closed his throat so tightly his voice is a whisper as he glares at the black sky and calls out, "Why?"

It's the best and worst question in all of life. And yet we can't stop asking it, screaming it, and sometimes praying it. But all too often the answer is just silence.

CHAPTER 5

MARTIN ROLLED AND STRETCHED, his body hanging precariously over the side of the couch. Groaning, he slid away from the edge. The sudden movement soured his stomach and brought a blinding pain to his head. Shielding his face with his hands, he opened one eye. The early-morning sun streamed through the blinds into his office.

He rubbed his hand over his face and immediately pulled it away. His palm and fingers were sticky and stained with a dried crud. Running his tongue over his teeth, his lip curled. His mouth tasted like something had died in it. Grabbing the back of the couch, he sat up, his foot bumping the empty whiskey decanter on the floor lying on its side. He put his head in his hands and stared at the carpet, trying to get the room to stop spinning.

He grabbed the bottle off the floor and stood up. He needed to do something about Rachel's recording—if she actually had one.

Glancing around the floor for the decanter's stopper, he saw it lying on the bar. He shuffled toward the guest bathroom.

Twenty minutes, four Advil, and a long, hot shower later, Martin was dressed and headed into the kitchen. Feeling like an intruder in his own house, he snuck to the cabinet and grabbed a travel coffee mug. He couldn't remember a thing after going into his office.

Footsteps sounded in the hallway, and his son, Lucas, jogged into the kitchen. "S'up, Dad." Lucas yanked open the fridge, grabbed a water bottle, and stared at his father.

Martin glared at his son. Lucas was the spitting image of him at eighteen. Six feet, with a trim runner's body and thick brown hair, he was a good-looking kid with no manners. "Is that my shirt? It is my shirt. Put it back."

Lucas pulled on the red and white jersey. "I'm going out with the crew to watch the game at O'Lindey's."

"I don't care if you're playing in the game, put it back."

"Yah, yah," Lucas said in a way that told Martin the kid had no intention of obeying, then headed over to a cabinet and took out a protein bar.

"Give me one of those."

Lucas tossed the bar to Martin, who managed to catch it.

"Where did you go last night?" Lucas asked.

Martin froze. "What? I didn't go anywhere."

Lucas took a big bite of the protein bar and flashed a smug grin. "I beg to differ, Your Honor. I heard you leave, and your car is blocking Mom's car in the garage. She's letting me borrow her car today. Do you want me to move yours?"

Martin blanched. Did he go out last night? No. With how much he drank, he would have been out of his mind to drive.

"Dad? You zoned out. Do you want me to move your car?"

Tiffany came into the kitchen, looking ready to seize the day. Her new pixie-cut brunette hair framed her heart-shaped face. She worked out and was still quite athletic for someone closing in on fifty.

"Are you going out?" Tiffany asked.

"Yes. I've got a few issues to deal with at work."

Tiffany's smile faded.

Lucas's phone rang. "Dude! Hold on." He looked at his mom. "You cool with me taking the car? I need it all day."

"Have fun." She handed him the keys but stared at Martin. "There's no place I need to go."

"You're the best, Mom." Lucas snatched the keys from her hand, kissed her cheek, and hurried toward the stairs. "We're all set, dude. I'll be leaving in, like, fifteen minutes."

"Where did you go last night?" Tiffany asked.

"Dealing with a lot at the courthouse." Martin snatched his car keys from the hook by the fridge. "I just needed to clear my head."

Tiffany opened her mouth, but Martin didn't give her a chance to respond. He yanked open the door to the garage and jerked it closed behind him.

His golf cart took up the first bay of the garage, followed by the Jet Skis and Tiffany's BMW convertible. However, his parking space was empty.

Martin swore and pressed the button to open the garage door.

The chain clanked, and the door rolled up. His Audi was parked outside at an angle, blocking Tiffany's BMW. He nervously circled the car, checking the bumper for any damage, bushes, or bicycle parts. Relieved that he found none, he opened the door and wrinkled his nose at a metallic odor. A half-empty pint of whiskey lay on the passenger seat. He grabbed it and walked briskly back to the garage, holding the bottle down by his leg in case Tiffany was watching out the window.

He lifted the trash can lid and stopped. Dropping the lid back down, he put the whiskey bottle in the tool cabinet on the top shelf in the back.

Martin returned to his car. The engine started right up, and he grabbed the steering wheel. It was sticky. Martin scowled. He'd deal with it later. Right now, he needed to get over to the salon and get that recording from Rachel.

Martin backed out of the driveway. He glanced in the rearview mirror. Tiffany and Lucas were standing in the kitchen watching him go.

If that tape ever got out, it would cost him everything. He wouldn't let that happen.

CHAPTER 6

THE DENT ON THE front of Bones's unmarked Dodge Charger is still there. I notice it as he inexplicably ignores the open parking spaces and parks off to the side of the restaurant. What a metaphor for his life—rusty and dented but still works and gets you where you need to be. I'm glad South Carolina no longer has vehicle inspections, because his car would not pass. And why can't he use a regular parking spot like everyone else?

Captain Rick Denton is different and takes his sweet time getting out while I wait beside my car, parked in a normal spot. I've been here for at least fifteen minutes, and I'm starting to drool at the irresistible odor of bacon emanating from the small diner and straight to me. As he approaches, I shake my head and hold out a twenty-dollar bill.

"What's this for?" he asks without a smile.

"Bones? Is that you?" I lay it on thick. "Seeing how you haven't bathed or shaved and look like you spent the night at the Downtown Rescue Mission, I mistook you for a poor, homeless soul looking for a handout."

Bones doesn't even crack a grin. Judging by his red-rimmed eyes, he might still be under the influence of last night's bourbon. "Been dealin' with my ex," he says.

"Which one?"

"Does it matter?" He looks around the parking lot, scoops a pack of cigarettes from his coat pocket, and lights one.

"Thanks for meeting me, Colm." He takes a drag. "Janelle came over last night."

It's been a while since I heard him say his first wife's name. "I can't imagine it was a social call."

"Why do I always pick the crazy ones?"

"Not to act as her defense attorney, Bones, but you're the one who asked her out, dated her, got engaged, married, and had a family with her. So, if she's a nutcase, what does that make you?"

"Thanks for always taking my side, brother."

"All kidding aside," I say, "the kids are grown, and the alimony is over. What's left to fight over?"

Bones shrugs his massive shoulders. "Fighting and loving ain't all that far apart, but I didn't bring you here to discuss my marriages. Let's go in and eat."

"Have you been here before?" I ask.

"Long time ago," he says.

The Junction was a single-story cinder-block rectangle that someone, twenty years ago, tried to make look like a train station. The sign was faded, but the paint wasn't peeling. More importantly, through the large row of front windows, the place looked clean, and there was a steady stream of regulars coming and going. The location isn't ideal—Gowensville—in between Spartanburg and Greenville, and close to the North Carolina line. But loyalty matters in these parts and the customers are willing to make the drive.

I open the door for Bones as he lumbers past and follow him inside. The Junction is the sort of place where you seat yourself and the laminated menus are already on the table—slid between the packets of jelly and the salt and pepper. The menus are sticky with the syrup from other people's pancakes, but then again, most of their customers know what they came for without having to look.

The place is crowded, but we find a booth in the corner. Bones wedges his massive frame into the seat. He would make a lumberjack feel small.

"I heard you got called out to that salon murder. I thought you were quitting this morning."

"That was the plan but . . . I don't know if I'm going to follow through with that—not yet at least."

For the first time this morning, Bones smiles. "Good. You're too young to retire and too old to work at Burger King."

What can I say? If I admit there was something about Rachel that reminded me of Ally, he'll think I'm crazy. But that's the real reason. If someone had done that to Ally, there's no way I could walk away.

"I've never quit a case." I look around the restaurant for the waitress, so I don't have to meet Bones's doubtful stare.

I stare across the room and see a waitress talking to an elderly customer. The man is smiling as he holds his fork in his shaking hand. His other arm is in a sling. The waitress is chatting away with him as she cuts up his ham. Something about her seems so out of order with her being in this place—like finding the *Mona Lisa* hanging in a gas station.

Bones starts to raise his arm to get her attention, and I kick him in the shin.

"What the hell did you do that for?"

"She's helping the elderly man with one arm in a sling."

Bones sits back. "I didn't notice that. And you don't have to say it like I'm a creep."

"Don't be so soft."

The waitress zigzags across the restaurant, topping off coffee cups with her right hand and refilling water glasses with her left. They were either short-staffed or unusually busy.

She makes it to our table and smiles down at me. "Good morning, gentlemen. My name is Belle. I hope you are having a wonderful start to your day. What can I get for you?" She has a sweet Southern drawl that tells me she's from around here.

I answer before Captain Denton can give some cynical or sarcastic reply.

"Coffee for both would be great. And you look busy today, so what if we save you an extra trip and go ahead and order, if that would help?"

"Sure, whatever suits you—I'm ready if y'all are."

Denton shifts his bulky body in the booth. "I'll take a double country breakfast and a glass of skim milk if you have it."

"Yeah, Bones—by all means, get the skim milk. Get the biggest, most calorie-laden thing you can find on the menu and then mitigate it with skim milk."

"Look who's talking? You should order the fat bomb special. You're so skinny I could save you from drowning by tossing you a fruit loop."

Belle looks on like Switzerland, not knowing whether to get involved and on whose side.

"Egg white omelet, no cheese," I say. "And do you have any avocado?"

"I'm sorry, we don't."

"That's okay," I say.

A customer at another table waves her over.

"I'll put your order right in." She smiles and moves away.

"I may have just met wife number four," Bones says.

"Please, Bones, she's light-years out of your league."

"I don't know, some women like men in uniform."

"That's true, but it's been about two decades since you had a uniform that fit."

Bones balls up the wrapper from his straw and throws it at me, but I deflect it.

"What's the deal with Travis Hendrick? How come you didn't catch the case? You're not on the outs with Lloyd again, are you?" I ask.

"No, but that's why I wanted to talk to you. I need your opinion on something."

"If it's about marriage, I recommend you not do it again."

"Funny. But that's not why I want your opinion. I was invited to be on a federal drug task force."

"Wow, that's great. Are you going to accept?"

"Considering everything—I don't know," Bones says. "The hours are good. But it's drugs."

"From a lifestyle standpoint, it's a good gig. No victims asking for updates. But I'm telling you, it's more boring than being a captain. I guess I'd ask you whether you want excitement or predictability. Do you want to work weekends, or fight a war on drugs that can't be won?"

"I'm good at wars that you can't win." He gives a bitter laugh.

For a few minutes, we discuss the pros and cons of him being on the task force. Belle brings us our food, refills our coffee, and asks if we need anything else.

I don't, but we aren't through figuring out his career path, so I order a side of bacon.

Bones looks at me like I've grown an extra head.

"Sure thing. One side of bacon coming up."

As we start on our second cup of coffee, I ask him where the idea to join the task force came from.

"The sheriff called me into his office and said the feds, DEA, and the U.S. Attorney's Office were looking for a local cop who knows his way around state and federal court and has some CIs. They need someone who can go get subpoenas from a state magistrate or, if need be, a U.S. magistrate. Probably mainly they want my informants, I'm guessing."

"It's a young person's gig, Bones. Running around chasing drug dealers, having to stomach FBI and DEA agents and their fights and territorial disputes and egos. Where are you in life, I guess, is what I am asking."

The wrinkles and bags under his eyes seem to pull him down to the floor. "Tired is where I am, Colm. Tired."

"You'd be good at it. Kim Lewis just started at the U.S. Attorney's Office and could use a friendly face. How long did they say the detail would be?"

"Twelve months, with the likelihood it'll be re-upped for another twelve," he says.

I nod. "It also gets you on the doorstep of retirement. I think you should go for it, but I can't decide for you. I would miss you if I were staying, but that's selfish and I'm not staying, not past this beauty salon case."

"I was sorta hoping you would decide. That way I'd have someone to blame if it goes wrong."

I finally see a glint of the old Rick Denton in his eyes.

"Do it, Bones. Do it to help Kim. And do it for yourself to have a better lifestyle."

Belle returns with a side of bacon. "I'll leave this bill with you. Take your time, and you can pay at the cash register or here, whichever you prefer."

"We both need to get going, so I'll leave the payment here at the table," I tell her.

"So nice to meet you both, and I hope you're able to come back again soon."

I glance at the check and notice a mistake. "Belle? You forgot to charge me for the bacon."

She hurries back and whispers, "It's on the house to make up for not having avocados."

Bones reaches over and takes half the bacon in his meaty hand. "I'm doing you a favor. You'd have some kind of fat overdose if I let you eat it all." He glances over his shoulder and watches Belle head into the kitchen. "Free bacon. She knows the way to a man's heart."

"You want the other half, Colm?"

"No, I was stalling so we could finish our talk. What do you think about Travis Hendrick?" I ask.

"He seems to be a good kid. He was a smart cop."

"How did he end up leading a murder investigation?"

"You're asking the same question I and everyone in the department have been wondering. How's he doing on the case?" Bones asked.

"Seems a little green."

"That boy is more than green—he's a seedling. There's no way he should have been assigned that case. You've been around enough to steer him in the right direction. Besides, the more you help him, the more you help yourself."

"DAs don't steer cases, Bones. We course correct."

"You know what I mean. Make sure he toes the line."

"Speaking of toeing the line, I have an appointment with Cindy." I take out my wallet as we slide out of the booth.

Bones's hand darts out, and he steals the last piece of bacon and flashes a childlike grin.

I search the inside pocket of my wallet, remove my emergency hundred, and leave it on the table.

Bones's lips press together, and he raises his eyebrows. "I mean, she's pretty and all, but a hundred dollars for breakfast?"

"Kind people deserve to be rewarded. She was literally cutting a man's breakfast up for him. It's the least I can do."

"I bet if she wasn't beautiful and kind, it would be twenty dollars, not a hundred."

"Wrong, Bones. It's what's inside that counts. Keep that in mind while you're courting wife number four."

After saying goodbye to Bones, I head to my car. I'm about to get in when the diner's front door bashes open.

"Sir! Sir!" Belle shouts in a high-pitched voice as she hurries down the front stairs and runs across the gravel. "You left your change on the table."

I wave her off and say, "No, ma'am, I didn't. That's for you."

"Sir, it's one hundred dollars for an eleven-dollar breakfast."

"It is," I say. "But you were unnecessarily kind. So, you earned it. Now, don't go sharing it with your co-workers. That's for you."

Belle stands there speechless for a moment and finally says, "Thank you, sir. You have no idea. Bless you, but no promises on the not sharing part," she says, mixing a smile with blinking tears.

I get in my car, and as she hurries back in the restaurant, she turns and waves.

I reach out to close my door, and a cold wind blows across the back of my neck.

"Colm."

I get back out of the car and look around. I could have sworn someone said my name, but no one is nearby. I must be hearing things.

CHAPTER 7

MARTIN'S KNUCKLES TURNED BRIGHT white as he gripped the steering wheel, speeding down the road to Rachel's salon. As a judge, he mocked defendants who stood before him and offered "passion" or "heat of the moment" or "inflamed emotions" in some failed effort to mitigate their crimes.

"I don't know what came over me. I would never hurt her, but I wasn't in my right mind."

Every excuse sounded cliché until it was his own voice uttering it.

The sign for the storage place came into view, and the world stopped the way it did when your plans finally confronted reality. Martin was having trouble breathing. He couldn't even blink. He could only stare at the surreal scene.

A sheriff's cruiser was parked in front of Rachel's salon, and police tape blocked off the front door. A sheriff's van was parked out back. Two men were photographing the ground.

Martin's foot lifted off the gas. His car slowed.

A deputy stood beside the cruiser and gazed down at the phone in his hand. The young man lifted his head and turned to stare at Martin's car. His eyes narrowed.

The steering wheel shook, and the car shuddered as the tires hit the rumble strip on the side of the road. Martin swerved back into the lane and sped up. His hand trembled as he jerked down the rearview mirror and angled it over.

The deputy was still watching him but hadn't moved.

Martin's heartbeat hammered in his chest—once, twice, three times.

The deputy returned to looking at his phone.

Martin felt sick and his mind raced. Last night was a blank, but he didn't . . . he couldn't . . .

"Where did you go, Dad?" Lucas asked him.

Martin hadn't gone out, but Tiffany said she heard the car, too.

He wiped his sweaty forehead with the palm of his hand. Maybe there was an accident.

Macon! Martin thought. Rachel's ex had been violent with her in the past. Maybe he showed up at the salon and started another fight.

Martin licked his lips. He had no idea what took place.

Lloyd would know.

Martin reached into his pants pocket for his phone, but it wasn't there. He swore. He didn't remember taking it this morning. He glanced around the car and saw it wedged between the seat and the center console. Tugging the phone out, he dialed Lloyd.

Small, dried flakes fell off the back of the phone as he held it to his ear. He must have spilled some liquor on it.

"I've been trying to reach you all night," Lloyd said.

"I had my phone on silent. What's going on?"

"Before we get into that, I need to ask a few questions. You and I go way back, Judge, and I need you to be honest with me. Where were you last night after five o'clock?"

Martin swallowed. "I came straight home from work. Tiffany made me dinner. I was home all night. Ask Tiffany and Lucas. Why? What is this all about?"

"There was an incident on Ender Road at this beauty salon where your, umm, friend worked."

"What friend?"

"You know that girl I saw you with at the Outer Limits? I saw your name in her appointment book. It had a gold star next to it."

"What happened?"

"I can't officially comment because it's an ongoing investigation, but off the record, Rachel was murdered. I'm sorry."

"Murdered? How? By whom?"

"We don't know, and I can't get into that anyway right now. But you should know your name appears several times in her appointment book."

"Well, I got my haircut there, Lloyd. Of course my name is in the book."

"Rachel also recorded the lengths of the appointments. Three hours is a long time for a haircut, Judge."

"Where's the book?"

"I have it for now, but I did that as a courtesy to keep your name out of this initial investigation."

"Did you get rid of the book?"

"I can't get rid of the book. The best I can do is make those pages disappear, for now at least. But I do need you to convince me you had nothing to do with this."

"For God's sake, Lloyd, is that a serious question? Are you really asking me if I was involved in her death?"

"No, I am asking you if there is anything connecting you with her that I should know about?"

"No, we had a casual relationship, not unlike a few you've had. I was home all night, and Tiffany and Lucas were there with me. I can't believe you would even ask me that."

"I'm not asking you anything, Martin, other than to assure me I am not jamming myself up while protecting you."

"I had nothing to do with whatever happened to her. I swear it. I actually cared for her. This is hard for me to process right now. I sure don't need more complications with my name being dragged through your investigation."

"So, you're telling me Tiffany and Lucas will vouch for your whereabouts all night?"

"Yes! Yes, they will."

"Okay, Martin, I'll take care of keeping your name out of it."

"I can't thank you enough." Martin started breathing again. "I'm sure you are looking at her ex-husband, aren't you? You know they were in a bitter custody dispute?"

"Yes, Martin, we do know that, but the question is how do you know that? See, that's sort of my point. The less you talk, the less you react, the easier this is going to be for both of us. I don't mind covering up an affair, but beyond that, you're on your own."

"How did she die, Lloyd?"

"I'm not releasing any details that only the killer would know. Plus, it's not in your best interest to know. Is there anything else that could possibly tie you to that girl?"

Martin gasped and glanced around the car but the burner phone he used to contact Rachel was nowhere in sight. That phone held texts and videos between him and her that he'd never want anyone else to see. "No. Nothing. I swear."

"You need to be smart on how you react to this when someone else tells you, Judge. You need to start working on that now. The fewer people who know about you and this girl, the better it is for both of us."

"Yeah." Martin nodded. "I will."

Lloyd hung up, and Martin stared at his reflection in the blackness of the phone screen. Something was smeared across his forehead. He grabbed the rearview mirror and angled it so he could see himself.

His face was stained with what looked like blood. Was he seeing things?

Slowly, he turned his hands over and stared at his sweaty palms. They were covered in blood, too.

CHAPTER 8

I PARK IN THE BACK parking lot of the Twelfth Circuit Judicial Center but don't get out of the car, instead choosing to watch the faces of the people on the sidewalk heading inside this monument to what is supposed to be fairness. They represent the complexity and contradiction of life. Some are here seeking justice, others hope to avoid it, while most would rather be anywhere else. Some have chosen to make this courthouse their life's work, coming every day for forty years to process court filings, or handle child support payments, or transcribe master-in-equity proceedings. For yet others, this will be the only time they ever set foot in this courthouse.

Through the crowd, I recognize Cindy hurrying down the steps. Dressed in a crisp navy suit, she has her lightly streaked gray hair pulled into a bun. This no-nonsense, born-and-bred Southern DA overcomes more injustice and inequity in a month than any DA I've known. If it fazes her, you can't tell. But she does more, with better results, and within less time than her counterparts.

I hurry out of the car. "Morning, Cindy."

Cindy stops short. "Colm. I didn't think you'd be here this early." She gazes back at the courthouse and then at me. "I have a budget meeting with the mayor. And I'm late. But it's great to see you back where you belong."

"No worries and thank you. We'll touch base later. I'll go get situated."

Cindy's mouth opens and quickly closes. She smiles, nods, and hurries to her car.

Did she want to say something and catch herself? The budget meeting probably has her rattled. They are, after all, the opposite of Christmas—people meet and take your presents. They don't exchange them.

Walking through the doors of the Judicial Center was like coming home, except to a dysfunctional family. Yes, there was familiarity, but the old cliché rings true: "Familiarity breeds contempt."

I had a love-hate relationship with this building. Courthouses are similar to hospitals, clinics, and counseling sessions in one respect— broken people come here to be healed. But there is no healing. Everyone leaves with some type of scar—one left either by a perpetrator or by the system, but they all leave with a mark reminding them that nothing is ever restored to its original state. Closure may be the greatest lie ever told. There is no closure. The collateral consequences of crime are a life sentence, just outside the prison walls. I make my way up the marble steps and through the double doors. There's no line for the metal detector and, as I approach, a sour-looking deputy who looks like Barney Fife—skinny as a rail but standing with his chest puffed out and both hands resting on his gun belt—launches into his "please remove all items from your pockets" speech.

I pass through and take the stairs to the second floor, head to the end of the hallway, and open the door to my office. It's almost exactly as I left it—my desk is in the corner with a great view of Barnet Park across the road with its gently rolling hills and beautiful, albeit man-made, waterfall. My file cabinets line the right wall, but the certificates on the wall, while similar, have the wrong names and schools on them. The pictures on the shelves aren't mine either. And some guy a little younger than me, with dark hair, a blue suit, and a puzzled look, is sitting in my chair, talking on my phone, and staring at me.

"Wait, wait, wait a second. Some guy just walked right into my office." He covers the phone with his hand and looks at me like I'm tracking in mud while trespassing. "Can I help you, sir?"

"I was about to ask you the same thing. I'm Colm Truesdale, the assistant DA. Did we remodel and I missed the memo? This is my office."

The man says into the phone, "Hold on a minute." He sets the receiver down and stands. "So, you're Truesdale. Dillon Bickler. I was hired to handle your caseload. I'm a lateral from another circuit." He circles the desk and extends a hand. "They moved your office while you were gone. I'm sorry no one told you."

I can feel my face tightening into what my mother always referred to as my Clint Eastwood scowl. I can't help it. But it's not his fault, and I don't blame the messenger. Instead, I look for the source of the bad news, the person who set the whole thing in motion. "We can figure this out after I meet Cindy in the afternoon."

"It was Cindy's decision to move your things. They set you up in a new office two floors below. B9 is where you are, I think." Dillon moves back behind the desk.

Things are coming into focus a little clearer now. His touch of contrition is really condescension. I didn't think my position was at risk while I was on the injured reserve list, but this guy wants to be the starting quarterback.

"Nice to meet you, Colm. I've got to get back to this call." Dillon picks up the phone, sits down, and swivels in his chair so his back is to me.

I take a deep breath and remind myself that I'm meeting Cindy at two. Heading into the hallway, I take the closest stairs and descend to the basement. This is where the old records were kept before everything became digital. I'm expecting a concrete tunnel when I open the stairwell door, but instead it feels like I stepped through a time machine and into the old building.

The first two floors had been renovated, and it appears they left the basement alone. The tiles are thick porcelain, the light fixtures are metal, and the door to my office is solid wood with a handle that gives me a sense of security when I grab it.

I turn on the light and reality hits. There are no windows. The room feels like a crypt. It's half the size of my old office, but the desk and furniture are deep mahogany, which grounds me a little. It's a demotion, but with nicer furniture.

Boxes are stacked on the desk, and when I notice what's inside, my heart sinks. The first picture is of Jaci sitting up in her crib. She has Ally's eyes and her smile. Jaci had me wrapped around her finger the moment she looked at me. The photograph beneath it is of Ally and me on vacation in Nova Scotia. She wanted to hike along the coast, back when the math was simpler—she wanted it, so we did it. Such is devotion. You don't ask why because you don't care why. You just do it.

I remove the photograph like I am holding the most fragile thing on earth, which, in some way, I am. Then I see that the frame is chipped in the upper right corner. What means the most to us is just another picture to someone else. I set Ally's picture on the built-in shelf behind me. My first instinct is to march back to my office and drag Dillon down the steps and show him what he'd done.

My rage simmers as I unload my other personal possessions, which are also haphazardly jammed into the box. I lift a small set of scales out—a law school graduation gift from Ally. The chain holding the left scale is bunched up, but after some gentle wrangling, I manage to straighten it.

"Always be fair. Fairness is a virtue more treasured than beauty," she used to say. "Fairness is beauty, Colm. Always remember that."

My phone buzzes in my pocket. A text from Travis. He wants to know if I want to be there when he interviews Macon Greer.

"ON MY WAY," I respond in all caps.

I hurry out of the office, pulling the door closed behind me. As I climb the stairs, memories assault me. I'm hiking up the hill after Ally along the Celtic Shores Trail. She reaches the crest and raises her arms above her head, as the sun clears the clouds and bathes her in light. It's so blinding that I have to look away, and she's gone.

So, too, is the memory.

I grab the railing and start climbing again. I couldn't help Ally when she needed it, but maybe I can do something for Rachel.

CHAPTER 9

ARRIVING AT THE SHERIFF'S Department, protocol dictates I visit the boss's office first. Lloyd is a lesson in what power can do in the wrong hands, both to the holder of that power and to those in the periphery. In truth, power impacts people in different ways, but it always changes you. For Lloyd, power inflamed his ego. He likes the trappings of the title, the fact that people defer to him, fear him, invite him to parties outside of his previous social stratosphere—he just doesn't like actually doing real police work.

But the best cops don't win races for sheriff, like the best lawyers don't win races for district attorney or attorney general. Fame trumps competency—nearly every time.

I knock on the open door and step inside.

Lloyd jumps, the wider-than-normal papers in his hand crumpling. "Colm!" His voice rises in surprise. I stand in the doorway as he turns the papers he was reading frontside down and tucks them into a folder.

"I came by because Travis is interviewing the ex-husband," I say.

He nods. "Good to see you. I keep forgetting some prosecutors like to be more, shall we say, 'hands on' than others. Travis's cubicle is down the hall on the left."

It's not so much "hands on" as ensuring that the arrest becomes a conviction, but I keep my mouth shut. Lloyd was never a real cop or even attended the police academy. And if he was ever in a courtroom, it was to observe, not participate, so Cindy likes us to keep a close eye on cases his department makes.

"While I have you, do you remember a lawyer named Frank Hastings? Defense attorney, I think."

"Yes. I had a few cases with Frank. One of my first trials was against him. Why?"

"Probably nothing, but Frank's brother filed a missing person report on him."

I shrug. "Haven't heard his name in a long time."

"Thanks for checking in, Colm. Good to have you back at work."

Making my way down the row of cubicles, I see Travis hunched over his keyboard typing with two fingers. I knock on the cubicle wall.

"Oh, hey, Colm. One second." He pecks at a few more keys, clicks the mouse, and stands up. "We have a little bit of a problem. I thought you should know. There was apparently some disconnect in booking. They didn't give Macon a DUI test or draw blood."

"That's not a *disconnect*, Travis. That's a calamity. There are only a couple of things a cop needs to remember in a DUI or public intoxication case. Administer a Breathalyzer, do field sobriety tests, or get an order to draw blood. You can't win a DUI case or a public drunkenness case when you can't prove impairment."

"I'm trying to figure out how they screwed up."

"'How' doesn't matter. We lost our best justification for holding this suspect. Striking a prosecutor is one thing. Simple assault at best. But driving under the influence—especially as a repeat offender—that would raise his bond to a number he might not be able to reach."

"As soon as I found out, I considered sending him for a blood test this morning."

"And? Did you?"

"No. The Sheriff thought too much time had passed. And he said that if Macon went to the hospital now, it would only highlight our mistake."

I stopped before I said something I would regret, like, *This is what happens when you send the JV squad to a murder scene.* "If we had given the blood test as soon as we realized it wasn't administered, that would've been best. Since we didn't do that, we can't pursue the DUI charges or public drunkenness, or else we expose our own incompetence, and that perception may bleed into areas where we did some good police work."

"I agree. Sorry, didn't know until it was too late," Travis said, lifting his chin.

"You're the lead detective on this case. It's your job to ensure everyone else does his or her job correctly. Juries aren't into chain of command. What they care about is pretty simple: Did you do what was supposed to be done or not?"

Travis's eyes harden.

I meet his stare with a cold one of my own. This is not a battle he wants to pick or one he can win. We have reached a critical juncture in this nascent relationship. He's either going to see his mistake or justify it. He's either a learner or an excuse maker.

"You're right, I was wrong. I should have returned to the Sheriff's Department and made sure Macon was processed correctly. It won't happen again."

"Fair enough, lesson learned. Are you ready for this interview?"

"Yes. I pulled Macon's rap sheet and incident reports. In addition to the case you prosecuted against him a few years ago, he has a history of drunk and disorderly conduct, public intoxication, driving under the influence, and a domestic violence case that was dropped."

"None of that is admissible at trial, but he probably doesn't know that, so harp on the fact that he's a recidivist, and maybe he will fall for it."

"Okay, Colm. There's something else. We haven't been able to locate Rachel's phone, so I'm working on a warrant to the cell phone provider to try and ping it."

"Let me see the warrant before we send it, but in the meantime, let's keep looking for it the old-fashioned way."

Travis nods. "I'm going back to the salon personally, and I sent two deputies out this morning to search off the road."

"Good. You take the lead on this interview. I'll be there if you need me. Just look my way, okay?"

Travis nods and starts walking down the hall. "We're in interrogation room two."

"I'm sorry again that they didn't run the tests. I told Rob, a deputy, but he thought Macon was only being charged for striking you."

"What matters is whether we have enough to hold him while we check out any alibi he might offer. Striking an assistant DA might be enough to do that, but the last thing I want to do is waste my time filling out victim forms since I'm not letting that go forward."

"What? You're not pressing charges?"

"No. If Macon didn't kill Rachel, then he's a man who just lost the mother of his child. The bruise on my face will heal. The child won't. He needs a parent—even if it's not a great one."

Travis leads the way as we enter the interrogation room. He walks past Macon, sitting on the side of a metal table fixed to the wall, and parks himself in the far chair on the opposite side, closest to the audio recorder. Two cameras on the ceiling at either end capture a clear view of the room.

I've participated in hundreds of interviews, knowing they were recorded and would be put under a microscope by supervisors, defense lawyers, jurors, and judges. Everyone acts a little differently on camera. The key is to act better.

I take the other free chair and slide it away from the side of the table, so nothing separates me from Macon. I prefer to interview suspects this way.

Travis reads a standard interview opening from a card, including Macon's Miranda rights. He fills in the date, time, and other details as he speaks. He passes the interrogation form and waiver to Macon for him to sign.

Macon slides it back and says, "I'm not signing anything, not yet at least."

Travis clasps his hands loosely on the table, unsure what to do next.

"Go ahead and start, Travis," I say.

While Macon didn't sign the waiver, he didn't invoke his right to remain silent either.

"Why don't we start with where you were last night before you came to the salon?" Travis says.

I try to mask my disappointment with Travis's opening. What happened to building a rapport with a witness or suspect?

"Why don't we start with where's my lawyer," Macon fires back.

This is not good. The goal of an interrogation is for the interviewee to do the talking, not the detective or the prosecutor. It's not show-and-tell. It's more like a scavenger hunt. Lie, bluff, distort—all of that is fair game, just keep the suspect talking.

Adding a defense attorney would at best slow this down and likely end it. So, I had to intervene.

"Yes, Macon, you're entitled to an attorney. It will cost you at least ten thousand dollars to get a decent one and you will sit here in jail until he or she gets up to speed on the case. On the other hand, you can help us clear you, save yourself ten grand, and I'll drop the assault charges on you for striking me."

"Why would you do that? Why would you drop those charges?"

"Because I want to find out who killed Rachel and not waste time on a simple assault case against the one parent your son has left."

"I don't have ten thousand dollars, and I don't need to sit here missing work."

"Well, then help us clear you. Give us a reason to let you go."

"I was home. When I heard something might have happened at the salon, to Rachel, I drove straight there."

Travis shakes his head and clicks his tongue like a disappointed math teacher when a student gets a question wrong. "Lying is not a good way to clear yourself, Macon."

Macon's eyes are bloodshot. I suspect some of that is from the booze, but it also appears that he's been crying.

"What are you talking about, Travis? You asked me a freaking question, and I answered you."

"First off, Mr. Greer, it's Detective Hendrick. Secondly"—Travis slams his hand down on the table—"you're lying to my face. Your own mother said you weren't at home!"

"Who are you callin' a liar?" Macon leans forward, his complexion turning a splotchy red. "You asked me where I was before I came out to the salon. I was home! I had been fishing, but when I came home, nobody was there. I went next door, and Liddy said my mom was worried about Rachel." Macon jabs an accusatory finger at Travis. "So, watch who you're callin' a liar!"

Travis is committing the cardinal error of interrogations, at least those with no jury around to watch. He's trying to show how smart he is rather than letting the suspect dig a grave. *Shut up and let Macon talk* is what I am thinking, but saying that would undercut Travis in front of a suspect.

"Let's hit the reset button again," I suggest. "First of all, we're all sorry for your loss and that of your family, Macon. I don't have the words, and even if I did, I wouldn't know how to use them. It is the worst cut that life can deal us."

Macon takes a deep breath through his nose and gives a curt nod.

"You said you went fishing. Where'd you go and was anyone with you?"

"Honeywell Dam. They open the sluice at two. I got there a little after one and stayed until at least six. More like seven."

"You don't know the time?" Travis asked.

Macon bristled. "No. I don't know the time. I didn't think I'd be quizzed on it when I put the poles in the bed of my truck, Deputy."

"It's Detective. Isn't there a clock in your truck? What about your phone?"

"Yeah, Detective, there are clocks on both, but they don't much matter if you don't look. I was fishing. The last thing on my mind was creating a timeline for someone to ask me about."

The interview was going south, and unnecessarily so. But it needed to be salvaged with a different tack and no defense attorneys involved.

No one really believed Macon killed his wife, except for the fact that the husband or boyfriend is exactly who usually kills women. The men who claim to love them. So, he has to be eliminated as a suspect and, for that, we need his full cooperation. "Did you purchase bait?" I ask.

"No. I use jigs and minnow traps."

"What about stopping some place for snacks or beer? Gas?"

Macon's eyes widen. "Wait a second. This isn't about me punching you or drinking and driving, which I regret, by the way. Do you think I had something to do with hurtin' Rachel?"

"You need to calm down," Travis says.

"Screw you! I would never hurt her. I loved her." Macon pounds the table.

"Then why were you arrested for domestic violence?" Travis says.

Macon plants his feet flat on the floor. I'm half expecting him to leap over the table, so I keep my arms loose and get ready to tackle him.

"She lied about that. I gave a little push, but she told the cops I smacked her. I didn't. I pushed her face away outta mine, that was it. She hit me way more times than I ever hit her, but the woman ain't never arrested. Always the man. If I had hit her, she wouldn't be here right now . . ." His voice trails off, and the words hang in the air.

"Why don't you tell us a little about the current custody suit," I suggest. "What started it? I thought you guys had worked out something."

Macon exhales and glares at the ceiling. "Look, I never wanted it to come to court. I didn't want no divorce. I never even signed the papers. I wanted to recon, umm, reconsider, whatever the word is—you know, get back together."

"But Rachel wasn't having anything to do with that, was she?" Travis presses.

"You don't know that," Macon shoots back.

"Was she seeing someone else?" Travis asks.

Macon's hand balls into a fist. "I think so. I don't know who, but she'd go out at night a lot."

"How did you know that?"

Macon glances back and forth between Travis and me. "I just knew."

Travis makes a face. "You're not a psychic. You were driving by her house."

"It's our house."

"But prior to her death, would you drive by the salon to make sure she was okay?" I ask.

"Yeah." Macon sets his elbow on the table and rests his head against his hand. "How did she die?"

"We aren't releasing the details on the cause of death, and the medical examiner is the one who does that anyway." It's a lie, but a small one to keep him talking. "Macon, it's obvious you still care about her, so why did you and Rachel split up?"

"It was mostly 'cause of me chasing after other women. Me getting arrested didn't help nothing either."

"Did you have an affair?" Travis asks.

"No. I had a few different one-night stands, but I never had no affair."

"What's the difference?" Travis asks.

"Well, an affair is 'cause you really like the other person, and it lasts a long time. The other is just someone you meet in a bar, and you go out to your truck, and it doesn't mean nothing."

"But you believe that Rachel was seeing someone at the time of her death? Do you know who? Anything at all, even if it's gossip. It could help us find who did this."

Macon shakes his head and to my surprise, his lower lip quivers. Tears roll down his face. "I swear to God I had nothing to do with it, but you better find the bastard who did before I do."

CHAPTER 10

MARTIN PULLED INTO THE Soap & Suds self-serve car wash bay, shifted the car into park, and wiped the sweat off his brow with his sleeve. Rooting around the car like a squirrel searching for a nut, he searched everywhere for his burner phone. It wasn't there. That meant it was either in his office at home or at the courthouse.

He took a deep breath, closed his eyes, and let it out.

"*State v. McDermott*," he muttered.

Martin's eyes snapped open. He'd been the judge in that case. Edward McDermott had killed his wife after a fight outside a restaurant. He stuffed her body in the passenger seat of the car, drove her to the edge of town, and dumped her body in the river.

At least that was the prosecution's theory. The problem was they found no evidence in McDermott's car. McDermott was still convicted because, with all the pretrial publicity, a witness came forward whose dashcam caught McDermott dumping what looked like a body over the guardrail.

Still, he might have gotten away with it because he cleaned the car so thoroughly. In most murder cases there are only two witnesses. One can't talk and the other doesn't have to. So, it boils down to science.

Martin had to get rid of whatever was inside his car.

He scanned the rows of cleaning solutions, cloths, and disposable scrub pads before realizing they all required payment in quarters. He stuck a twenty-dollar bill into the change machine, eighty quarters poured out, and his pockets were soon bulging.

After purchasing an assortment of everything and cradling the supplies in his arms, he rushed back to his car. Yanking the door open, he got inside and pulled it shut.

A knock at the window startled him.

Martin froze.

A woman stood outside the driver's side door. She cupped her hand to her forehead and tried to peer into the vehicle.

Martin opened the window a crack and said, "Yes? What do you want?"

"Do you have change for a ten? I only need a couple of dollars' worth of quarters."

Sweat rolled down the side of Martin's face. He dug into his pocket and pulled out a handful of quarters and held them through the gap in the window. "You can have it. I've got plenty," Martin said.

"Really? Thanks so much."

Powering up his window, Martin decided to start with cleaning the steering wheel first. He opened one of the pre-foamed scrub pads and began to run it along the curved surface. Within seconds the yellow foam turned pink and then nearly red. Bloody soap bubbles fell onto his pants and the floor.

Setting the scrubby down on the center console, he stared at the mess. Through the windshield, he noticed the woman he gave the quarters to speaking with a man. She pointed at Martin's car.

Martin jammed the car into drive and quickly pulled out of the bay. His hands were slick with what looked like bloodied soap. This will never work. Forensics is too good now.

Martin might not be able to clean it, but a professional could. Right next to the Audi dealership was a detail shop. But now he needed to clean the car up a little before anyone saw it. It can't be too obvious. A little work before the real work.

Martin made his way to the nearest convenience store. He pulled up to the gas pumps, shut the car off, and began using one of the wipes he'd purchased to get the blood and the soap off the steering wheel. Grabbing all the cleaning products up into his arms, he got out of the car and ditched them in the trash can.

As he reached for his door handle, he stared at his blood-covered hands.

He swore. What could he do to clean them now? He'd just thrown everything away. On either side of the trash can, a squeegee sat in a dark liquid. Using the container like a disgusting wash basin, he rinsed his hands and flicked them dry. He didn't dare wipe them on his pants until he remembered the blood from the soap bubbles had already dripped onto them. He'd have to wash his clothes as soon as he got home. Or throw them away. Or burn them.

He opened the door, started the car, and zipped out of the parking lot.

After a nerve-racking fifteen-minute drive across town, he pulled up to the detail shop. To his relief, the lobby was empty. He walked inside, running over his fabricated story in his mind one more time as he approached the bored-looking man sitting behind the counter.

"Good morning," Martin said. "I'm looking to have my car detailed. My son borrowed it and he and his buddies had a little accident, and I need to get it cleaned up."

"We don't do any bodywork," the man said matter-of-factly.

"Oh, not that kind of accident. They were playing pickleball or something, and one of them hit the other with a paddle. Bloody nose all over the seats. I tried to clean it up but it's a mess."

The man turned to the computer. He wiggled the mouse, the screen came to life, and he asked, "What did you say your name was?"

"John. John Stevens."

"We don't have an appointment for a John Stevens, and we're booked to the end of the week."

Martin's fingernails dug into the palms of his hands. He was about to let the guy have it when he noticed the poster on the back wall—an ad featuring Beau Landry, a local businessman, philanthropist, campaign donor, and longtime friend.

"I didn't know Beau owned this place. He's into darn near everything, isn't he?"

"Yep. Mr. Landry is the proprietor, but I run it."

"I'm a friend of Beau's."

"So is everyone else who comes in here, sir."

"Well, why don't you call Beau and see if he might be able to squeeze me in, or would you like me to?"

"I already am." The man held up his phone. "Sorry to bother you, Mr. Landry, but there's a John Stevens here who says he's a friend of yours."

Martin swore under his breath. "Please, give me the phone."

"Hold on, sir." The man looked uneasy but still handed the phone to Martin.

"Beau? Sorry about this." Martin walked over to the corner of the room. "It's Martin Weber," he whispered. "I didn't want Tiffany to know that I spilled something in her car, so I gave the guy a fake name."

"I understand completely, Judge," Beau said, his Cajun accent thick and charming. "Your secret is safe with me. Wives don't need to know everything." He chuckled. "I'll let them know to give it the works."

Martin exhaled. "Thank you, Beau. Really, thank you. I owe you one."

◆

A few minutes later, Martin paced the lobby waiting for the car to be detailed. He'd only solved one of his problems. What was he going to do about that recording Rachel alluded to?

He doubted she had it—like a lawyer bluffing during negotiations. But he couldn't take that chance.

He stopped and stared out the window to the parking lot.

The police would leave once they finished their job. Once they did, he'd slip inside, find the recording, and leave.

The door to the office opened and the clerk hurried out. "My apologies again for earlier, sir. Our deluxe deep clean will take several hours."

"I can't wait here that long."

"No need, sir." The attendant strode around the counter with a set of car keys in his hand. "Mr. Landry instructed me to give you access to our loaner vehicle parked in front. Use it as long as you need."

Martin glanced at the new BMW, which cost twice the price of his current car.

"Compliments of Mr. Landry."

Martin stared at the keys dangling from the man's hand. Judges are not technically supposed to take gifts over two hundred dollars, but this was a borrow, not a gift.

Martin took the keys.

It wasn't like he was making a deal with the devil, after all.

CHAPTER 11

"I'M A DETECTIVE. I don't need a babysitter," Travis says as he gets out of his car in front of the large yellow colonial set back from the curb.

After the way he handled the interview with Macon, I wasn't so sure. I let the comment slide.

"You're talented," I lied. "But talent and experience are different. You can't rush experience."

I smiled, trying to buck him up further. "Not only do I want to see you do well, I need to see you succeed. Making an arrest doesn't do us any good if it doesn't end in a conviction. Look, I was an awful prosecutor when I began, but I listened, and I learned from those who were better than I was. Good prosecutors are thieves. We steal from one another. I'm sure the same is true with law enforcement. Do your best, learn from your mistakes and mine too, and 'borrow' from the cops you respect the most."

"I appreciate that," Travis says.

"I've known Shauna Phillips for years. Since she may have been the last person to see Rachel alive, other than the killer, of course, we need to hear whatever she has to say. She's our best lead right now."

Her house is in the oldest part of town—Hampton Heights. It's a small house on a small lot but was constructed to last for centuries. There's a unique charm about these old brick homes on tree-lined streets with elegant, simple names like Maple and Mills, and the one Shauna lives on, Plume.

We're halfway up the brick walkway and I'm noticing a couple of loose bricks that could use some extra mortar, when the front door opens. Shauna is dressed in a long brown skirt, a light tan blouse, and dark brown sandals. She sees me, squares her shoulders, and lifts her chin. "I wasn't expecting you, Colm."

"I'm so sorry for your loss," I say as I climb the stairs and hug her. "Shauna, this is Detective Travis Hendrick. He's the lead investigator on Rachel's case."

"Thank you for seeing us, ma'am."

Shauna leads us inside. The living room is simple, with modern furniture. Travis and I sit on the couch while Shauna takes the recliner.

"Anything to drink?" Shauna asks.

Both Travis and I politely decline.

Travis leans forward. His voice is surprisingly empathetic. "I understand how upsetting this must be for you. Can we start with how you knew Rachel?"

"I was her mentor, I guess is what you would call it. I also considered her a friend. We met through the business fellowship I run. It's a nonprofit aimed to help start-ups and those struggling with small businesses."

"When did Rachel first come to the business fellowship?"

"About six months ago. She was so focused and driven. All she did was ask questions. She was street-smart and motivated—what she needed was a little encouragement and direction."

"You were listed in Rachel's appointment book two days ago."

I shift on the couch, pleasantly surprised that Travis's line of inquiry is spot-on.

"Rachel actually asked me to come over. She said she wanted to give me a cut and color on the house." Shauna dabs at her eyes with a tissue in her hand.

"Did you notice anyone or any other cars in the parking lot when you pulled in?"

"I was on my phone like usual. I parked facing the storage units. I don't remember seeing anyone."

"You didn't see any other car in the parking lot?"

Shauna shakes her head. "I'm sorry but I can't recall. I never in a million years thought it would matter."

"How was Rachel when you spoke with her?" Travis asks.

"Fine. Excited. Happy. She didn't seem to have a care in the world."

"Did Rachel ever speak about her ex-husband or anyone she was seeing?"

"No, Rachel was all business whenever we spoke. Plus, I wouldn't be the one to ask about romance advice," she added with a smile, "as you can tell by the fact that I live alone."

"Did she ever mention any friends or family, in a good or bad way? Anything that might help us?" Travis asks.

"She wasn't especially close with her father or mother. I don't think they approved of her first marriage. She insinuated that a couple of times. They were also relentless in their insistence that she go back to school. Rachel would say, 'There are two ways to major in business, and I'm doing it my way.' So, the only family she had was her son and of course she relied on her ex-mother-in-law for some childcare. I don't recall any specific friend or confidante. I'm so sorry. I wish I could be more helpful."

I place my hands on my knees, lean toward Shauna, and ask, "This will sound unusual, but it's important. Do you recall what kind of jewelry Rachel was wearing?"

Shauna angles her head and glances up at the ceiling. "Let me think for a second. She had small diamond stud earrings, another hoop earring in her left ear. I remember that because I complimented her on how pretty she looked. Her hair was behind her ears, so I could see the earrings pretty clearly. What else? Give me a second. A gold chain with a heart pendant, and a tennis bracelet that was quite stunning."

"In what way?" Travis asks.

"Well, I don't mean anything negative by this, but the bracelet seemed more expensive than something Rachel would buy for herself. It certainly wasn't something Macon would have, or could have, bought. It was a solid circle of diamonds encased in rose gold. Really gorgeous. Maybe it was costume jewelry. It's hard to know, but it sure looked real."

Travis continued asking questions for another fifteen minutes, but we didn't get much else. After wrapping up the interview, Shauna walked us to the door.

On the way back to our cars, Travis says, "With what she said about that tennis bracelet, maybe we need to reexamine the robbery theory."

"One thing Bones always says is never rule anything out. Just set it aside where you can pick it up again if the facts change."

As I get into my car, I've got to agree with Travis. He did a good job in this last interview but, the deeper we get into this case, the more I wish Bones was the one doing it with me. Something feels wrong—like I'm looking into what should be the shallow end of the pool, but I still can't see the bottom.

CHAPTER 12

"WHAT IF HE'S HOME?" Knox asked as he turned onto Colm's street.

"He isn't." JD pointed at the empty driveway. "Calm down. Everything is delivered to people's homes now. No one will suspect a thing."

"I don't like getting this close. Someone could see our faces."

"Pull your hat down." JD and Knox both tugged the rims of their baseball caps lower.

Knox parked the van alongside the sidewalk so as to not block traffic, even though there was next to none in this tranquil neighborhood at this hour. "I still don't like it."

"We don't have a choice. The video feed died again. I'll be right back." JD got out of the van carrying a cardboard box.

Strolling up the Tanner's driveway, JD cut across the backyard to Colm's. A large pine tree with an old birdhouse screwed into the bark provided a perfect view of the rear of Colm's house.

JD pulled on a pair of latex gloves, opened the birdhouse, and removed the concealed trail camera. It took less than a minute to switch the batteries out.

After checking to ensure the camera was working, JD hurried across the yard to Colm's porch. Reaching beneath, JD's fingers closed around the box of the hide-a-key and pulled it out.

JD climbed the steps, unlocked the back door, and slipped inside.

The house was quiet and still. JD crept through the kitchen and into the hallway. The thin carpet muffled any footsteps on the way to the bedroom.

The door creaked as it opened. A light layer of dust covered everything. Had Colm ever come back into the room?

JD smiled and crossed to the nightstand. The holster for the .38 was still there, but the pistol itself was back in the cabin. JD placed the box of ammunition in the drawer and shut it.

After backing out of the room and down the hallway, JD stopped in the kitchen. A picture of Colm with his wife and daughter was held in place by a heart magnet. Next to it was a photograph of Colm and Bones at the Glendale Shoals waterfall. JD took the pictures and snuck out the back door.

CHAPTER 13

ANOTHER TRIP TO THE crime scene can't hurt, plus, it will give me time to think. Route 29 is the only road leading that way. Whoever killed Rachel would have had to take it, from either the east, which I had already driven the night before, or the west. There is an eeriness knowing you are driving the same road as a killer. But nearly every road in this town reminds me of some path taken at some point, for some reason, by some killer.

The best homicide prosecutors try to feel like a victim and think like a killer. The dualism wrecks you. You aren't getting inside a killer's head so much as they are taking up residence in yours.

Someone I love warned me to get out before it's too late. But it's already too late.

Even this peaceful drive is now consumed with wondering if Rachel's murder was premeditated or a crime of passion. The weapon tells you a lot. Guns are for killing at a distance. Impersonal. Strangulation, well, the human hand has so many nerve endings, so much feel, you would literally feel the life leave, and face-to-face, you would see the eyes go dormant.

Knives, scissors, screwdrivers, and sharp objects are more personal than strangulation. What could possess someone to lift a sharp object and plunge it into a person even once, let alone time after time after time? Blood splattering and plaintive cries for help. I shake my head involuntarily, trying to get the thought of her last words out of my mind. *Why are you doing this? Please stop. I won't tell anyone. Let me live.*

Mercifully, my thoughts are interrupted as I pass an out-of-business gas station and see the storage sign ahead. I slow down and pull into the parking lot, where Travis is speaking with another deputy.

I park beside his unmarked Charger and meet him at the front door.

"You drive too slow," Travis says, glancing back over his shoulder. "Tom had another kid, and I couldn't handle another baby picture."

"Technically, Travis, Tom didn't have the kid; his wife did. But I get your point. Have the techs finished yet?"

"Almost." Travis unlocks the door and ducks under the crime scene tape.

I follow him inside as the lights and mirrors conspire to bring the room back in a full blaze of detail. At some point, a jury might be standing right here. They will want to know why. Actually, they will want to know it all. Who, where, and why? How did it begin? Was it an innocuous meeting gone tragically wrong? Was it a botched robbery? Was it spontaneous or planned? It's not healthy to dwell on this too long, but it's also the only way to convince people who haven't dwelled on it at all.

"We solved one mystery." Travis points at the salon chair covered in plastic. "The new chair was for a new hire."

I glance at the precise spot where the killing took place. Her body is gone but her blood remains. Her last moment of life reduced to a mere stain on the floor. The evidence has long since been bagged, removed, and sent for analysis and processing. The appointment book is gone as well. Fine dust particles from the fingerprinting powder are everywhere.

"Besides the bracelet, nothing else missing—not that we can identify," Travis says. "She had a small jewelry box in the bedroom, but only her prints were on it, and it was closed. A hundred and twelve dollars was still in the cash register. There was also a photograph on the nightstand next to her bed." He holds up his phone and shows me the picture he took. "Look at her wrist."

In the photo, Rachel is holding her son's arm as he waves at the camera. A beautiful diamond and gold tennis bracelet dangles from her wrist.

"That fits the description Shauna gave. Good work, Travis."

"Thank you."

I walk over to the dried pool of blood. Blond hairs cover the floor and stick out of the blood in clumps. My mind moves to the trial and how little is ever presented about the nature of the character of the victim. Legally speaking, I guess I get it. It's against the law to murder a bad person just as much as it is murdering a good one. But still, I can't help but wonder what Rachel was like? What did she dream of? The jury won't hear any of that, but they will wonder. And of course, what was her last thought when she knew life was ending? That one I can probably answer: her son.

From the immaculate way Rachel organized her shop with not a dust bunny in sight, she would have been mortified by the powder and hair strewn across her establishment. My eyes follow the trail of dried blood leading to the back door.

"Looks like the killer headed straight out the back and didn't go into any other room," Travis says. "We searched the office and bedroom, but they don't look disturbed."

"Did the techs photograph, video, and document everything, and I do mean everything?"

"Yeah."

"Good, juries aren't only interested in what you did find. They'll be reminded by defense counsel of what we didn't find and, more importantly, what we didn't even bother to look for. Now is the time to scour this crime scene for every conceivable piece of evidence."

"You made your point, Colm."

"It's not my point, it's *the* point. You checked yourself? You watched the video from the crime scene techs yourself? We can't afford another Macon Breathalyzer mistake."

The muscles in Travis's jaw flexed, and he scowled. "I'll make sure. I haven't had a chance to check behind everyone else yet, Colm. I've been too busy doing my own job."

Clearly, he is agitated at me, which is good. I'll press the gas pedal a little more to make sure his anger turns into work. "There is no 'my job' or 'their job' at trial, Travis. The government speaks with one voice—and I'm going to be the person having to explain it all to the jury. Do the little things now and there's less to explain away later."

"I get it, I get it, I will triple check." He looks away and points to the back room. "We may have caught a break. Forensics found a handful of bloody, wadded-up tissues partially under the shelves in the back room near the door. I already sent it for DNA testing."

"Good. In stabbings, the knife frequently slips, and the killer cuts their own hand, but we need to make sure if they're connected to her murder at all. Hopefully, the DNA will match hers or the killer's."

Travis carefully walks to the side of the bloody shoeprint trail. "We did get a match on the shoes. They're men's Doc Martens, size twelve." He stops and shines his flashlight on one print in particular. "Scott, the camera guy yesterday, said that the missing part of the print is likely from a cut in the tread or a rock stuck in there. If we can find the shoes, there's a decent chance we can get a definitive match."

Small pieces of the puzzle are beginning to click.

"Let's talk about next steps," I say. "There's a security camera facing the street at the storage place across the road. Interview the workers, the owners, anyone who may have been there. Who knows, maybe for once a surveillance camera was actually working. And we'll need to finish the evidence sweep. Head east and west down both sides of road and search at least ten yards on either side, in case the killer tossed the murder weapon or any other evidence out of the vehicle. There's a closed gas station, neighbors to be interviewed, and—"

"Hold on." Travis is frantically typing into his phone. "I know all this. I want to cross-check what you're saying in case I miss anything."

I run my hand through my hair. This stuff is obvious. I shouldn't have to tell him, and he shouldn't need to take notes.

"Okay. Thanks." Travis smiles. "I appreciate it. How far on either side do you think we should search the road."

"Ten yards on either side and a mile in both directions."

"That's what I was thinking." Travis shoves his phone in his pocket. "I just wanted to make sure we're on the same page."

Truth is, I'm not even sure we are in the same book. Most of this is elementary. Experienced homicide detectives don't need to be told. Someone other than me needs to help Travis. Someone from the Sheriff's Department with real experience. Good facts make good lawyers. Good investigators find good facts. Forty-eight hours is the magic window. Most murders are solved within that window. After that, the odds go down dramatically.

We're approaching the witching hour, and I'm afraid my lead detective can't tell time.

CHAPTER 14

TRAVIS LEFT HIS CAR in the salon parking lot and crossed the street to the Hill Brothers Self Storage Center. A chain-link fence topped with barbed wire rings the property. Inside were several single-story cement buildings with orange roll-up doors. The building closest to him was different, however. There was a single window with the blinds drawn and a door with the word OFFICE printed in faded white. There was a light on inside.

Travis stopped at the front gate. A security camera was mounted on the corner of the closest building and aimed at the entrance. From the angle of the lens, he hoped it recorded the salon, too.

A keypad stood next to the driveway along with a sign that read, CALL FOR AN APPOINTMENT, followed by a phone number.

Travis dialed the number as he walked along the fence toward the office. The call went straight to voicemail, so he cupped his hand to his mouth and shouted, "Hello! Anyone here!"

A car sped past on the street behind him.

"Sheriff's Department!" he yelled as loudly as he could. "Anyone in there?"

The sound of the car's engine faded in the distance.

Travis walked back and double-checked the number on the sign. He crossed over and grabbed the roll-away gate. It slid a foot and a half to the side and stopped.

Pushing it harder, he slipped through. He dialed the number yet again as he headed to the office. Gravel crunched beneath his feet. When he reached the door, he heard the phone inside ringing.

"Hey, this is Detective Travis Hendricks with . . ." Travis's voice trailed off when he looked to the end of the building.

A squat pit bull stared at him. Its ears flattened on top of its head.

"Sit? Sit!" Travis glanced back at the gate. It was over twenty yards away. There was no way he'd outrun that dog.

The dog barked and sprinted forward. Its paws raked the ground, sending gravel flying in the air behind it. Spit flew from its jaws, and its eyes widened at the thrill of the chase.

Travis grabbed the doorknob, turned, and pushed. To his surprise and utter relief, it opened. Falling inside, he spun around and slammed the door shut.

Outside, the dog barked ferociously, its claws scraping off the metal door.

Travis caught his breath and heard one of the more ominous sounds in life. The sound of a shotgun shell being chambered.

"Put your hands up nice or I'm gonna put a hole the size of a pumpkin in your belly."

"I'm the sheriff . . . with the sheriff. I'm a deputy," Travis stammered as he raised his arms.

"That's a funny sheriff's uniform you're wearing. Turn around nice and slow, boy."

"I'm a detective." Travis kept his arms up as he turned.

An older man with long, white hair and thick glasses held a Mossberg 590A1 pump action shotgun in his shaking hands.

Travis swallowed. "You can see my badge on my belt. My name is Travis Hendrick. There's a big dog outside."

The man lowered the gun. "I'm Ethan Hill. Don't worry none about Cletus. He wouldn't hurt a squirrel. He likes company. I'm guessing this is about whatever's going on next door?"

"Yes sir, it is." Travis lowered his arms. "I noticed the security camera and was hoping to get a copy of the footage."

Ethan's wrinkles deepened. "What happened over there?"

Travis took a deep breath. "There was a murder."

"A murder?" Ethan asked, as he moved toward the desk and sat down. He placed the shotgun against the wall. "Rachel?"

"Yes sir, I'm sorry to be the one to tell you."

"Oh my, she cut my hair. What happened? Was it a robbery or something?"

"We're looking into everything, sir. Did you happen to be out here two days ago, late afternoon to evening?"

"No. I'm getting over a stomach bug. What the hell happened?"

"I can't get into the details. I'm sure you understand, but we would welcome anything you can remember, even if it seems insignificant."

"I'm sorta in shock right now, to be honest. She was such a sweet girl. Can't say much good about her husband, but I assume you already know that."

"What makes you say her husband wasn't much good?"

"They used to fight a lot. You'd hear him all the way over here. Big mouth. Liked to drink and swear. She was tiny, and he was a big slob. I don't know what she ever saw in him."

"Have you seen him around much lately?" Travis took out his phone and took notes.

"Not really, just dropping some kid off. I guess he's theirs. It breaks my heart to think that little boy lost his momma."

Travis handed Ethan his card. "How can I get a copy of that surveillance video?"

"My nephew handles that. Bright kid. I'll give him a call and one of us will bring it by the Sheriff's Department."

"I'd appreciate that, sir."

After Ethan put Cletus on a leash, he showed Travis to the gate.

Travis got into his car and headed down Route 29, stopping at every house along the way. The story at each home was the same—no one saw anything, no one heard anything—except rumors and gossip. No one had any surveillance cameras, security cameras, or doorbell cameras.

Travis pulled into the closed gas station and stopped in front of the building. Besides some graffiti, the building was cleared out but looked secure. A green dumpster sat next to the corner of the building, and an air pump, which was missing its hose. *People will steal near anything,* he thought.

Travis glanced inside the dumpster and flinched. It was filled with old trash. All of it appeared moldy, like it had been there for more than a little while, but as nasty as it was, he'd still have to search through it—piece by piece. He took out his phone and texted Jimmy, the patrol sergeant on duty:

SEND A COUPLE OF DEPUTIES TO THE GAS STATION
ON 29 EAST OF THE SALON. GOING THROUGH A
DUMPSTER. BRING SOME DISPOSABLE GEAR.

Next to the gas pumps were two trash cans. He crossed over and peered into the closest trash can. It was empty, but the one on the opposite island had a crumbled beer case poking out the top. The cardboard wasn't soggy, so it had to have been discarded not too long ago.

He lifted it out of the trash can, his mouth dropped open, and his heart skipped a beat. Partially visible beneath a fast-food bag was a blue vinyl glove crusted with what appeared to be dried blood.

His hands shook as he snapped pictures. As he did, something wasn't right. He counted the fingers again and stopped.

"How can it be a six-fingered glove?" he muttered.

Travis leaned down and realized there were two gloves stuck together. Beneath them, he noticed the gleam of metal.

He took several more pictures and called the sheriff to relay the news.

"Listen, Travis, I need you to contact the crime scene boys and get every last thing in that trash can analyzed. And get some dogs out there to see if they can pick up the scent of anything else that might have been thrown out or away. Is there a forensics team still at the salon?"

"I think so."

He stared back into the trash can. Latex gloves do conceal fingerprints, but the thing about the latex itself is that it often holds the DNA of whoever wore them.

"Get them there immediately and don't touch a thing."

Travis hung up. He was expecting a little more praise and excitement from his boss, but even a tepid response did nothing to dull his excitement. He may well have found the murder weapon and bloody gloves.

CHAPTER 15

I'M BREATHING HEAVILY AS I jog down Elm Street. Running this late at night, I should wear something reflective, but I'm in a black T-shirt and stick to the subdivisions surrounding my own. I grew up in this neighborhood—a few streets over from where I now live. I could probably run these sidewalks and streets with my eyes closed.

Running started as a friend when I was young and has now become my therapist. Running is a lot easier these days than closing my eyes. Lying in bed, staring at the ceiling is useless, but sleep is worse sometimes. That's when the nightmares come. Or worse yet, dreams about what used to be, and when you wake up, the real nightmare is being awake.

When I was a kid, I feared that ghosts were in the closet or under my bed. Now they have moved inside my head. Whether it's work or loss, the back side of my eyelids are a rolling movie screen. And I am powerless to turn off the projector. Running and exercise are temporary distractions. Alcohol helps, but you can't stay drunk all the time. You can try, and I have, but I have to work—at least a little while longer. I've thought about taking Mae up on her offer for a prescription, but the best medicine would be to move; move away from the memories and hope they stay put.

I reach the end of my street and sprint. My legs are churning, and my lungs are burning, and I don't slow until I reach my yard. I double over with my hands on my knees as I try to breathe. Sweat drips off my hair and onto the tall grass that's long overdue for a cut. I used to be so conscientious about how our yard looked. Now, I don't care.

I lift my gaze to the window. The wind brushes the branches of the oak tree behind me, making the shadows it casts on the window move. For a second, I think someone's inside. Hope might be the most dangerous drug of all. For someone who has dedicated his professional life to following facts, why do I still succumb so easily to the false illusion of hope?

It's not her. It's never going to be her.

I head for the garage. The previous owner was going to make it a woodshop and add a loft, but I installed climbing holds around the top instead. After chalking up my hands, I'm dangling by my fingertips as I make my way around the room, trying to keep my feet off the floor.

One lap turns into three, and then four. They say grip strength is an indicator of how long you'll live. I don't care about that anymore. I drop to the ground and lean against the wall.

Maybe that will do it. Maybe that tired me out enough to rest a little. I make my way around the dusty car parked in the middle and bump into a case of beer I bought for a Fourth of July party that never happened.

After a shower, I mix a protein shake with water, since the milk went bad. Giving up manifests itself in so many different ways. Overworking. Not caring about what used to be considered essential, like food and fresh milk. Apathy is just a slow, socially acceptable form of suicide.

I head to my makeshift office on the first floor. Besides the desk, an office chair, and the recliner I dragged in there, the room is empty. It's the only room in the house that isn't full of what used to be memories but now seem more like ghosts. Memories can't be erased but the things that trigger them can be moved, so I did. I moved everything into the guest bedroom. All the photographs, knickknacks, plants—everything.

The other rooms haven't been touched, but I need a place to live, to work, and occasionally sleep. The living room wasn't an option for my office because we used to lie there and watch TV. The kitchen was Ally's favorite room in the house. I can still picture her standing there smiling, making us a meal. Forget the bedroom. I haven't even opened the door since, well, since the last time I opened the door and life as it was just stopped. And I can't even get near Jaci's nursery.

What I really need to do is move, but I can't bring myself to do that. It feels disrespectful.

I power up my laptop and stare out the window to my backyard. I'm glad it's night or I'd have to pull the blinds closed. If it weren't dark, I'd see her sitting on the ground in the garden, smiling as she planted what she called "beauties" and pulled what she called the "uglies."

It's all weeds now.

I open the desk drawer and take out the bottle of Johnnie Walker Black Label. I pour a glass, down it in a shot, and start working on my computer.

The computer beeps with a message and link from Travis. The heat from the whiskey fuels my excitement as I read about what Travis has found. Maybe the lecture helped. He did something right. Gloves, possible murder weapon, and the surveillance video from the storage facility across the street. I pull the video up and click Play.

The camera is focused on the gate, but you can see the left half of the salon and the front door. My hope takes a hit when I realize what poor quality the picture is. It is so distant and grainy, I can't even read any of the letters on the CUTZ FOR ALL sign. On top of that, the camera is motion-activated, and the range that sets it off is limited to a car passing by the gate closest to the edge of the road.

I pour another glass and watch a few passing cars to make certain, but it's true. If a car is driving on the side of the road next to the salon, it won't set off the camera, but if it is on the storage facility side it will. Once the camera turns on, it records for five minutes and automatically shuts off.

I rewind to the beginning of the day. I grab my notebook and start writing down time stamps and vehicle descriptions. As we reach the time of Shauna's appointment, a motorcycle triggers the camera. A red sedan that matches Shauna's car is parked facing the storage unit. Behind it, a silver two-door sedan is there. The sedan drives off and a minute later, Shauna gets out of her car.

I rewind and watch the tape again, but it doesn't record the person getting into the silver car. The windows are tinted.

Two and a half hours later, a sheriff's cruiser passes by, triggering the camera. The parking lot to the salon is empty, but the lights are on. Headlights flash behind the trailer, but the house blocks the view of the car.

I note the time, 5:34 p.m.

The headlights turn back on. The time stamp continues to count up, telling me that the camera is still recording, but the car behind the salon doesn't move.

"Come on. Drive. Drive."

The recording stops.

I swear and take a sip of my whiskey. The camera starts recording again at 5:50.

A white van triggered the camera. The headlights glow from behind the building, but I still can't see the car. Suddenly, the car appears from behind the house. It's moving so fast it's a blur. The only details I can make out are that it's a silver two-door car.

The van's brake lights blaze an angry red as it skids to a stop. The logo on the side of the van is blurry but familiar. I pause the video and rack my brain for where I've seen that logo before.

I note the time and switch over to my email. I attach the video link and password and send it to the best digital forensic examiner I know— Jen Cramer. If anyone can clean up that logo so we can read it, she can.

Travis nailed this one. I'll give him a word of encouragement tomorrow. This is the best lead yet.

I power the recliner all the way back and yawn. Outside, the moon peaks through the clouds. Something gleams on the side of the pine tree at the edge of the backyard. I start to sit up until I notice the old birdhouse. Ally had put it up after a blue jay kept trying to make a nest in the umbrella out in the patio. The moon was probably shining off a hinge or something.

It was nothing to worry about.

CHAPTER 16

JD STARED DOWN AT the photograph of Colm and Bones while the video feed from the trail cam outside Colm's house played on the computer monitor. Colm sat in his home office recliner and worked on his laptop.

"You should see his house," JD said. "He hasn't changed anything since it happened. Except for clearing out his office, that is."

"Why do we have to wait so long? Every day we do is another day Larry rots in jail."

"If we listened to you, we'd all be dead trying to bust Larry out. I told you this is going to take time. Good things do. Besides, Truesdale needs to suffer. Not just die, but suffer."

Knox stomped over and flopped on the couch. "There was nothing on the police scanners about our lawyer. I don't think they found him yet."

JD leaned back in the chair. "That's fine. I wanted Frank to ripen a little first. I told you I'll handle that part, too."

"What am I supposed to do, just wait?"

"Yes." JD picked up the photograph of Colm and Bones. "But don't worry. Your part is coming. Be patient."

Knox scowled.

JD picked up the new deck of playing cards and fanned them out on the table until locating the King of Hearts. Tearing the card in two, JD placed them in an envelope and addressed it to Colm Truesdale.

Knox sat up. "Are you going somewhere?"

JD smiled. "I need to mail a letter."

CHAPTER 17

THERE'S NOTHING IN THE house to eat, and even though there are a hundred places between my home and Gowensville, I head toward The Junction for breakfast as the sun is starting to rise. I went years and years without even thinking of the place, and here I am going twice in one week.

I seat myself in the same booth Bones and I shared.

The waitress, Belle, is standing three booths down and speaking with a middle-aged couple. The woman shifts uncomfortably in her chair and eyes the door. The man points at his eggs, theatrically turns his hands palms up, and shrugs. Even without hearing what he's saying, I can read the body language. He isn't happy and he's taking it out on the closest person to him. That is something I will never understand. Why do people feel entitled to berate or belittle people in certain lines of work, whether it be restaurants, airline personnel, or even clerks at the courthouse? Some people feel it's okay to try to make others feel small.

It bothers me, but it doesn't faze Belle. She listens patiently and politely nods. Whatever she says must have worked because the wife relaxes, and the man finally calms down.

Belle heads my way. "It's so nice to see you here again. Where's your friend Bones?"

"You have a good memory. I'll tell him you asked about him."

"What can I get you this morning?"

"Well, I can assure you it will be easier than whatever that couple over there was having," pointing in the direction of the unhappy duo.

"Oh, that was nothing. His eggs were a little too scrambled for him, so I gave him the pancakes for free."

"How can scrambled eggs be too scrambled?" I ask.

"Well, you know, sometimes folks are just having a bad day. It's okay. Everybody's happy now. By the way, how are you? Forgive me for saying, but you look tired."

That catches me off guard. I find myself equal parts sorry she noticed and grateful she cares. I want to tell her the truth and say, "No, Belle, I'm not sleeping at all. I'm working on a horrible murder case," but why would I ruin her day by talking about murder? "I'm great." I work up a smile. "I'm pretty boring and predictable, so I'll go with the same thing as last time. Egg omelet, no cheese, please."

"With avocado? We got some in."

"You're kidding? You did? That's a surprise, but a nice one. Yes, that would be wonderful." I don't know why I get so happy about avocado, but I do.

"Nothing else? No bacon?"

"You do have a good memory. I wish you were working on some of the cases assigned to me."

"You're a lawyer, right?"

"I'm a prosecutor. I work out of the courthouse. Enough about me. Tell me where you are in life."

"It's neither hard nor terribly exciting, I'm afraid. I work here, of course, and am finishing up at Greenville Tech."

"What are you studying?"

"Belle?" An older man in the corner raises his coffee cup and waves her over.

She blushes. "I lost track of what I was supposed to be doing. I'll get your order placed and out as soon as I can." She hurries over to the customer. "Sorry, Mr. Grant. Here you go."

Twenty minutes later, I shovel the last bite of avocado into my mouth.

Belle drops the bill off and says, "It was nice seeing you again. I'm afraid I'm late to take my morning break, so you'll probably be gone by the time I get back. Have a great day at the courthouse."

"I sure will, and you do the same." I'm savoring my last half cup of coffee when someone shouts my name.

"Hey, Truesdale!" Angus Greer, Macon's brother, is standing in the doorway flanked by two heavyset men. Angus is tall, wide, and weighs close to three hundred pounds. The men with him place a hand on each arm, but Angus shrugs them off and stomps over. "You've got some nerve, boy."

I slide out of the booth and stand up. "This isn't the time or the place, Angus. If you want to have a conversation with me, come to the courthouse."

"I'll do what I please, when I want and where I want. My brother is in jail because of you. The only thing he did wrong was not hit you hard enough." Angus's hand clenches into a fist.

"Your brother didn't need my help to go to jail. He's always been good at that."

"That's a load of crap." Angus shoves the man trying to hold him back. "You turn around and arrest a guy when he just lost the love of his life?"

"I'm a prosecutor, not a cop. I can't arrest anyone, and I didn't arrest your brother."

"You're a hypocrite and a callous bastard."

"Angus, if you want to have a civil conversation about what happened and why, we can. If you want to make a scene, you will be riding in the back of a squad car in less than fifteen minutes, and you'll be sitting in the cell next to your brother. It's your choice."

"Okay, Mr. Fancy DA. What do you think I don't know?"

"Macon was drunk and hit me, which means you don't pass Go. You don't collect two hundred dollars. You go straight to jail. I'm a little more sympathetic than you think. I'm not pressing charges on Macon. I understand what he's going through—better than you do. So, get your facts straight before you come screaming in a restaurant and make a fool out of yourself."

Angus steps back speechless. I wait for him to say more but he doesn't. He turns on his heels and stomps out of the diner.

By this point everyone is looking at me, so it's time to head on. I leave the money for the meal and a tip on the table and glance around for Belle. She must be on her break. I'm glad she missed the drama.

I'm heading to my car when I notice Belle, bundled up in a coat, sitting at a picnic table off to the side of the restaurant with a book in her hands.

She glances up and waves.

Curiosity gets the better of me, and I head over to see what she's reading. "We haven't formally met. I'm Colm Truesdale."

"Belle Atkins."

"What are you reading?"

She covers it up quickly and says, "Oh, it's nothing."

"I'll have you know I am a highly trained investigator, and I'm pretty sure I saw a book of some sort."

She laughs again and holds up *The Scarlet Letter* by Nathaniel Hawthorne. "I'm a business major, so this assignment is a bit of a stretch, but it's quieter out here."

"What brought you to The Junction?" I ask.

For the next fifteen minutes, Belle gives me the thirty-thousand-foot overview of the last couple of years of her life. "I grew up in Greenville. I finished high school and always wanted to go to college, but ... well ... my parents are both disabled so I wanted to stay close. It's the best of all worlds. I get to go to college—the first one in my family actually. It's a blessing really."

"How much longer do you have before you finish your degree?"

Belle's phone beeps. "Shoot. My break's over." She stands and so do I. "Thank you for listening and for talking to me. You must have more important things to do than talk to some waitress at a diner."

"Actually, I don't. This has been the best part of my day so far."

Belle laughs. "Well, it's early. Hopefully your day improves. But anytime you want to talk, you know where to find me." She waves and walks toward the diner.

My phone buzzes with a text from Bones.

GOT AN ANGLE ON SIMONE CASE 2 CHECK. BRINGING TRAVIS W/ ME. K?

I text back, "Sure. Thanks. Want me to ride shotgun?"

NAH. IT'LL BE A LEARNING EXPERIENCE FOR HIM.

I laugh. I've got a feeling that Travis has no idea what he's in for.

CHAPTER 18

TRAVIS PULLED INTO THE parking lot, eager to give his report to the sheriff. This was a huge day for him. This should quiet all the whispers about his mom and the sheriff and how he got the promotion. He's on the verge of solving his first homicide, and he did it by old-fashioned leg work. And then he noticed Captain Rick Denton leaning against that banged-up Charger he was so fond of.

Denton took a long drag off his cigarette and let the smoke slowly curl out of his mouth, only to be swept away by the chill fall breeze. With an angle of his head, Denton summoned him over.

"Morning, Captain," Travis said, stopping a few feet away.

"I've got a lead I want you to run down." Denton let the cigarette dangle from his mouth as he took a folded-up paper out of his pocket.

"You'll need to give that to someone else, sir. I'm meeting with the sheriff to let him know I've almost solved the beauty salon case."

Denton slowly raised his gaze until his brown eyes locked with Travis's. The older detective's mouth pressed into a thin line and his forehead showed every hard-earned crease. "First off, you haven't *solved* anything, Travis, unless there was an arrest made overnight and I somehow missed it at roll call this morning. You had a good day, but to really solve a case you need a series of good days, and then you need a conviction. Don't forget, I pass out assignments. That's what 'Captain' means. Lastly, it's not the 'beauty salon' case. The salon wasn't murdered. Rachel Simone was." Denton handed the folded piece of paper to Travis.

Travis squinted his eyes to read the tiny print on Clint Fisher's rap sheet. It was a long read. Clint had been arrested multiple times for breaking and entering, theft, larceny, robbery, aggravated assault in the first degree, and a host of other charges. At the bottom it read PAGE 1 OF 9.

"There's a lot of pages from the report missing," Travis said.

"I didn't feel like carrying a novel in my pocket. It's more of the same. Fisher's been in and out of the system since he was fourteen. He's the poster child for why people hate the criminal justice system. Did you see where he was arrested for stabbing a woman?"

Travis rescans the page. "That charge was dropped."

"Clint cut a plea deal. The stabbing occurred during a break-in. You'll notice Fisher's last known address?"

"It's just down the road from the beauty salon; I mean from where Rachel was killed. Did you hear I may have found the murder weapon? And a pair of bloody gloves."

Denton took another drag and nodded. "You looked in a trash can, Travis. I think the better question might be why it wasn't done the night of the murder during the neighborhood canvas? You'll have to forgive me if I don't get too excited when a cop does exactly what he's supposed to do, but he's a day late."

"Late is better than never . . ." Travis wanted to reel the words back in as soon as they left his mouth.

"Homicide is the big leagues. You screw this up, a killer walks and the victim's family lives out their days with no justice. You got any idea what that feels like?"

Travis stared down at the paper. "I'll check this out."

"One more thing, Travis. Malcolm Truesdale is not just a personal friend. He's the closest thing I've ever had to a brother. He's our best. Watch his back. We clear?"

Travis eyed Denton. "You don't have to worry."

Denton dropped his cigarette and ground it. "Good. Get in."

"What?" Travis cocked an eyebrow. "I was going to go speak with the sheriff."

"Why? So he can give you a pat on the head?"

Travis blinked rapidly. "No. I want to give him a progress report."

"Get in the car. You can call him from the road, if you want, but I got a tip that Clint is home, and I don't feel like grabbing a uniform for backup." The car rocked as the large man sat down.

Travis glanced at the report in his hands and frowned. He wanted to prove to the sheriff that he was up to the job. Bringing in a suspect might be a great way of doing that, too. Travis hurried around the car and got in.

"Are you wearing a vest?" Denton asked as he started the engine.

"No. Do you think I need one?"

Denton tapped his chest, and his knuckles thumped off the Kevlar plate. "I always wear one."

"Really. Why?"

"People have a tendency to shoot at me." Denton grinned as he sped out of the parking lot.

CHAPTER 19

I SET MY NOTEBOOK AND case file on my desk as someone knocks on my office door.

A woman in her mid-twenties holding a tablet marches in, stops at the corner of my desk, and stands at military attention. Her brown hair is pulled back in a tight bun, and her serious facial expression is only off-set by glasses that make her eyes appear larger than they are. Even with heels, she is barely five feet tall, but I've seen flagpoles less rigid than her spine. Her presence is commanding, even if diminutive.

"Good morning, sir. My name is Irene Scruggs. I'm your new assistant. I emailed your itinerary for the day, but you haven't responded yet, so I wanted to see if there was some kind of issue."

I clear my throat and say, "I haven't had a chance to check my emails yet this morning, Irene."

"Yes, sir, but I sent it yesterday at ten forty-four a.m. Have you checked your spam folder?"

Did I join the Marines in my sleep, or did I get a new boss while I was out in the field?

"I'm pretty sure I just haven't seen it yet. I'll log in here in a second and check. Thank you for your attention to detail."

"Certainly." Irene remains at attention and begins to read the afore-mentioned email to me from her tablet. "Dear Mr. Truesdale, please find your schedule listed below. Ten a.m. interviews with potential Victim Advocate candidates. We had several qualified applicants, and their résumés are attached, listed as a VA attachment."

As she continues to speak, I open her email on my monitor. She has broken down my entire day into color-coded time chunks.

"At one p.m., assuming a noon lunch break, you are to review potential candidates to round out your investigative and paralegal team. And—"

"Wait, hang on a second. Did you serve in the military?"

She looks vexed and annoyed at both the interruption and the question. "I never had the privilege of serving, sir, but my father is a Marine. We only have ten minutes before your appointment with District Attorney Porter. May I continue?"

"Hang on, Irene. I have a meeting with Cindy this morning? As in ten minutes from now?"

"Yes, sir. I was getting to that, sir."

"That might have been the best place to start."

"Yes, sir."

"Hold whatever next thought you have and please call me Colm."

"Yes, sir." She catches herself and contorts her face into a failed smile, clearly not liking the informality that most of the rest of the world would treasure. "How do you like your coffee, Colm?" She sounds like a robot working as a barista.

"You don't have to make my coffee. You're going to be busy enough with more important things."

"Thank you." Irene smiles. I'm stunned. I had not seen her teeth to that point, but at least we are making a little progress.

"Great job with the schedule. Call me ten minutes from now. Okay?"

Irene looks confused but agrees.

I use the rear stairwell. There's something about this meeting that bothers me. Cindy and I have been friends for ages. I even golf a few times a year with her husband, Dominic. Then it hits me. So why hasn't Cindy stopped in to say hello? Is it because I've been relegated to the basement, or is there another shoe waiting to drop?

I reach the top floor, head down the hall, and walk into Cindy's waiting room.

"Colm!" Amanda Beauchamp rises from behind her desk and hurries over. The sweet woman is the epitome of Southern grace. "It's so good to see you." She wraps her arms around me and hugs me like a long-lost brother. "Oh, my goodness. You've gotten so thin. Are you eating? Your clothes are two sizes too big for you!"

"It's good to see you, too." I smile. We both know why I have lost weight, but neither one of us wants to talk about that. There's nothing really to say.

She means well. She cares. I love her for that. But I don't want pity. I think briefly about when my mom dragged me to Sunday School, and the story of Job. The people who meant the most to him never said a word. Presence is enough. Sympathy or empathy is enough. People do not like silence, which is why so many people wage war against it. But silence is actually the mark of a close relationship. It is a sign that you can communicate without words. That is especially good when there are no words to say.

"I am happy to cook something for you, Colm."

Cindy's office door opens. "Colm." Cindy glances at her watch and smiles. "Right on time."

I thank Amanda for the offer, follow Cindy into her office, and shut the door behind me.

Cindy's office is spacious, with high ceilings and large windows that let in natural light. Such are the benefits of being the boss. It's still not worth it. Having to run for office, fielding calls from cops, victims, family members of defendants, judges, and the media. I note the irony that the top prosecutor in any jurisdiction never actually has the time to prosecute any cases. He or she is really just an administrator with a law degree.

The far wall is lined with wooden shelves filled with certificates and framed awards. The main accomplishment of an elected DA is getting elected, but people like to give plaques. At the center of the room sits an enormous mahogany desk that Cindy crosses behind.

I sit in a comfortable, cushioned chair facing her.

"Welcome back, Colm."

"I'm afraid I'm a little unprepared to give you an update on the Simone case."

Cindy waves a dismissive hand. "My wanting to see you wasn't about that. I wanted to let you know that I'm here for you. As a boss and a friend. We all are, in whatever way you need. I've met with HR and their counseling program is—"

"I'm good, Cindy. I am," I say, staring her squarely in the eye. "Thank you for everything; for the time, for the space, for the concern. I mean it. You have been great. But I'm fine."

"Well, if you need it, the resources are there for you." Cindy glances at the computer monitor on her desk. "I hope Irene is going to work out for you. I'm trying to figure out the office situation by juggling some folks around, but space is limited due to the judges wanting more room for their clerks, and they say they are adding a new judge down in family court, so I am having to be creative."

"Space is limited" actually means that I won't be getting my old office back. I nod and try to let it go, but I get an ominous feeling this conversation is heading somewhere uncomfortable.

"What I really wanted to discuss with you," Cindy continues, "is how I can help you transition back to work, not only as your supervisor but as your friend. In discussing how to handle your return, we thought it would be best for you to ease back in."

"Who is 'we,' Cindy?"

"Let me finish, Colm, which is why I need to apologize face-to-face." Cindy places both hands on her desk. She pauses, tilts her head to the left, and raises her eyebrows, adopting that look of pity that I can't stand. "I didn't catch that your name was placed on the on-call duty roster. That should never have happened, and I'm sorry. I'm assigning the Simone case to Dillon—"

"It's already my case. I've been on it since the night it happened, working with the detectives, passing out leads. I'm fine and more than capable of handling it."

"I'm sure you are," Cindy says, sounding more like a parent comforting a child than the DA. "But you'll also agree that you don't even have a team right now. Don't you think it would be best to build the plane before you try to fly it?"

I take a deep breath and think about my rebuttal for a microsecond before launching into it. *I don't have a team because you dispersed them* is what I am thinking, but thankfully not saying. Instead, I opt for "I'm going to take you up on your offer of doing anything you can to help me."

Cindy leans back in her chair and relaxes. "Good."

"What helps me the most right now is doing what I used to do, putting cases together and winning them at trial. You say you want to help me; this is what helps me."

Cindy smiles with her mouth but not her eyes.

Before she can counter, I switch subjects. "How's Dominic doing? I was planning on calling him to see if he wanted to play a round of golf."

While she brings me up to speed on her husband, and before she can circle back around to the case, my phone rings, and I quickly stand up.

"I'm sorry to cut this short, but it's imperative I take this call. It's about Rachel's case. Thank you, again. Give my best to Dom." I stride out of the office, lifting my phone to my ear. "This is Colm. No, that's not great. You understand me?"

"Understand what?" Irene asks.

I wave at Amanda and head into the hall. Once I am out of earshot, I respond. "Meet me in my office. We have a lot of work to do."

CHAPTER 20

TRAVIS AND BONES PARKED across the street from a three-story, rundown hotel. The whole place was painted yellow, trimmed in a bleary, jaundiced off-white.

"This hotel is a meth clinic, except the people who check in aren't trying to get off meth, they are dying to stay on it. Literally," Denton said.

"How could they name this place the Hilton Plaza?" Travis wondered aloud. "Isn't that copyright infringement?"

"Because it's the Hillton Plaza. Two Ls." Denton pointed. "Clint's in apartment ten, three over from the end."

"Are you sure I shouldn't go back to the station and get a vest?" Travis asked.

"No, but you should have it with you all the time. That way you don't have to go looking for it. It should be part of your daily routine, like shaving and brushing your teeth." Denton stubbed out his cigarette. "Don't worry about Clint. He's a stabber, not a shooter. And if he had a gun, it wouldn't be here long. He would have sold it, pawned it, traded it, or had it stolen."

"You're not making me feel better about not having a vest."

"Vests don't stop knives anyway. The blade cuts the fibers. Besides, you're going to be covering the back door. I doubt he'll make it out of the apartment. If you see him coming, get low and brace your foot at the bottom of the door. The door opens out, so if you do that, he'll bounce off, and I'll scoop him up."

"We don't have a warrant," Travis pointed out.

"A warrant?" Denton scoffed. "Are you serious? This isn't the police academy; this is real life. Clint will give us a reason to arrest him, trust me. I might even help him."

"And if he doesn't?"

Denton shrugged. "Let me worry about that. Take the sidewalk on the right and circle around back."

Travis exited the car but didn't shut the door. "What are you going to do?"

"I'm going up and ringing the doorbell." Denton grinned.

Travis shut the door, crossed the street, and started walking. Part of him wished he'd gone in to give his report to the sheriff. Denton had a reputation of being much more like Rambo than Columbo. They said he liked to act and then think.

The sidewalk circled around to the rear of the building. When Travis reached the corner, Denton's Charger raced across the street and skidded to a stop in front of the hotel. The huge detective shoved open his door and got out. He'd taken off his suit jacket, vest, and collared shirt. Now wearing only a white tank top, he looked truly menacing as he stomped up the steps and pounded on the door.

"Bobby! Get your sorry butt out here now." He thumped on the door. "Bobby? I know you're home."

Travis stood there for a second, wondering who this Bobby was that Denton was yelling for. He hadn't said a word about anyone named Bobby. Then Travis realized it was a ruse to lure Clint into opening the door.

Travis bolted down the sidewalk and ran around back to get into position. He approached Clint's apartment. Through the window, he saw a medium-built man with long brown hair inside, standing with his back to Travis, looking through the peephole in the door.

"Open the door, Bobby, or I'm kicking it in. I want my money!" Denton shouted.

"There's nobody named Bobby here, so go to hell," Clint yelled back.

"Tell him to come out, or I'm coming in."

Clint opened the door until it hit the security chain. "I'm telling you, man. There's no Bobby here."

A woman Travis hadn't noticed jumped off the couch and stared out the rear window. She looked like a zombie with pallid skin, greasy hair, and stained clothes. Her sunken eyes met his. She raised a gaunt arm, pointed at him, and screamed.

Clint slammed the front door and fled through the kitchen.

Bones broke the chain on the door like it was a strand of hair and rushed inside.

Clint ran for the back door, busting it open, and charged straight through Travis.

Travis tumbled backward, tripped, and landed on his back in the grass.

A second later, the back door broke off its hinges as Denton smashed through it. The door flipped once and landed on the grass beside Travis.

As Travis scrambled to his knees, Clint sprinted down the sidewalk.

Denton outweighed Clint by a hundred pounds, but the detective ran with the speed of a rhinoceros. He quickly caught up to Clint, grabbed his shoulder, and yanked him to the ground.

The woman from the apartment slammed against Travis's side and clung to his back. A fist pummeled his face. The woman screamed like a banshee as she wailed away on his head.

Travis blocked one punch and seized her wrist.

Like a zombie, she opened her mouth wide, revealing rotting teeth, and tried to bite his face.

He managed to grab hold of her forehead as they fell onto the ground.

Denton loomed over them, carrying Clint by the back of his belt like a toddler throwing a tantrum. After dropping Clint, Denton grabbed the woman's left arm, slapping a handcuff in place before cuffing her right and jerking her back to a sitting position.

"Calm down, Destiny. What's wrong with you, attacking a cop? I thought you would be smarter than that by now."

Destiny's wild eyes lost their fire, and she sat calmly, staring at Denton. "I didn't know if you were real cops." She pointed at Travis. "With that cheap suit, I thought he was a banger looking to shake us down."

"We can talk about that at the station." Denton helped Destiny to her feet and jerked Clint up.

"You can't arrest me," Clint said. "Do you have a warrant?"

"I don't need one. You hit my deputy with your door. Now get moving." Denton steered Clint down the sidewalk.

Travis brushed the dirt off his jacket and stared at Destiny. "I paid a lot for this suit."

She rolled her eyes. "You got ripped off."

"Get moving, Travis," Denton called out. "I want to find out what they know."

CHAPTER 21

MARTIN BACKED THE LOANER car out of the garage and sped down the driveway. He rubbed his bloodshot eyes and chugged his coffee. Last night was brutal. He'd tossed, turned, and stared at the ceiling trying to figure everything out. He searched his office but there was still no sign of his burner phone. He must have left it in his chambers at the court-house. He'd have to get it later.

Right now, he needed to know if Rachel had made a recording of their conversation. He raised himself up in the seat and scanned the front parking lot of the salon as it came into view. There wasn't a car in sight.

Exiting the car, he climbed the steps. Police crime tape covered the door. He reached out his hand. The door was locked.

"Hey!" someone shouted as footsteps crunched the gravel behind him.

Martin's arms flailed around in circles as he struggled not to fall.

A sheriff's deputy stomped forward and stopped. "My apologies, Judge Weber. I didn't recognize you."

Martin wet his lips and swallowed. "You startled me, Deputy."

"Sorry about that, Judge. Just preserving the crime scene." The deputy glanced at the BMW and raised an eyebrow. "What are you doing here, by the way? Is it something official? Should I notify the sheriff?" He reached for the radio on his shoulder.

"No. That won't be necessary, Deputy." Martin hurried back down the steps. "I . . . my son gets his hair cut here. I saw the crime scene tape and was curious, that's all. Keep up the good work. I'll be sure and let the sheriff know how diligent you are."

The deputy smiled and nodded. "Thank you, sir."

Martin got in the car and forced himself to calmly drive out of the parking lot. He leaned back in the contoured leather seat and tried to think. His sweaty fingers tightened on the steering wheel of the loaner car, and he gasped.

"Beau!"

Martin reached for his phone and dropped it like he'd picked up a rattlesnake. He couldn't call Beau. This was too important for a phone call. No, this was something you had to discuss face-to-face. Beau needs to know this is important. Plus, for all he knows, Beau records his own calls. He was a slippery, shady guy.

Should he take the risk? If he asked Beau for help, Beau would know about Martin's affair with Rachel. But Beau probably already knew. He'd seen Martin and Rachel enough at the Outer Limits to put two and two together.

But Martin did have a trump card he could play.

Martin took a left at the light and sped across town to the Outer Limits. Beau had several businesses and different offices at each one of those businesses, but Martin hoped that the large club was his castle.

- Parking out front, Martin hurried to the door and rang the bell.

After a minute, a poised woman in an elegant black dress strode down the steps and unlocked the door. Her long, dark hair was pulled back in a ponytail. She wore no jewelry or makeup, nor did she need it. Her dark eyes locked with his. "Judge Weber. Welcome. Please come with me."

Martin followed her inside. "I was hoping to speak with Beau Landry."

"I assumed as much, Your Honor. This way." She climbed the steps, crossed the lobby of the club, and held open a plain door. A long corridor stretched out before him. There were no posters on the walls and the floor was concrete. "Mr. Landry's study is at the end of the hallway. Good day to you, sir." She closed the door, leaving him alone.

Martin glanced at the door handle. Something made him want to check to see if it locked. What a ridiculous thought. He was getting paranoid if he believed that Beau would trap him in here.

As he neared the door at the end of the corridor, a wiry man opened it from inside. He wore black shoes, black suit pants with a matching jacket, and a red shirt opened at the collar. His crow-black hair was long and slicked back. But his most distinctive and disquieting features were his eyes. His right eye was a brilliant pale blue. But it was his left eye that made Martin gasp. It was an opaque gray that Martin had only viewed on a corpse.

The man stepped out of the way.

Beau Landry stood in front of a wall filled with books. The room was warmly lit. Next to the wall with the door was a leather couch. Gas fire logs crackled and heated the room. A small table with a reading lamp on top and two recliners on either side sat in the far corners of the room. The walls, all except the one with the door, were lined with bookshelves filled with various works.

"Martin. To what do I owe this surprise?"

Beau's greatest asset wasn't his looks, it was his effortless charm. People gravitated toward him, and he took full advantage of it—and them.

The man with the dead eye closed the door.

Martin swallowed.

"Care for a drink? My friend here is Jean Boucher. He's the head of security for all of my ventures. There are no secrets. Everything stays with us."

Boucher poured two whiskies and brought them over.

The ice in Martin's glass clinked as his hand shook.

Beau motioned Martin over to the chairs in the left corner. "I can't imagine what a small businessman could do for a judge that he could not do for himself, but whatever you need, say it. What are friends for?"

Martin gulped his drink. "I met a young woman here at the club. Our relationship was purely platonic. She had some custody issues, so she wanted some advice. In the end, it was a mistake. The woman thought I was interested in something more, which I was not. I am married, after all." Martin tapped his wedding band for emphasis. "She wasn't pleased with that response. In fact, she insinuated that she had made a recording of me and would make it public unless I changed my mind."

Beau settled back in the chair and nodded sagely. "'Hell hath no fury,' isn't that what they say?" He turned to Boucher and they both grinned. "That is an unenviable situation. And you say you met her here? In my club?"

"Yes. Rachel Simone. She was a hairdresser."

Beau stared down into his glass. "That certainly is a predicament. A lot more challenging now given that she's dead, isn't it?"

Martin nodded. "Yes, she's dead."

"Murdered, I believe, is the right word, Your Honor."

Martin nodded and finished his drink.

Beau remained silent, staring at Martin like he was studying a painting.

"I had nothing to do with it!" Martin said, his voice rising.

"Well, Judge, with all due respect, if people think you were having an affair and she was secretly recording you," Beau said matter-of-factly, "that might be motive enough, to some at least."

Martin coughed and set the empty glass down on the coaster. "Yes. And I am telling you that I had nothing, absolutely nothing, to do with any harm coming to that woman."

"Of course you didn't, Martin." Beau sipped his drink. "But you still have a serious problem."

The warmth of the whiskey spread into Martin's chest. "And so do you—The Shops at Willow Creek."

"You are referring to my zoning issue? We're waiting for the result of the appeal."

Martin forced himself to lean back and try to appear calm. "As it stands, your appeal will be rejected, but only due to a technicality. And would it be fair for a multi-million-dollar investment that is sure to benefit the city be squashed because of a trivial matter that I could assist with?" Martin's heartbeat drummed in his ears. He tried to swallow but his mouth was so dry he couldn't.

The silence was broken when Beau said, "Excellent. Let us speak no further on either subject."

Martin sat in his chair unsure if Beau had agreed to the deal or not. "So, you'll get that recording? How?"

"Do you want to know how it's done or just that it's done?"

Martin didn't know whether to cry or cheer. He stood up and thrust out his hand. "I can't thank you enough. Really. And I assure you, I had nothing to do with what happened to Rachel."

Beau rose and placed a hand on Martin's shoulder. "Yes, you have mentioned that already. Stop talking about that. Let's stop talking about any of this. Not a word to anyone." Beau led him to the door. "You have my word; you don't need anything else. Boucher himself will handle this with discretion."

Boucher stepped forward. His chilling eyes narrowed.

Martin backed out of the room. "I'll hold up my end."

"I'm certain you will. Good day, Judge Weber." Beau smiled and closed the door.

A lock clicked, the sound of it echoing down the narrow hallway. Martin broke into a cold sweat.

What had he done?

CHAPTER 22

IN THE INTERVIEW ROOM, Travis sat across from Clint Fisher at a steel table bolted to the wall. Bones sat next to Travis, glaring silently at Clint. They had already gone through the formalities of starting an interview, including the reading of rights, but Travis was hesitant to begin. He was unsure if Denton wanted to lead the interview or if he should. Travis slid the pre-printed Miranda waiver form across the table to the suspect, but Clint pushed it away unsigned.

"I've heard them all before, but I'm not signin' nothin'," Clint said.

The uncomfortable silence grew until it became unbearable.

Clint leaned forward and said, "Whatever you guys think I did, I didn't do. I ain't saying nothing else. So, you two can stop with your good cop, bad cop game. I've seen it all before and I ain't fallin' for this 'psycholiminal' silent treatment."

Bones leaned back in his chair and crossed his massive arms. "For a guy who claims he isn't saying anything, you sure do talk a lot."

"I know how you guys are. But I didn't do nothin'."

"You sound like a guy with a guilty conscience, Clint," Denton said.

"Why am I even here? What is it you think I did that I didn't do?"

"Let's start with, Where were you two nights ago?" Travis asked.

Clint shrugs. "Sittin' home with Destiny watching TV, I guess."

"She said you went out that night," Denton fired back.

Travis reached for the pen to cover his surprise. They hadn't spoken to Destiny yet.

Clint glared at the ceiling and muttered, "Stupid bi—"

"Don't say it, Clint." Denton leaned in. "I don't like that word. Where were you?"

"I was out, but not doing nothin' illegal, illegal."

"What exactly does that mean, Clint? 'Illegal, illegal'?" Travis asked.

"I kinda-coulda been using a little somethin' to medicate my pain. My back hurts. That's why I can't work."

"We want to know what you were doing around Ender Road," Travis said.

Clint shrugged. "I was at Mo's."

"What's Mo's real name?" Travis asked.

"Lester."

Denton's hand slammed down on the table so hard that Travis and Clint jumped. "The fun is over, Clint. This isn't about drugs or how tough you think your life is. There's a dead woman, and we think you know something about it."

"Whoa . . . whoa, wait a minute, I don't know nothin' about that." Clint swallowed and scratched at his neck. "I wasn't jokin'. His name really is Lester, but we've been callin' him Mo since junior high. Jenkins. That's his last name. Lester Jenkins."

"And he lives over near Ender Road?" Travis wrote down the name. "What street?"

"Highland. It's his mom's house."

"How do you know Rachel Simone?"

"I went to high school with her. She cut my hair but—" Clint stood up and pointed at them. "No way. You're not pinnin' that on me. No. No. No."

"Sit your butt down, Oswald," Denton said, and Clint obeyed. "No one's trying to pin anything on you. We want to know what you saw. So, think."

"I liked Rachel. Always did, always will. I didn't touch her."

"Good. Then you won't mind taking a lie detector test," Travis said.

"Not a chance. No way. All you've gotta do is turn the knob a little, and it'll say I'm lyin'."

"But you're willing to give a DNA swab?" Travis pressed.

Clint's eyes widened and his voice rose. "I told you I got my hair cut there. My DNA is probably all over the place!"

"Have you taken a look in the mirror lately?" Denton said. "You haven't had a haircut in a year."

"That don't mean nothin'. They get DNA from frozen dead elephants. If their DNA lasts that long, mine would last a year. But I swear on my mother's grave that I would never hurt a woman."

Denton scratches his chin. "Funny hearing that from you, Clint. If I remember right, you did time for breaking and entering where you did stab two people, including a woman."

"That's crap and you know it."

"You pleaded guilty," Travis pointed out.

"You guys stacked charges. I was lookin' at thirty years, or I could take a deal for two. Of course I took the deal."

"Does that mean you did or didn't stab them?" Travis asked.

"Mo grabbed a bat so I grabbed a steak knife, but I never intended to stab Stacey. I was tryin' to stab Mo, but Stacey got in the way."

Denton ran his hand down his face. "Are you telling me you've got two friends named Mo?"

"No. It's the same guy. Lester Jenkins. We made up. But I didn't mean to stab either of them. I'm doin' my home detention and haven't failed a drug test yet."

"That's probably because you haven't been given one. How 'bout we call probation in now and see how well you do on tests?"

"Come on, man. I had nothin' to do with hurtin' Rachel. Why would I?"

"You've got a chance to prove that to us, Clint. You can take a lie detector test and DNA." Clint opened his mouth, but Denton cut him off. "Or I'm calling probation. Your choice."

Clint rolled his eyes. "Fine. I'll take the test."

"Sit tight." Denton rose and motioned for Travis to follow him out of the room.

Once they were in the hallway and shut the door, Travis said, "Hold on a second. Is that it? We're not going to keep questioning him? He admitted to being in the area."

"We can always pull him back in, but he didn't do it. Lie detectors make good threats but lousy cases. They aren't admissible anyway. Plus, I don't like him for this."

"So now what?"

"Now it's time for you to do your job and keep looking."

CHAPTER 23

WISPS OF BLACK SMOKE rose from the charred remains of Rachel's salon and home.

"What happened?" I ask, getting out of my car.

"There's good news, bad news, and undetermined news. Which do you want first?" Travis asks.

"Give me the bad first."

"Rachel's trailer burned to the ground last night. The fire examiner thinks something was left plugged in, possibly a curling iron. It's a total loss, along with everything in it."

I rub my temples with my index finger and thumb as my brain tries to take it in. "A curling iron? Are you serious?" I glare at the shell of the building. "I sure hope you and forensics got everything of any evidentiary value out of there before this happened."

"We did, but we never found Rachel's phone. It's still missing."

"If we haven't found it by now, we probably won't. It's at the bottom of some lake with the SIM card removed. Now we've lost the chance to reexamine the crime scene and lost the chance for a jury view if there's ever an arrest and a trial."

"What's a jury view?" he asks.

"It's when the jury comes out to the scene of a crime. The lawyers don't go—only the judge and the jury, but that chance went up in smoke with the rest of her salon."

"There is a possible silver lining to this fire." Travis takes out his phone and scrolls to a photograph. "One of the firefighters discovered this hidden in the wall. It was next to a water pipe that ruptured. The case melted onto the tablet but that and the water may have protected the memory chip. I doubt we get anything off it, but I've asked forensics to try to recover any data."

I glance at a photograph of a partially scorched computer tablet. "Why would Rachel have a tablet hidden in the wall?"

Travis shrugs. "I don't know. If forensics can recover anything, we may find out."

"Is this the good news, a tablet that probably can't be restored hidden in a wall?"

"No, the good news is that your friend enhanced the logo on the van that cut off the suspect's car. It belongs to Breathe Right Heating and Air Conditioning."

"That's where I saw that logo. It's a cloud mascot, right?"

Travis nods. "I spoke to the van driver. The only details about the car she can remember are that it was silver, looked expensive, and had dark, tinted windows. But we caught a huge break. She remembered part of the license plate, 'N2G.' It's short for "Not Too Good" in texting, so it stuck out to her."

"'Not too good' is good news, Travis. Very good, actually."

Travis scrolls through his phone, reads his note, and says, "When I get back to the station, I'll start cross-checking plates. It's not a lot to go on, but it's something and takes a little sting out of the burned-down trailer."

"Between this and finding the gloves and knife, we're making steady progress, Detective."

Travis smiled. "Thank you."

"You ready for the morgue?"

Some of the color drains from Travis's complexion and he swallows. "Sure."

CHAPTER 24

BEAU LANDRY PACED THE floor of his hexagonal office adorned with vibrant colors and patterns. From the bold Caribbean blue walls to the colorful Mardi Gras masks hanging on the walls, Beau wanted whoever was in the room to feel his power and mystique. He reveled in being well known but not well understood. He had worked hard to cultivate an image as an out-of-the-picture power broker in the Upstate of South Carolina—the kind you would invite to all the right parties, but he never bothered to attend.

The office furniture was a mixture of wooden chairs and tables with intricate carvings. Plush velvet couches with rich embroidery faced each other, with a long coffee table set in between.

"You don't believe his story, do you?" Beau asked.

Boucher shrugged as he walked over and handed Beau a thumb drive. "Not after watching this video of Martin and Rachel having sex in the Marquis lounge. They were good enough to do it right under the chandelier."

"But I'm not sure about the murder. He acts guilty, but what did the coroner's report say? Something like she was stabbed nearly twenty times. I don't see Martin getting dirty and bloody like that. A gun, sure. Poison, maybe. He's guilty of something, but I don't know that it's murder."

Boucher walked behind the bar, took out the bottle of Rhum Clément Liqueur d'Orange, and held the label out.

Beau nodded.

Boucher poured two glasses. "A man like that wouldn't sully his hands. He'd use a gun, shoot once, and leave. Or he may be dumb enough to try to hire someone else to do it, you know, create that layer of deniability that never works out in murders for hire."

"What about in the heat of the moment?" Beau took the drink and raised his other hand theatrically. "I wonder if this hairdresser developed a conscience, maybe found out he was married, or maybe Martin wasn't able to help her like he said he would. A woman who looks like that is not going to be interested in Martin Weber except for money, status, or help."

"Considering he's a judge, he's not used to hearing 'no.' "

"Judges have huge egos. It makes sense. He's standing there in the salon and flies into a rage. He grabs the nearest thing he can, a pair of scissors and . . ." Beau raised his imaginary weapon over his head and plunged it down. "A crime of passion? Manslaughter and not murder?"

A wicked grin spread across Boucher's face. His blue eye shone brightly while his dead eye gleamed like a full moon on a starless night.

"What are you smiling at, Boucher?"

"You can't spell *manslaughter* without the word *laughter*, no?"

Beau forced a chuckle. To Beau, murder was a sometimes-necessary compliance tool, but for Boucher, it was a hobby, a sport he derived pleasure from.

"I still think he's too soft," Boucher said. "But who knows? Every man is capable of killing someone if he is pushed hard and far enough."

"It doesn't matter to me whether he did it or not, except for extra leverage. It's a pity you couldn't find the recording. But this video from the club," he said, holding up the thumb drive, "should be enough to get his attention for the rest of his judicial career. We don't have to help him any more than we already have. And he's agreed to solve our little problem with Eagle Point."

"Still, if we had something connecting him to the murder, he'd never get off our hook. He may run for the Court of Appeals or Supreme Court one day. Who knows?"

Beau smoothed back his hair as he crossed the room and sat on the closest couch. "I recognized the girl's photograph when I saw it in the paper. Beautiful young woman. When I spoke with the Sheriff, he indicated it looked more like a robbery gone wrong."

Boucher rolled his eyes. "Lloyd is a fool. Why would a robber stab someone nineteen times? Why would a robber take a single piece of jewelry and leave the cash, the TV, and other valuables?"

"Good work, by the way. Well done."

Boucher shrugs. "Easy enough. The trailer burned down to the frame."

"I have a lot invested in Martin Weber. He's not telling us everything, and that concerns me. For now, stay close to him."

"When do you want me to start?"

Beau glanced at the door.

Boucher frowned. He downed his drink, set it on the table, and rose. "Understood, boss. When have I ever let you down?" Boucher doesn't wait for a reply or even look back for one. He pushed open the door and shut it after himself.

Beau sipped his drink and smiled. With a sitting judge beholden to him, all of his plans were coming to fruition.

CHAPTER 25

I PARK IN FRONT OF the Edgar J. Murphy County Administration Building and shut off the engine, but I don't get out. The morgue never bothered me before—not like most people—but I'm not sure I can handle it now. A lot has changed. I stare at the modern, two-story complex that houses all the forensic labs and the medical examiner's offices and think about letting Travis handle this one alone.

I drum my fingers on the steering wheel. But I can't pass off this responsibility. Letting someone else do something this important is not my style. I have never been good at delegating significant tasks, and this one is essential.

Travis parks and we head for the entrance. The front doors of the building swoosh open as we approach. I lead the way to the elevators and the basement. I press the button and notice Travis has turned a little paler and is noticeably quiet. The bell dings, the doors open, and a chill sweeps into the elevator. The air is dense and cold, seeming to press in from all sides.

Exiting the elevator, I knock on an office door with an engraved metal plaque: DR. ARDELL SHARP, MEDICAL EXAMINER.

A moment later, the door opens, and Dr. Sharp greets them. "Good morning, Colm."

"Ardell, this is Detective Travis Hendrick."

"Nice to meet you." A short man, Ardell's white hospital coat nearly touches the shiny linoleum floor. "Rachel Simone case?"

"That's correct," I say.

"I like to present my findings in three ways, with varying levels of detail depending on how squeamish you are. If you want the most thorough walk-through of the autopsy report and have a strong stomach, I can explain what I discovered while we review the body together."

I glance at Travis, and he nods confidently.

"Certainly." Ardell motions for us to follow him down the hallway. "We keep the morgue as clean as possible, so please scrub and put on gloves, booties, paper gowns, and respirators. Changing room right through here."

Ten minutes later, we're back in the morgue. An earthy smell hangs in the air, tinged with the scents of unknown chemicals. Ardell pulls the sheet off Rachel's face, and Travis loses all the color in his.

"The deceased is female, white, twenty-six years old. I estimate the time of death between six and eight p.m. Based on the responding EMT's recording of body temperature, lack of rigor mortis, and lividity, I could narrow the window. There was no food in her stomach, so we can't use digestion to help us there. The official cause of death is the severing of the carotid artery. The victim had been stabbed nineteen times with a four- to five-inch, single-edged knife."

"Were you able to match it to the knife Travis recovered?"

"We're still testing the knife, but my preliminary examination would say there's a high probability of a match." Ardell takes a penlight from his lab pocket. He angles the light down to Rachel's neck. "You'll notice the bruising against the skin. The knife has a distinctive guard and left a bruise around one of the chest wounds. I should be able to match that to the weapon definitively by this afternoon. The scissors were impaled into her chest postmortem."

Travis clears his throat but doesn't say anything.

"And we already identified the shoeprint as a men's Doc Martens, size twelve." Ardell aims his pen light to the wound on Rachel's chest. "The killer used the scissors to cut off the victim's hair before plunging them into her chest. I recovered several strands from inside the chest cavity. I'm afraid that's all I have so far."

"What about the bloody tissues found near the back door?" I ask.

"We did a preliminary blood screen and the blood on the tissues is type A, while the victim was type B. We've sent it to the state lab for DNA testing, but they warned us it will be a couple of weeks."

"Was there any evidence of alcohol or drugs in Rachel's body?" I ask.

"None."

I shake Ardell's hand. "Thank you. We'll let you know if we have additional questions."

"I'll finish the written report and get that to you as soon as possible."

I stare down at a beautiful young mother reduced to a cold corpse on a steel table. Why? For what? Ardell did everything in his power to uncover the secrets Rachel's body held. Now it's my job to make sure whoever did this to her is held to account. As awful and soul-wrecking as this whole process is, it's the only reason I've found worth having a law degree for.

CHAPTER 26

BONES PARKED HIS CHARGER beside the sheriff's cruiser and an older BMW. Standing outside what looked like a small fishing cabin with the North Pacolet River as a backdrop was Deputy Michael Jenkins. Jenkins was close to retirement after more than thirty years on the force. He had literally seen everything there was to see, so his pale complexion wasn't a good sign of what waited inside that cabin.

"What do we got, Mike?" Bones asked.

Mike reached into his pocket and tossed Bones a tin of Vicks VapoRub.

"That bad?" Bones asked.

Mike slowly nodded.

"We got a call from some fisherman who noticed a peculiar smell coming from the cabin. I ran the car when I got here. Comes back to a Frank Hastings. Hard to say who's inside but that's probably where I would start."

Bones opened the tin and put a streak of VapoRub beneath each nostril. "Hard to say" is police talk for significant decomposition or damage.

Once inside, Bones realized why Mike looked so peaked. Slumped over a table in the center of the room was a body and what was left of a face. A revolver lay next to his hand.

Flies buzzed over Frank and the dried blood covering the table and floor. A TV with a hole in the screen and shattered glass sat in front of him.

"His brother reported him missing," Mike said. "I'm not one to speculate, but this was someone pretty committed to killing himself."

"Isn't everyone who takes their own life committed?"

"I suppose, but he wouldn't take no for an answer." Mike pointed to the ceiling and a broken rope dangling from a beam. A noose with a frayed end lay on the floor.

Bones moved closer to the corpse. The head was heavily damaged but dark bruises and scrapes ringed Frank's neck.

"I see what you mean," Bones said.

"But why shoot the TV?" Mike said.

"Who knows. I heard Elvis shot a TV, too," Bones said, leaning down and peering at the revolver. "Three shots."

"What?"

"There are three empty casings in the revolver. He could have shot something before he got here or shot the TV more than once." Bones crossed over to the wall.

"A .38 would have gone through the TV."

Bones's flashlight beam stopped on a hole in the dark oak directly in line with the TV. "That's the one that went through the TV. I bet we find the other in the ceiling." He shined the light along the wall and stopped at another fresh hole in the wood.

"Maybe he missed the TV the first time?" Mike suggested.

"From five feet?" Bones shook his head. "I wouldn't think so."

"There's a suicide note." Mike pointed at the pad of paper on the table. Bones read it:

I didn't adequately prepare for the trial. I didn't subpoena the right witnesses. I conspired with other attorneys to defraud clients of their money.

I'm sorry,
Frank Hastings

"Did you touch anything?" Bones asked.

"Of course not."

"Call forensics. Tell them to get here stat."

"For a suicide?" Mike asked.

"Better safe than sorry. It's probably exactly what it looks like, but we only get one chance to process the scene. It's worth a little extra time and inconvenience to remove that one percent of me that thinks it's all a little too neat and tidy."

"Maybe you're the one who should think about retiring. You sure you aren't seeing a killer around every corner? Seems pretty open and shut to me."

"Except for the three shots and a suicide note that seems written for his malpractice insurance carrier. So, yeah, I got a few questions that I want answered before I sign off on this."

CHAPTER 27

LATER IN THE AFTERNOON, Travis and I are summoned to a conference room in the county courthouse reserved for attorneys. So much of our justice system is based on history, precedent, and practice. Who sits where in a courtroom, who speaks when and in what order, even which conference room is used. There are no signs assigning one room to prosecutors and another to defense counsel. It's always been a certain way, and lawyers honor these unofficial traditions.

Judges are extremely reticent when it comes to ex parte communications. They want both sides present so they can hear both arguments side by side and make a decision. But some decisions are within the exclusive province of the prosecution or the state, and there is no defense counsel present, especially at the investigative, pre-charge stage.

Travis is leaning forward with both hands on his knees. His face is pale, and every once in a while, he swallows.

"Do you know what 'robitis' is?" I ask.

Travis shakes his head.

"It's what happens when some lawyers get promoted to judge and put on a robe. A few become humbler and more introspective with the gravity of their ascension to the bench. Others, however, confuse themselves with God."

The door to the judge's chamber opens, and I'm shocked to see Martin Weber standing there. He's a trial court judge. These ministerial tasks are usually delegated to magistrate judges. Rarely, if ever, does a trial judge hear an application for a search warrant.

I rise and nudge Travis's shoulder. "Good morning, Your Honor." I cross over to shake his hand and turn back to Travis. "This is Detective Travis Hendrick."

"Why don't we have a little chat in here." Martin leads the way through the door into his office.

The judge's chamber is a cavernous room, lined with bookcases filled with thick, leather-bound law books. The wooden paneled walls are adorned with somber portraits of past judges, which stare down condescendingly. The windows are covered with heavy, dark drapes.

Martin positions himself in a large, high-back, ornate chair behind a wide mahogany desk. He motions to the two chairs in front.

Travis and I sit. My knees rise higher than normal because these chairs are so low. I stare up at Judge Weber, realizing immediately the not-so-subtle power play. He's using the height difference to demonstrate who controls the authority inside the room.

He picks up one document sitting on the desk and begins to read silently.

This waiting game is another example of him setting the stage, letting us know that he also controls our time. He was once a trial lawyer himself. They usually make pretty good judges, unless, of course, they catch "robitis."

Judge Weber sets the document back on the desk and looks to me, then Travis, and back to me. He lifts up his right hand and sets his index finger down on the center of the page dramatically. "This, gentlemen, is a civil case waiting to happen. Before you say anything, let me explain something. Actions have consequences. The lack of action, the lack of preparation, well, that, too, has consequences." The judge stares at Travis, who in turn looks perplexed. "This should serve as a lesson to you, Detective Hendrick, that I do not allow shortcuts or bypass fundamentals, like standing and expectations of privacy. I am rejecting this application for a search warrant because the underlying affidavit for the warrant is fundamentally flawed as written. If you get more evidence or better evidence, you are welcome to come back."

I sit bolt upright and lean forward. It takes a lot to shock me. Denying a ministerial request for phone records would be one of those things. "Your Honor, this is a standard application for a search warrant for the victim's cell phone records. There is clearly probable cause these phone records contain or may reasonably contain relevant information to the investigation. I—"

"That is one area where you and I will have to agree to disagree, Counselor. You have failed to provide sufficient probable cause as to how there is a reasonable likelihood that evidence of a crime or the identity of any purported defendant is contained on this phone record and will be uncovered. According to the affidavit, the victim was killed in a botched robbery, therefore rendering any information contained on the phone record as purely speculative at this point. If you get more evidence, you are welcome to come back and we can try this again."

"Excuse me, Judge, I never reached a conclusion about the crime. This isn't a trial. This is literally the lowest standard of evidence we have— mere probable cause."

"We aren't claiming we're a hundred percent certain it was a robbery—" Travis began saying.

"Did you or did you not write," Martin picks up the warrant and flips to the second page, "in addition to the above-mentioned information, we are looking for photographs, texts, emails, and any and all information regarding a tennis bracelet that was stolen during the criminal offense?"

My knuckles turned bright white as I squeezed the arms of my chair to keep myself from backhanding Travis. I never included that verbiage when I created the document.

Travis looks to me, and from the helpless expression on his face, it's clear that he did.

"In addition to that," Martin continues, "the phone in question actually belongs to Macon Greer, not Rachel Simone. He has the privacy interest, not her. I see no waiver from him. But then again, why should he cooperate since he, too, has been charged?"

"The sole user of the phone was Rachel Simone, Your Honor," I point out. "And since she is dead, it's hard to get her consent, but I'm sure she wouldn't mind us trying to find out who killed her." I knew it sounded like a smart-ass comment as soon as it came out, and I was okay with that. This is a ridiculous ruling, and the judge and I both know it.

"Macon bought the phone and paid the bills. Additionally, since he has pending criminal matters in your office, this could be construed as you forcing him to give testimony against himself or, at a minimum, circumventing his right not to produce evidence against himself, which would be a clear violation of his Fifth Amendment rights."

"Your Honor, with all due respect, the record belongs to the phone company. It's not testimonial from Macon. It's literally a business record. We are not seeking the contents of any texts or phone calls, simply the metadata. We have done this a thousand times without any incident at all, Your Honor."

"Well, there's a first time for everything, Mr. District Attorney. This is a murder case. Every item is going to be scrutinized by the appellate courts, and I will not have my good name besmirched by a reversal on a motion to suppress because you did not do your job."

"Well, Your Honor, we will use a taint team. If there are any calls made by Macon on Rachel's phone, those can be kept from us. All we want is a record of who Rachel may have been in contact with before her death."

"I've ruled. I understand you are disappointed, but I'm not going to circumvent the Constitution, even for something as significant as a murder investigation."

"We aren't asking you to circumvent anything, Judge. We're asking that you approve a warrant for phone records, which is routinely done. Maybe we'll just use a grand jury subpoena."

"Be careful, Counselor. I don't take well to threats to go around me. And while I'm at it, I'm deeply concerned with your handling of this case, Detective Hendrick. Concerned enough that I will speak to the sheriff, noting these shortcuts and looseness with the facts and the omissions from your affidavit."

"While you're making calls, Your Honor, you may as well call Cindy, too. I reviewed this affidavit and application, and there is no requirement that Detective Hendrick put exculpatory information in an affidavit for a search warrant."

"Don't push me, Colm."

"I'm not pushing you, Judge, but I am pushing forward. This ruling is wrong, and we are going to use every lawful means to access relevant information. You did what you thought was right. We're going to do the same."

"You can try that, and it will still wind up here on a motion to quash the subpoena from either Macon, the lawyer for the phone company, or both."

"I guess we will have to hope for a different judge if that happens, Your Honor."

"I would not threaten me with judge shopping, Mr. District Attorney. I have quite a good relationship with your boss."

"So do I, so call her," I dare him. "While you're on the phone with her, I'll look up the number for the Supreme Court on where to register judicial complaints."

"What did you say to me?"

"I think you heard me. This is not even a close case on this warrant. You are looking for a reason to make this harder than it should be or needs to be. And both of us can play that game."

"Sir—" Travis begins to say, but I nudge his foot in an attempt to shut him up.

Judge Weber looks at me, cocks his head to the side, and bites his lower lip before saying, "In the light of everything that's happened in your life, Colm, I'm willing to let this go as a good faith difference of opinion on whether this affidavit is sufficient for what you are seeking. You want both the metadata and the details of what's on her phone. I can't allow that in a potential capital case. I will not allow shortcuts."

"Thank you for your time, Your Honor." I glare into his pompous eyes, nod curtly, and march to the door. I hurry through the waiting room, and I'm halfway down the hallway by the time Travis catches up to me.

"Colm, wait a second. There has to be something we can do to re-submit the affidavit."

I stop and stare daggers through him. "He rejected it for no reason other than he can. There is no legal basis for his ruling. He's intentionally erecting barriers and we need to find a way around them."

"Maybe he's right." Travis groans. "Maybe I am too inexperienced to be handling this case."

"We need those phone records. Without them, we don't win."

CHAPTER 28

THE FOLLOWING MORNING, I'M heading to what has the makings of becoming a new routine—at least in terms of eating a real meal. It might be the only one of the day. I used to crave structure and predictability and daily ritual, but marriage and parenthood upended all of that. There is something therapeutic about this drive through the farmlands of upper Spartanburg County. Much of this used to be peach trees, but that's a tenuous way to make a living, so it's slowly being converted into smaller farms for horse lovers. The line between city life and farm life is a thin one in terms of geography.

I pull into the gravel parking lot hoping that what I consider "my booth" is open. I angle the rearview mirror down to see if I look as bad as I feel. Last night was rough, but I rationalize my drinking with what Judge Weber had done to our investigation. He went out of his way to wreck our investigation, so I went out of my way to wreck myself. It didn't change his ruling, but it took my mind off of work for a little while. A couple of aspirin when I woke up and some breath mints now will hopefully cover my tracks.

Walking up the wooden stairs toward the front door, I make a mental note to check on Mae. I'm not the only one feeling loss and grief. She knew Ally a lot longer than I did. Sibling love is no less real than romantic love, it just manifests itself differently. I know I should see her more often, call, answer her calls, talk it over, focus on the happy times . . . I know I should, but I keep putting it off.

I walk in and smile to myself and how life is constructed through small ecosystems. If this were a diner close to the courthouse, it would be full of lawyers and court personnel and cops. But drive twenty minutes and no one recognizes you, or if they do, they leave you alone. Being left alone feels pretty good right now, and my booth is open.

A different waitress, Maddy, comes over. She's a little older than Belle and doesn't have quite the effervescence.

"And how are you, sweetie?"

"I'm doing great. How are you?"

"Tired, overworked, underpaid, my hose are too tight, and my feet are killing me, but otherwise, I'm fine. Thank you for asking." She smiles when she says all of that. "Based on Belle's description, I would say you're the lawyer. Figures she would leave the cute part out. You want your egg-white omelet with avocado, am I right?"

"That's my usual order, but there may be more than one customer who likes that."

"Nope, because we don't carry avocados for anyone but you. Belle felt bad we didn't have any so she bought some with her own money."

"I wish she hadn't done that."

"Doesn't surprise us one bit." As Maddy heads to the kitchen, I try to process what I just heard. Gratuitous acts of kindness do happen, I know that. But I'm not in a line of work where I get to see it often.

Maddy brings my order, refills my coffee, and gives me a small glimpse into her life—"Two kids and two jobs, one for each kid," she says laughing. "You know the drill. You can pay here or at the register. Suit yourself."

"I'll leave it here, but I'm going to leave a little extra and please give it to Belle. I don't want her spending her money on something for me."

"She won't take your money, so you can save yourself the trouble. Plus, you may see her before I do. She was headed to the courthouse today."

"Courthouse? Which one?"

"I didn't know there was more than one. I heard her ask the boss if she could switch with Lisa because she needed to get some forms from the courthouse."

"I'm there every day or, if it's federal, right across the street. I would have been happy to help and get whatever she needed. I wish she had said something."

"Yep, and the better you get to know her, the more you would know she never would. But, I'll let her know you were here and offered to help. How's that?"

I pay the bill, leave a little extra for Maddy and a little extra for Belle, despite being warned it was a waste of time.

That small act of kindness motivated me to do more than just think about my sister-in-law, but to actually do something about it. Sixteen minutes later I'm in her driveway. I spend about an equal amount of time sitting in my car debating whether this is the right way to start the day. Eventually the prospect of doing something unexpectedly kind wins out.

Mae Jennings is a forensic psychiatrist with a small private practice specializing in major depressive disorders. She also teaches an adjunct class at the local university on abnormal psychology and is often retained in death penalty cases by the defense. That used to place us on opposing sides during trials—at least until I married her baby sister. She is the best I've ever seen at cutting through the fog and the defense mechanisms and forcing you to confront yourself, especially the places you want left alone. That's probably why I keep avoiding sit-down visits with her and rely on texts and voicemails.

I trudge up the walkway and hold the railing as I pull myself up the four cement steps.

She opens the door, hugs me, and we walk inside to sit down in her living room. Nothing has changed. I sit in my usual recliner.

I glance at an old family photograph from their youth—even before I met Ally. Mae feels the loss as deeply as I do, we just process it differently.

One of Mae's cats jumps on my lap, which is a welcome distraction. "Which one is this?"

"Clarice. She's the friendly one."

"I like her name," I say. "Where are Hannibal Lecter and Multiple Miggs?"

Mae rolls her eyes. "I see living alone hasn't been good for your humor."

"It hasn't been good for anything, to be honest. Too much time to think. Too many memories."

"You want to talk about it? Not a day goes by that I don't cry at some memory of them."

"I think I'm about all cried out, to be honest. I just work and drink and try to make sense of how I missed all the signs."

"There were no signs, Colm. Ally was crushed after losing Jaci to SIDS, but you, me, everyone, thought that she was getting better. She poured herself into volunteering, she went to therapy . . . I'm trained to look and there were no signs she'd take her own life. Have you thought about maybe moving to another house, one that doesn't hold so many memories?"

"You know, the funny thing is that ninety-nine percent of the memories are joyous ones. There was so much laughter and happiness in that house. It's just that two calamities triumph over all the joy. You're the psychiatrist, not me. It seems there is a limit to how happy we can ever be, how high we can ever get, but there is no bottom. We keep plunging deeper and deeper."

"Do you think you are abandoning them? Is that why you stay? It can't be good for you to be in that house alone all the time."

"Yeah, I probably do liken it to abandonment. It's like, if I leave, I am leaving them behind, even though she would tell me to go live my life, live it to the fullest. She would tell me to go be happy. It feels like a betrayal to me. So, I stay in a self-constructed prison. I don't know how else to put it."

"Does getting back to work help at all?"

"Maybe it will. Maybe you can help. Can I get your professional opinion for a minute?"

"Of course you can, but only if you promise to come eat dinner with me once a month—that's my price."

"Deal."

"Tell me what you have."

"It's probably easier to show you. Here are the crime scene photos from a murder at a beauty salon," I say, passing my phone to Mae.

"How many times was she stabbed?"

"Nineteen. And the killer stabbed her with the scissors, which wasn't the murder weapon, after cutting her hair off, postmortem."

"Hmm." Mae hands the phone back to me and picks up Clarice. "It's clearly overkill. It's not trichotillomania but it's a close cousin. That is pulling one's own hair and eating it. This is cutting someone else's hair off and spreading it around. So, what was it about the victim's hair that set the killer off? Or was the hair symbolic of something else? Clearly, it was designed to humiliate her. Do you have any suspects at all?"

"We have two, but honestly, neither is very good. The ex-husband seems pretty broken up by the whole thing, and Bones picked up a serial petty thief who's done some B&Es in the neighborhood."

"How long ago was the divorce?"

"A year. But they're in a custody dispute."

Mae shakes her head. "That level of rage is extremely personal. The killer plunged the scissors into her heart. That's significant, and so is stepping on her face afterward. Whoever did this wanted to belittle her. It was the final act of proving superiority. Like standing on a vanquished foe."

I brush my hair back and exhale.

"You don't agree with my assessment?" Mae asks.

"I completely agree," I admit. "We are running through that magical forty-eight-hour window, and we don't have a great suspect in mind yet. But I am going to keep at it until we find whoever did it."

"You look so tired and thin, Colm. Can I at least get you something to eat? You can take it with you or drop it by your house and save it for dinner."

I shake my head. "I'm fine."

"Are you?" Mae sits on the edge of the couch and sets Clarice down on the floor. "How are you acclimating back to work life? You can always press the pause button if you need to."

"Work is work. I probably should not have come back at all. I probably need a complete change of scenery. It feels like . . ."

"Like what you said, that you are abandoning them." She finished my sentence.

"I definitely can't stay. It's not sustainable, long term. I need a little more time, I suppose."

"Where would you go?"

"I don't know. Aruba, Alaska, Albania—I may go through the alphabet."

Mae doesn't laugh. I look at the cream loveseat she's sitting on and remember the moment Ally and I picked it out. We'd been married for less than a month and didn't own a single piece of furniture. I wanted to tell Ally it was too expensive, that we didn't need to buy something brand-new at that trendy store, but her excitement made me reach for my credit card. We gave Mae the loveseat right after Jaci was born.

"I don't have everything planned out yet," I tell her, hoping she falls for it and doesn't press for more details.

"You're serious, aren't you?" she asks, her voice sounding in a state of alarm. As the firstborn of four girls, she was a decade older than Ally, the baby of the family. Mae was part mom and part older sister to Ally, and in turn has become the same to me. For several moments she quizzes me, and her questions are a lot better than my answers.

"Mae, I love you and I am listening to you, but I don't want to keep doing this. Not now. Not for the foreseeable future. It's one thing processing loss when it happens to other people, but this is different. I can't work my way out of this."

"Two things," Mae says as I try to brace myself for what's about to come. "You aren't just leaving people—friends, family like me. You're leaving what I truly believe is your calling. It's the reason you were put here. So few find their interest and their acumen aligned. So few marry what they love with what loves them back. You were put on earth to advocate for people who cannot advocate for themselves. That's your gift. You put yourself in the shoes of those who were marginalized, abused, hurt, and even killed. To do that to yourself—volitionally—is a gift to others. I know it takes a toll. A toll on top of the toll you have already paid."

"Life has taken a toll on both of us, Mae. It wasn't just me."

"Well then, do what I did. Take a break, take a long break. And when you come back, I don't care what you advocate for, so long as you advocate. It is what you were made to do."

"I used to believe that," I say. "I'm apathetic about life right now. I'm not suicidal. You don't need to worry about that."

"I'm not done yet, Colm. Now for my second point."

I laugh. "Are you gonna bill my insurance for this? This is like the longest time I've ever spent listening to a psychiatrist without objecting."

"I'm not like family. I am family. Not by genes, but by choice. Because I choose to love you like a brother even though the person who connected us is gone, the commitment is not. You know, I sit there staring at families sometimes, and it always strikes me that the only two people who are not genetically linked are the parents. All of the children are connected biologically. But not the two who started it all. The parents are committed. The rest are connected. And sometimes we give short shrift to the commitment. But I do not."

She leans over toward me and clasps her long hands together. I can imagine her doing this on a daily basis with strangers.

"You and I do not have a single gene in common," Mae tells me. "We are here by choice. That type of love is no less real, no less strong, no less eternal than the love of blood and genes. So, yes, I don't want you to leave for good, but I am okay if you leave for a good reason. Have you told Cindy?"

"No, because she would take me off this case, and right now I need a reason to get up. I need a reason to think and work and leave the house.

"Take a leave of absence after this case. Travel. Move to another part of town. Move to Greenville. Go to the U.S. Attorney's Office. Run for attorney general. You'll never outrun the grief, but you can change the framing, change the picture, and change how you process the grief. Don't give up your gift, Colm. That's all I'm asking."

I'm halfway down the steps when Mae calls to me and I stop.

"I don't know why they sent it here, but you got some mail."

She hands me an envelope with my name on it.

I open it and a King of Hearts that's been torn in two falls out. "Did someone drop it off or did it come in the regular mail?"

"It was in my mailbox. What does that mean?"

I shrug. "I don't know. Not the first suicide king I've gotten sent to me. I started getting them after Ally. Someone wants to remind me I have a broken heart."

"Have you told Bones? He could investigate."

I put the envelope and the card in my pocket. "That's a great idea, Mae. I'll do that. Nice seeing you."

I hate lying to her, but if it makes her feel better, what's the harm? It would take Bones the rest of his career to hunt down the list of people with an axe to grind against me. Besides, a torn playing card isn't going to kill me.

CHAPTER 29

TRAVIS SAT AT HIS desk, waiting to be summoned by the sheriff. He took a long sip of his Red Bull, something he'd been living off of for days now, and set it back on his desk. He stayed up too late again last night thinking about this case. The line between thinking and obsessing was getting blurry.

He stared at his computer screen, scrolling through the evidence sheets listing everything that had been collected or accessed in the Rachel Simone case. Those telephone records were crucial to see who she had been in contact with, in terms of both metadata and content.

If he couldn't access the phone records, he needed another way to find out about Rachel. But Rachel's ex-mother-in-law knew almost no details about Rachel's current life. And her ex-husband knew even less.

Travis switched to the image folder of Rachel's appointment book. The techs in the lab had photographed each page and downloaded them into a shared evidence folder. There were days where Rachel's schedule showed dozens of appointments, but these people were customers, not necessarily friends. How much would they really know about her, and who should he even start with?

He stopped scrolling and looked at one page filled with names. Rachel recorded the client's name and phone number, appointment time, the service she was providing, the charge, and how they paid. The more he looked, the more he noted her business was more than scissors and shampoo; hair extensions, coloring, balayage, eyelash extensions . . . He had to research what balayage even was: hand-painted highlights for a soft and natural look. The average price was over a hundred dollars, but Elana Garcia was listed as getting that for free.

Travis sat back in his chair. That's quite a gift. Why the generosity?

A quick records search revealed only one Elana Garcia in town. Grabbing his car keys off the desk, he glanced down the hall at the Sheriff's Office. Lloyd could wait for now.

◆

Punching Elana's address into his GPS, Travis pulled out of the parking lot and headed that way. It was a twelve-minute drive to the Spring Hill Apartments. He parked in a guest spot in front of building three, unit one, and rang the doorbell.

The door opened and a young woman in her early twenties with dark hair and frosted highlights answered. Her green eyes showed a mixture of surprise and annoyance as she asked, "Can I help you?"

"I'm Detective Travis Hendrick with the Sheriff's Department. I'd like to ask you a few questions if you have the time."

"I need to leave for work in ten minutes. Can I ask what this is about and whether it can wait?"

"It's about Rachel Simone. Would it be possible to discuss this inside?"

Elana touched her chest, and her shoulders slumped. "For her, yes. But I really can't be late for work, so we have to talk fast. I need to leave in ten minutes. I open today, there's no one else to do it, and I don't need any problems at work."

"Understood. I'll make it as fast as I can, I promise." Travis follows Elana into a tiny, open-space living room. He sat on a padded stool while Elana took the loveseat. "Did you know Rachel well?"

"She was a good friend. I knew Macon, too."

Travis was feeling a tingle of success at finding Elana and tracking her down. "What can you tell me about her, him, or them as a couple?"

"Yeah, Rachel said Macon was the very jealous type, and his level of jealousy and suspicion depended on what he was drinking or smoking at the time and his own guilt."

"Guilt over what?"

"Mainly that he was doing pretty much exactly what he was falsely accusing her of doing, but then again, that's most men, isn't it? Even after they split up, he kept texting and calling—awful things."

"Did you see any of these texts or hear the voice messages?"

"No. Rachel just talked about them. She said he 'loved' her in his own twisted sort of way—whatever that means."

"Was Rachel seeing anyone that you know of—after she split up with Macon?"

Elana stared down at her hands. "I don't know. I don't know."

"This is important, Elana. I wouldn't ask if it wasn't. Anyone at all?"

Elana rocked back and forth. "Maybe. I don't know his name, but I think there was a guy that she met at a club. It's downtown off Pearl Street."

"The Outer Limits?"

Elana nodded.

"Did you ever see him? Or a picture of him? Or did she describe him—anything that might help us track him down?"

Elana shook her head and suddenly stopped. Her eyes widened. "The club has security cameras. They're all over the place. I'm sure there's video of them drinking or talking or doing whatever people do at the Outer Limits."

"How do you know there are surveillance cameras inside the club?"

"I would rather not say."

"Well, I would rather not be working on finding who killed her, but that's where we are, so how do you know that?"

"I'm not getting involved. Or else you might be working on my case next."

"What does that mean?"

"Just what I said. I don't want to get any more involved than this. I am telling you what I can without jeopardizing myself."

"You seem to know a lot about what they were doing. Are you sure you don't know the guy's name?"

Elana stood up but didn't look at him. "I'm sorry, but I gotta go to work. I've told you all I can, more than I probably should have. I don't get to carry a gun or wear a badge. I have to protect myself."

"If you feel unsafe, we can protect you, Elana."

Elana's eyes filled with tears. "Like Rachel? I'm sorry. That's all I have. The video will tell you what you need to know—if you can get it."

CHAPTER 30

I PULL INTO THE PARKING lot of the Outer Limits and Travis is standing beside his car waiting.

"You didn't need to come. I just wanted to inform you I had a lead."

"Give me a second to get out of the car," I say, waiting for him to step back so I can fully open my door and exit. "Great job tracking down Rachel's friend, but trust me, you don't want to go and interview Beau Landry by yourself. I don't think you even want to come with me. He's a shady character with lots of insulation. He's the largest donor to nearly every elected official in the area, including your boss and probably mine, too."

Travis crosses his arms. "Yeah. I've heard he's not the type of guy whose bad side you want to be on."

"I'm not sure you even want him on your good side, Travis."

"Why is doing the right thing so hard?"

"Because people don't agree on what's 'right.' Welcome to life, Detective. Nothing is ever free. There are always strings attached. The question is whether you can see the strings and who holds them."

"My grandmother used to say the strings were usually in the hands of the Devil."

"Around here, that would be Beau Landry."

"All we're asking for is to see the security footage. Why would anyone get upset at us for trying to solve a murder?"

"Because for the clientele of this club, anonymity is the number one consideration. Let me take the lead on this."

Travis thinks about it for a moment and nods. "But I'm coming with you."

"Sounds good. Ready to put your career in jeopardy?" I laugh.

Travis starts walking beside me, but he doesn't even crack a smile.

We reach the door, and I ring the bell. After a minute, a poised woman in an elegant black dress strolls down the steps and unlocks the door. Her shoulder-length dark hair is angled longer in the front and gets shorter as it goes back. "Mr. Truesdale, Detective Hendrick." She nods to each of us in turn. "Welcome. My name is Rain. How may I help you?"

"We'd like to speak with Beau Landry. Is he in?"

"He is. Please come with me."

We follow her through the lobby of the club. She enters a waiting room decorated in black and gold modern furniture. She crosses to an ornate door, knocks softly, and opens it.

"Excuse me, Mr. Landry. Mr. Truesdale and Detective Hendrick are here to see you." She moves to the side, holding the door open.

Beau Landry is seated behind a minimalist desk. The room is smaller than I expected but decorated in the same black and gold style as the waiting room. Beau rises to greet us and motions to the chairs in front of the desk.

Travis and I sit down.

Beau smiles and folds his hands on his desk. "How can I help?"

Travis relaxes in his chair and looks at me hopefully.

"Thank you for seeing us with no notice," I say. "We're working on a murder case involving a young woman who visited this club from time to time. We want to review any surveillance tapes you may have. We don't think there is any connection at all to your club, of course. We're trying to see who she may have been socializing with in the days or weeks leading up to her death."

Beau glances at Travis and back to me. "I see." He leans forward, placing his elbows on the desk and steepling his fingers. "Perhaps if you tell me who in particular you were looking for and the date that you believe she was here, it will help us know where to begin our search?"

I remove my phone from my jacket pocket and pull up a photograph of Rachel. "This is the victim, Rachel Simone. And we'd like to get all of the surveillance footage you have from the last month."

Beau raises his eyebrows and offers a doubtful smile as he hands the phone back to me. "I don't recall ever seeing her at the club, but we have so many guests, that would not be unusual. I did see Rachel's picture in the article in the paper about the murder at her salon. Heartbreaking. So young, and a mother, too. I'll reach out to our IT Department and have them gather what we have. I'm not sure how far back they keep tapes or what precisely is captured. There are privacy considerations, but we will see what can be found and turn over everything of use. Should I have them drop off what we find at Cindy's office?" He glances at Travis. "Or Lloyd's?" Beau maintains his stare.

I smile at him. "The Sheriff's Department will be fine," I say, unfazed by the casual familiarity Beau used dropping our bosses' first names.

"I'm crossing my fingers hoping it will be helpful. Since we opened the club five years ago, we haven't had an incident requiring police response. We cater to a low-key and well-behaved clientele."

"I'm sure you do, Mr. Landry. It probably doesn't hurt to have half the Sheriff's Department employed off duty either, does it? Regardless, we thank you for looking as quickly as you can and letting us know."

We all stand and shake hands.

"Detective, if you don't mind my asking, how did it come to your attention that Rachel was a customer?"

Travis opens his mouth unaware of what Beau is trying to do, but I interrupt before he can answer. "We don't mind your asking one bit, Mr. Landry. Just like I'm sure you don't mind that we can't answer."

"Very well, just curious. Rain will show you out. I'll be sure to call Lloyd and Cindy and let them know what a fine job the two of you are doing."

The door behind us opens, and Rain appears. She leads us out the way we came and locks the door once we're on the front steps.

Travis keeps looking over his shoulder as we head to our cars. "He's right, you know. I don't ever remember getting called out here when I worked patrol."

"Can you name any place that's open late and serves alcohol that doesn't ever have issues? Like every week kind of issues?" I ask.

Travis sticks his tongue in his cheek and shakes his head. "No."

"If the club isn't reporting issues, that means they have a private way of dealing with situations."

"Hopefully those video recordings can help us when we get them," Travis says.

"You mean *if* we get them. Did you notice what Beau said at the end? He said he would call if he finds anything *of use*. My guess is that Beau will decide what's of use and to whom. But I hope I'm wrong. Call me if you hear anything."

"Will do."

Travis drives away, and I get into my car. Beau knows more than he is saying. I'll need to alert Cindy that she might get a call from one of her campaign donors.

I glance back at the club. A man on the second floor in a dark suit jacket with his hair pulled back in a ponytail is staring down at me. The hairs on the back of my neck rise.

My phone buzzes with a text from Mae inviting me over to dinner next week.

I glance back, and the man in the window is gone.

CHAPTER 31

MARTIN PAID FOR HIS bottle of American Oak Kentucky Bourbon and hurried out of the store. He wanted to celebrate tonight. All of the loose strings had been tied—all except one. But the cell phone he used to call and text Rachel was bound to turn up. He just needed time and space to turn his courthouse chambers upside down, or get Tiffany out of the house long enough to look there.

Last night was the first time he rested with any semblance of peace. He didn't know if it was luck or because Beau Landry lived up to his name of Mr. Fix It, but regardless, whatever recording Rachel may or may not have made was now burned to a crisp.

He pressed his key fob and the lights on his Audi flashed. As he sat, the passenger door whipped open, and the man with one dead eye got in.

Martin gasped. "You startled me!"

"Judge." Boucher fixed him with a cold stare. "We need to talk."

Martin nodded. "I was just thinking of calling Beau," Martin lied. "To thank him."

"That's not necessary, and that's not the reason for my visit. There's another issue. Assistant DA Colm Truesdale and Detective Travis Hendrick stopped by the Outer Limits."

"Why? For what? Why would they come see you?"

"They were looking for video containing Rachel Simone."

Martin's mouth went so dry he couldn't swallow.

"We need to ask you—one more time for absolute clarity," Boucher continued. "Did you have anything to do with the incident at the salon?"

"No. No!"

"We need to know everything. We don't like surprises. We can't control surprises, and we can't fix what we don't know."

"I met Rachel at the club, but I never talked about it with anyone."

"Did she?"

"I don't know. I wouldn't think so. But I don't know her friends."

"We need to provide some surveillance video to the police or they will get suspicious. But what we will give them will be from limited locations, viewpoints, and times. Neither Rachel nor you will appear in any of the videos we find. I'm sure of that. But I have to turn something over to them without turning over anything useful. We're going to have to alter and edit what we find and release, and do it in such a way that no one, not even forensic experts, notice."

Martin felt like he was drowning. "Will that be the end of it? It was an affair—nothing more."

"If that's the case, and you've covered your actions, this matter should be concluded. Are you sure there's nothing else linking you with Rachel?"

"Nothing. I was discreet."

"Do yourself a favor, keep a low profile and stick to your normal routine. And whatever you do, needless to say, do not discuss this with anyone. No part of it."

"That's a great idea. As a matter of fact, I already have a vacation planned out of the country—"

Boucher scowled in disgust. "The last thing you want to do is leave town. Act normal and do nothing out of your daily routine for the foreseeable future. Is that clear?"

Martin nodded.

"Now, for your end of it, where are we with the promise you made to Mr. Landry?"

"I've already gotten the ball rolling. Any objections to Eagle Point will be dropped this week."

"Good. Fixing your issue has come at considerable expense to my employer."

"I know. Thank you. I owe Beau."

Boucher smiled and his dead eye gleamed. "Yes, Judge. You do."

CHAPTER 32

IT WAS CLOSING IN on 5:00 p.m. as I make my way down the row of cubicles toward the Sheriff's Office, hoping to catch him before he left for the day. Judge Weber threatened to call Cindy to complain about me and threatened to do the same with Lloyd about Travis. I could handle Cindy, but Travis would need some backup in dealing with his boss. The sheriff would not hesitate to throw Travis under the bus to save himself a lecture from a judge.

Lloyd's secretary, Helen, covers the receiver of the phone she's speaking into and says, "I'm sorry, Mr. Truesdale, but the sheriff isn't in. Is there something I can help you with?"

"No, ma'am, just saying hi. Thank you." I beat a hasty retreat and notice Travis sitting at his monitor in what looks like a catatonic trance. I head over to his cubicle.

On his computer monitor a deputy's body cam video is playing. The deputy had pulled into the parking lot of Cutz for All.

"Hey, Travis."

Travis jumps like a kid watching a horror movie.

"Sorta jittery today, aren't you?"

"Just looking at body cam footage from the night of the murder—to see if I missed anything."

"Smart thinking, Detective."

"I need something good to happen to me today. I think I'm in the sheriff's doghouse. He said he wanted to speak with me this morning, but I think he went home."

"Can't be too bad if he left for the day. Lloyd likes to chew people out. It's his weird way of feeling like he's contributing to the investigation. I wouldn't worry about him, Travis. He won't be the last unreasonable boss you have and . . ."

My voice trails off as I stare at the paused video. On the monitor, frozen in time, is the first responding deputy entering the salon. He's passing the desk with Rachel's appointment book on it. The book is opened to a page with a gold star, but that can't be right. What I remember seeing was the book opened to the page with Shauna Phillips's name on it. There was no gold star.

I stare at the screen. The appointment book is resting on top of another book, so it's angled away from the deputy's body cam. I can't read the writing on the page, but the gold star is clearly visible.

"Hello? Is anyone home?" Travis snaps his fingers.

"Sorry. I was going over the crime scene in my mind." I don't know why, but for some reason I decide not to share this new information with Travis. Instead I ask, "Can you send me this footage? Send it to my courthouse email. I want my own investigators at the DA's office to see this and maybe try to clean up the video a little. Great work, Travis."

"Sure. Thanks," Travis replies. "I'll email a link. Hey, why are you here?"

I don't want him to know that I came to run interference between him and Lloyd. But now I have a different goal. "I wanted to see how you were doing and say hi to Bones."

"He's not in either."

"Okay, well, when you see him, tell him I'll catch up with him later."

I make my escape and head for the basement and the evidence room. I sign in on the evidence log to protect the chain of custody and note, "Review evidence for potential use in trial," as my reason for needing to enter.

As I wait for the sergeant over evidence to retrieve what I requested, there's the angst that comes with knowing something isn't quite right.

He gives me a large cardboard box, which I carry into the conference room set aside for prosecutors. It's what the cops call "the cage" because it does resemble a cage. Wire fencing from floor to ceiling to make sure no one can come in without first being logged in and their name recorded on the chain of custody sheets. You cannot have gaps in the chain of custody when it comes time to introduce evidence collected as exhibits at trial.

I remove the wide book from its evidence bag and lay it on the table. I flip to the last page with anything written on it, and it's exactly how I remember. "Shauna Phillips" is written in black and circled in red with a heart next to it. Starting there, I flip over each page, hunting.

The pages for October 8 and several dates in July and September are missing, and no page has a gold star in the corner.

This is crucial evidence, and it should have been handled as such. Missing or spoliated evidence tanks cases because it raises doubts on what else investigators may have missed or gotten wrong.

I stare down at the book, and the words *reasonable doubt* course through my mind. Either someone in law enforcement was grossly negligent in preserving evidence, which isn't good, or someone in law enforcement tampered with and altered evidence, which isn't good.

I review the log. It shows the deputy who found it and marked it, and it shows the deputy who collected it and bagged it. It shows the deputy who transported the evidence from the crime scene to the Sheriff's Department. Someone, somewhere, somehow, royally screwed this up. And it's going to be me explaining it away to defense counsel, the judge, and ultimately to a jury.

So how exactly do I do that?

CHAPTER 33

SITTING IN MY HOME office, I'm reflecting on this murder case and admiring this balanced diet I have adopted: alternating between whiskey and protein shakes. As of late the alcohol has outpaced the protein.

An email comes in from forensic examiner Jen Cramer, but not the news I hoped for. The still photograph taken from the responding deputy's body cam wound up being too blurry and too angled for her to clean up. I curse under my breath.

Frustrated, I turn the video on yet again. I know by now there is not a clearer view of the book, but this inconsistency has to be explained. Perhaps the defense won't pick it up, but you have to assume a good defense attorney will find every weakness you have seen and maybe more.

I need to vent, so I pick up the phone and dial Bones.

He answers and says, "City Morgue, you kill 'em, we chill 'em."

"Not now, Bones. I'm not in the mood."

"I liked you better when you had a sense of humor. What's going on?"

I take a deep breath and fill him in on everything I've found out.

"Travis gave you everyone's body cam video. Can you use that to narrow the list of people who may have had access to the appointment book?" Bones asks.

"No. With everyone coming and going, I can only rule myself out. At least six people either came directly in contact with, or were in close proximity to, that appointment book, and they're all in law enforcement."

"I personally know four of the guys on the list, and I'll vouch for them. It's true Travis is a nepo hire, but why would he sabotage his own case?"

"Does the sheriff have access to evidence at the crime scene, in transport, or once it gets into the cage?

"Of course he does, he's the sheriff. It's his department, his building, his evidence room. But why in the world would Lloyd do anything to hamper this investigation? Unsolved homicides make it harder to get reelected. I think Lloyd's a politician masquerading as a cop, but tampering with evidence is serious. That's beyond simply politicizing a department. It's criminal."

"Not if you don't get caught, Bones. Look at the facts and lay aside the 'why' for a second. We know what page was there and present when the first deputy on the scene went in. By the time I get there, it's gone. And now it's gone gone."

"What are you going to do? Are you going to confront the sheriff based on flimsy evidence? Are you going to call the State Law Enforcement Division? Notifying internal affairs is a waste of time. Lloyd handpicks who serves in IA."

I stare at the video playing on the screen. "I'll sleep on it and see if I can come up with a plan in the morning."

"Want to do breakfast?" Bones asks. "We can meet at The Junction and talk it over some more."

"Sounds good. I'll see you there at eight."

The thought of adding some real food to my otherwise liquid diet brings a flicker of a smile to my face. But the motion on the computer screen refocuses my attention. The deputy I'm watching turns back toward the door and his body camera sweeps the salon. He stops, and my eyes widen.

I pull the laptop closer. The body camera is focused on a mirror on the wall and not the appointment book itself. In the reflection, the appointment book is visible from yet a different angle. I can almost make out the writing on my small laptop screen.

My hands shake with excitement as I capture the frame and send it to Jen.

I pour another glass of whiskey to celebrate and begin looking for another shot or angle with the mirrors reflecting the book. Alas, there isn't one.

An hour goes by, and my email beeps again.

It's Jen. She explains she adjusted the contrast, the perspective, and flipped the image, and that enabled her to clearly see the following...

By this point, I am on my feet, but my stomach hits the floor. The missing page is for October 8. MARTIN WEBER. 1:00–4:00. LIGHT TRIM. $0.

"Martin Weber!" I shout at the ceiling.

No wonder we got such a lousy ruling from him. And then the anger begins to seep in. If he was a customer, he should have disclosed that up front and recused himself from hearing any motions connected with the case. How can he justify presiding over a request for a search warrant when he was getting three-hour haircuts for free?

My anger gives way to prosecutorial suspicion. Why would Martin want to cut the hair he paid so much money to have planted on the top of his head? Martin doesn't have enough hair for a three-minute cut, much less three hours. What could he and Rachel be doing for that long?

The hairs on my arms rise. This isn't a bombshell; this is a nuclear explosion detonating right in front of my eyes. I take a well-earned swig of whiskey. Bones and I have a lot to discuss tomorrow at breakfast.

CHAPTER 34

MARTIN SLAMMED HIS CAR door shut and rushed into the house and toward his office. That stupid hairdresser was still causing him grief.

Shutting the office door behind him, Martin hurried to his desk and jerked open the top drawer. He shoved everything inside to the left and to the right. He raked through the contents like a drowning man looking for a life jacket.

"Where is it?"

He stormed over to the couch and felt down along each cushion. He grabbed the back of the sofa and dragged it away from the wall, but there was no sign of it. He couldn't have left it in the car. Everything they picked up while cleaning the car was placed in a little plastic bag, and they hadn't found the phone.

"Where is it?" he snarled.

The office door opened, and Tiffany stood there staring at his trashed office. "What are you looking for, honey?"

Martin made no effort to conceal or redirect his anger. "My phone."

She rolled her eyes. "Oh, stop acting like a teenager. You probably forgot it in the car. Dinner will be ready in about five minutes. I made lasagna. Do you want it in here or will you join me in the dining room?"

Martin rubbed his hand down his face. "I'd like to eat with you, but I can't tonight. I have to go to the office."

"At this hour? Why didn't you tell me? I made your favorite."

"I have to go." Martin raised his voice. "I'm sorry. Believe me, I don't want to, but it's an emergency at work."

Tiffany's smile faded. "I can wait for you to get back."

"Don't. Go ahead without me. I don't know how long I will be."

Tiffany nodded and quietly closed the door.

Martin grabbed his keys off the table. The last thing he needed was for that burner phone to fall into the wrong hands, and the wrong hands would be any but his.

CHAPTER 35

SITTING IN THE CORNER booth of The Junction across from Bones, I wrap my hands around my coffee cup, letting the warmth sink into my palms. It's a chilly morning after yet another restless night.

"Are you listening to me, Colm?"

"Of course I am," I lie.

Bones scowls at me over his coffee cup. "Weber is a judge. You might as well throw a grenade in a porta potty if you try bringing him in for an interview."

"Having his name on that address book is enough. He's a potential witness. But if I use that, it opens a whole other can of worms. There'll be an investigation into a cover-up by law enforcement, which maybe there was."

"You can't prove that yet, so what is the upside, given the hell that's gonna break loose?" Bones runs his hands through his hair and mutters. "I'm gonna need a bottle of antacid if you really are taking on the sheriff and a judge."

"I don't know if it was Lloyd who took that page. I've gone over that video a hundred times. There's no way for me to prove who stole or lost it. But I saw him put some large papers in the safe when I stopped by his office."

"If it was the sheriff, and I'm not agreeing with you that it was, what's the phrase you use in court all the time, 'assuming argando'?"

"Close. 'Assuming arguendo.' For the sake of argument."

"Okay. Whatever. There's a reason nobody speaks Latin anymore. Regardless, if Lloyd took the page, he's too smart to throw it away. He'd keep it as leverage or hide it somewhere and claim he was examining it and 'forgot' to put it back in evidence."

"Let's say you're right. Where would he keep it?" I ask.

"Probably in his office safe at the Sheriff's Department. Close enough for plausible deniability. Far enough away to keep anyone from actually seeing it. Lloyd is the type of guy who would cover for a judge, but if you're not sure—and you're not—how can you get a warrant to get into the safe?"

"Difficult, to say the least."

"Between the three hours for a haircut for a guy with fake hair, a gold star next to his name, and a bedroom in the back of the salon, you have a guy cheating," Bones says, "but murder is a whole other level. Do you think a judge would throw everything away—including his freedom— and kill someone?"

"It depends. Weber has always been ambitious and had higher aims. A sex scandal would derail all of that. Men have done more for less logical reasons."

Belle makes her way toward our table with her radiant smile. I'm sure she greets everyone like that. It seems to be part of her DNA—kindness.

"Sorry, I was in the back when you got here. Do you guys want your normal or switch it up today?"

"I'll take my usual, Miss Belle, and I'll emphasize skim milk again because it drives my little friend crazy," Bones said.

"The same thing as always for me. And thank you for the avocados. You didn't need to do that."

Belle put her hand on her hip. "Did one of my co-workers dime me out?"

"I wish I could say, but attorney-client privilege, you know," I say, shrugging my shoulders.

"Seeing how you left me a hundred-dollar tip and I bought a couple of avocados, it was nothing."

"It was extremely thoughtful, and I am very appreciative."

Bones looks on with bewilderment. "Have I missed something?"

"You missed everything," I say.

Belle laughs. "I'll get these in and back out as quick as I can."

I want to ask her about her trip to the courthouse, but not in front of Bones, so I take a pass.

The order comes. Bones reaches into his pocket. "You won't need the page to bring Martin in for questioning." He flips a folded-up sheet of paper across the table to me. "Weber has three vehicles listed in his name. A 2002 Ford F-150 red pickup, a sky-blue BMW convertible, and a silver Audi. Check out the tag." He shoves a forkful of sausage into his mouth.

I read the police vehicle report and sit up. "W8N2GLF."

"Waiting to golf." Bones sarcastically chuckles. "It matches the partial plate given by your witness."

"This is becoming a lot more than a set of coincidences and a judge trying to conceal an affair."

"Maybe, but you're going to need a lot more if you're going after him," Bones says.

"Forensics has great tire prints. If we can get photographs of the judge's tires, that could work."

Bones stops with his fork halfway to his mouth. "Which leads to my next question: What are you going to do about Travis?"

"Are you asking if I trust him?"

Bones nods and starts in on his pancakes.

"I can't conclusively rule him out for taking the page any more than he could rule me out, but he's given me no reason to distrust him. I was going to loop him in, but I wanted to ask you about something you said. You called him a nepo baby, but his father is a professor and his mother is a stay-at-home mom."

Bones set down his fork. "The issue is who his mom stays home with while the husband is at school. I'll give you three guesses and a hint. It rhymes with Floyd."

I almost choke on my omelet. "Seriously?"

"So the story goes, and I have no reason to doubt the source. A rookie deputy called me a few months back. He'd spotted a car parked next to Lawson's Fork Creek. When he knocked on the window, the sheriff and Travis's mother were in a compromising position and a limited state of dress. The rookie figured he was going to get fired and asked me what to do. I told him to shut up. He did. Haven't heard another word about it since. But I believed him."

I take a deep breath. "Travis hasn't given me cause to doubt him, and taking him off the case would result in questions and delays and fights and interagency squabbles, none of which I want or need right now. I'm going to loop him in and have him photograph the judge's tires."

Belle hurries over to our table, a little distracted but still pleasant. "They'll take that whenever you're ready. No rush. Hope you both have a wonderful day."

Bones turns to me and says, "Why does she always look at you when she talks to us?"

"I don't know, Bones. You should have seen the way you devoured your breakfast. Maybe she's afraid to get too close during feeding time."

I snatch the check off the table and Bones laughs.

"That was funny, buddy. And thanks for buying—again."

"Anytime." I tip more than Bones, so that's the real reason I reach for the bill. Plus, we're really coming here so often because of me, so why should he pay for my smile.

I settle the bill and Bones heads out. On my way to my car, I spy Belle at the picnic table outside, looking preoccupied. She sits with a tablet and phone by her left hand and a stack of papers and folders to her right. A yellow pencil is clenched between her teeth as she glares down at the form before her.

I think about heading on in to work, but this gentle, familiar voice in my head says, "Try to help, Colm . . ."

So, I do a mini-pirouette and walk toward the picnic table.

"You can eat the pencil if you want to, but the food inside is pretty good."

She takes the pencil out of her mouth and laughs.

"I'm not trying to insert myself, but your friend that dimed you out on the avocado also mentioned you had to do something at the court-house. I doubt I can help, but if I can, I'll try."

Belle sighs. "My father is a veteran who needs to go on disability, but I don't know what kind to apply for—VA or social security. It's so hard to understand these forms. And it's impossible to get someone on the phone, so I feel kinda lost."

"You could go to law school and still not navigate disability law. It's a pretty niche area. If you want me to take a look, I will."

"I could never ask for that and I wouldn't be able to pay you. I'm just venting. I'll figure it out."

"You didn't ask, I offered, and I couldn't accept a penny anyway. I don't practice in that area. But I know folks who do, so if you want me to take a look or have someone do that, just say the word."

"Well, I am lost—that much is true. If it were for me, I probably wouldn't take you up on it. But it's for my dad and I would like to help if I can."

"Well, then, let me take the forms and have a friend look it over. I'll bring it all back next time I'm out this way."

"That's too much. Maybe your friend could look, and I'll run by the courthouse and pick the forms back up. No sense in you making a trip out here for that. I'll write our home number down and if something happens, great, and if not, I really, really appreciate you even offering."

"Done! I'll report back as soon as I know something."

She was in the process of saying thank you for the hundredth time when her watch beeps. "Oh, shoot! I need to get back to work." She hurriedly gathers up her things into a pile and hands them to me. "I can't thank you enough."

"Belle, I'm happy to help. Really. You can thank me if we get it done."

She scoops up her notes and the book she was reading on disability and is gone, jogging up the side stairs into the diner.

A car honks. Someone swears. The real world is back—in more ways than one.

I take my phone out of my pocket and square my resolve. It's time to unleash the firestorm that may crash down on my head. I laugh at the thought that I might be taking Belle's place at the diner when she graduates college if I am wrong about Judge Weber, and I dial Travis.

"Hey, Buddy. We have a potential suspect. But you're not going to guess who he is . . ."

CHAPTER 36

TRAVIS SLOUCHED DOWN IN his seat as he tried to surreptitiously tail Judge Martin Weber's car along Main Street. Sweat stuck his shirt to his back. As they crossed town, he kept sufficient distance between the judge's silver Audi and his own unmarked police car. The traffic light ahead turned red, and Travis rolled to a stop. He took a swig out of his water bottle. His mouth was dry before he set it back in his cup holder.

"This is career suicide." Travis stared at his hands, which were unsteady. The Sheriff and Martin were more than golfing buddies. They'd known each other for years and probably had more than a few secrets between them. Once Lloyd found out what Travis was doing, he would go ballistic and fire him.

Colm had good cause, and if this were anyone other than a judge, he would not be giving it a second thought.

Martin slowed, took a right onto Rutherford Avenue, sped up, turned into the court lot, and parked in his reserved spot.

After slowly circling the building, Travis pulled into the lot and parked in a public spot. He stared through the windshield at Martin's car. With tinted windows, he didn't know if the judge was still inside or not.

Travis drummed his fingertips along the steering wheel and waited five more minutes, just to be safe. Finally, satisfied that Martin had exited the car and entered the courthouse complex, Travis grabbed his phone off the front seat and opened his camera.

Colm said the forensics tech had such high-quality impressions they could match them to photographs of the Audi's tires. Since both tires on the driver's side had several unique characteristics, he should concentrate on getting pictures of those.

Travis walked as calmly as he could across the parking lot as if he were heading toward the courthouse's rear entrance. When he neared the car, he readied his phone. The sidewalk was deserted, so once he got close, he bent down and began snapping away.

His hand shook as he took the first three pictures. Using a double-handed grip like he was shooting a pistol, he braced his left elbow against his chest and took several more. Keeping low, he moved to the rear tire and repeated the procedure.

"Excuse me?" a woman called out.

Travis almost dropped his phone as he jerked upright.

Standing on the sidewalk was a visibly angry middle-aged woman and a teenage boy who stared sheepishly at his feet.

"Do you know where the entrance to traffic court is?" she asked.

Travis directed her to the front of the building, exhaled, and stuffed his phone back in his pocket. He glanced at his scared reflection in the car's tinted window. The sun, riding high in the sky behind him, emerged from the clouds. Through the tinted window of the car, a silhouette of a man seated in the front became faintly visible. The shadow turned toward him.

Travis swore and stepped back.

The car door opened. "What in the hell are you doing?" Martin snapped as he exited the car and removed the headphones from his left ear.

All of Travis's well-laid thoughts on an alibi disappeared. Some people aren't built for fast lies or surveillance work.

"Hello, Your Honor. I, uh, I'm Detective Hendrick."

"I'm well aware of who you are, but what I don't know is why you are spying on my car!"

"I'm not spying, sir. I was hoping to apologize," Travis replied skittishly. "About the other day and the warrant. I wanted to assure you that will never happen again. Lesson learned."

Martin scowled. "Do you think coming here and accosting me in the parking lot will stop me from speaking to your boss, son?"

"No, sir. I wanted to apologize without Colm being here, and you do what you think is right about the rest of it."

Martin shook his head. "I don't know if you're aware of this, sonny, but your running mate, Truesdale, isn't wrapped too tightly." He reached into the back of his car and grabbed his briefcase off the floor, dragging a white paper mat protector with it. The large paper fell to the ground and blew sideways.

Travis scooped it up and handed it back to the judge.

Martin stuffed it inside the car and slammed the door. "Lloyd speaks highly of you. So do yourself a favor, and before you listen to Truesdale again, run whatever he's telling you by your boss. That's my career advice for you. Do you understand me?"

"Yes sir, Your Honor, I do." Travis nodded.

"Good." And with that, Martin headed into the courthouse.

Travis tried unsuccessfully to swallow and hurried for his car. His phone rang in his pocket. He took it out and glanced at the caller ID— Colm Truesdale.

Travis let the call go to voicemail. Colm was the last person he wanted to talk to right now.

CHAPTER 37

BEAU LANDRY RECLINED ON his deep tan leather couch as Benita removed a Cohiba Behike from the cigar box on his desk. Her slender fingers gripped the guillotine in her left hand while she sensuously ran the cigar beneath her nose and inhaled. She rolled the end of the cigar between her lips to wet the end and—snip—a perfect cut.

Benita danced to the slow, sexy salsa playing over the speakers. She swayed her hips as she held the lighter up and lit the flame. Slowly puffing on the cigar, she nursed it to life as she glided across the floor and over to Beau.

Beau inhaled deeply in anticipation.

Two sharp knocks sounded against the door.

"Not know, Boucher!" Beau called out.

The knocking continued.

"Do you not understand what 'not now' means?"

The knocking grew louder.

"Well, then, come in! But it better be an emergency," Beau yelled. He plucked the cigar from Benita's fingers. "Come back in fifteen minutes, honey."

Benita raised her shoulder, her dress sliding down over her tanned skin.

Beau's gaze followed her out of the room. "The world better be falling apart, Boucher." He puffed on his cigar.

Boucher was silent, his attention still focused on the door Benita exited through. His dead eye stared coldly while his blue eye gleamed.

There was something about Boucher that made Beau question if keeping someone that dangerous around was worth the risk. Even tamed tigers can bite the head off of the trainer.

"What is it?" Beau asked.

"There's a problem." Boucher crossed his arms. "Our judge is being tailed."

Beau continued to recline on the soft leather couch puffing on his cigar. "Police or sheriff?"

"Sheriff. The new detective, Hendrick. He took photographs of Weber's car tires."

"Pictures of car tires? Where and why?"

"It was pretty brazen, boss. Right in the courthouse parking lot. They must have tire prints from the crime scene and he's looking for a match."

Beau reached for his phone. The muscles in his jaw tensed. He was thinking he may well have made a mistake. He was a perfectionist. He did not tolerate mistakes—his or anyone else's. But crime, cover-up, and perfection are usually mutually exclusive.

"Five Diamond Detail," the man on the other end of the line answered.

"Let me speak with Eric."

"This is him. Who's this?"

"Beau."

"My apologies, Mr. Landry. I didn't recognize your voice, sir."

"Earlier this week, you contacted me when Martin Weber brought his Audi in to be detailed, right?"

"Yes, sir."

"Why did he bring the car in?"

"He said something about his son's friend getting hurt playing pickleball. Said the kid took a paddle to the face and it gave him a bloody nose. Did he complain or something?"

"No, Eric. Everything is fine. Good work."

Beau hung up and set the cigar in the ashtray. He met Boucher's cold stare and nodded. "I may have misjudged the judge. He may have had something to do with what happened. And he is making too many mistakes now."

Boucher shrugged. "The police are looking at him. If you ask me, cut your losses and feed him to the wolves, boss."

Beau rose and strolled over to the bar. "The police are looking here, too, Boucher. Someone told them to ask for the surveillance tapes. They did not come up with that on their own. We need to know where that tip came from and seal the leak. I've invested too much in Martin to walk away, especially now. We need to keep him afloat at least until he does what he promised to do. But we do need a tighter leash."

"No one can remove all the evidence, boss. There will always be traces left somewhere."

"You're right." Beau poured himself a bourbon and lifted the bottle toward Boucher, who shook his head. "Maybe we focused on the wrong thing. Perhaps we cannot remove the evidence. But can we remove the ones looking for the evidence?"

Boucher grinned sadistically. "That would bring a lot of attention, and not just local."

"I know. Right now, we need to send a message. Strong, not lethal. We need them to ease off their investigation or redirect their resources. I do not care about Martin so much as he has now involved us."

"The detective is an easy mark. He never even noticed me following him."

"He's not the one I am worried about. I want you to send a message to Truesdale. Nothing too harsh, but enough to make him reconsider retirement. He took one leave of absence—maybe it's time for another one."

"Your definition of harsh and mine vary. Hospital?"

"Not if you can help it, but make sure that Colm Truesdale understands that if he continues down the road he's on, there will be consequences. Try a graceful exit first, and if graceful doesn't cut it, we can move on to grave."

CHAPTER 38

I'M SITTING IN THE small conference room reserved for attorneys at the courthouse. Travis is pacing in front of the windows. With each pass, he stops, shakes his head, peeks out the window, and starts again. Nervousness manifests itself in so many different ways: talking too much, talking too little, movement, sitting like a statue. Travis has opted for movement, lots of it. I can't blame him. The last time we were here, Judge Weber threatened both of our careers. I didn't care. But it's different for Travis if this goes south. No Sheriff's Department in the state would hire him.

The door to the chambers opens, and Judge Aaron Harrison enters. In his late seventies, Judge Harrison's hair is dark silver, his thick glasses have bifocals, and his face bears the cynicism of presiding over a thousand trials. A thin man, his crisp white shirt with a dark tie appears two sizes too large for his neck. But he is impeccably dressed and hasn't lost a step mentally or physically. He firmly shakes my hand, then Travis's, and sits in the nearest chair.

"Thank you for seeing us on such short notice, Your Honor."

Harrison nods. He is relentlessly demanding of both sides of the courtroom. He is an equal opportunity abuser of both prosecutors and defense attorneys who do not meet his expectations. He does not tolerate shortcuts, discovery games, or courtroom shenanigans. He charged his own courtroom bailiff with contempt for falling asleep in court and had a deputy, who was a witness, led out of the courtroom in handcuffs when the deputy refused to follow his instructions on what he could and could not testify to.

"Your Honor." Travis nods so low that it resembles a bow.

I relax a bit when I notice that Harrison cracks a faint smile.

I take a deep breath before launching into my opening argument.

"The reason we wanted to meet privately and not prefile any requests or affidavits is because this is a very sensitive matter. When I explain it, you will see what I mean. I've never had a case like this one before."

"Sidestepping protocols is not something that I am particularly fond of, or known for, Counselor, so let me caution you before you begin that you better have a darn good reason for doing this ex parte, in my chambers, and without filing your paperwork. You could have filed it under seal, you know, if you were worried about public exposure."

"Yes sir, Your Honor. It's not just public disclosure that is risky here, sir. It's also sensitive within the confines of this courthouse."

Judge Harrison sat up a little straighter. He had seen and heard it all before, but this at least had the potential to be different. "Well, Counselor, at some point, my decision—no matter what it is—will be made public and thereafter reviewed by appellate courts, so I am going to review whatever request you have in an exacting way. With that said, do you still wish to continue?"

Before my heart beats twice, a hundred different calculations flash through my mind. The one fact that shouts the loudest is that if I show the slightest hesitation in my request, Harrison will sense the uncertainty and undoubtedly deny it. "Yes, Your Honor."

"Proceed."

"Detective Hendrick is investigating the murder of Rachel Simone at her beauty salon. She was stabbed multiple times, and the crime scene was gruesome. It was, Your Honor, what forensic psychiatrists call 'overkill.' As part of that investigation, we are requesting a warrant to obtain cell phone records, including all calls, text messages, and location data, for Judge Martin Weber's cell phone."

The silence was piercing. It seemed like an eternity.

Harrison's unflappable expression cracks and his eyes widen, but he maintains the uncomfortable silence. Since nature abhors a vacuum, and he had not ordered me arrested, at least not yet, I decided to keep going.

"There are a number of pieces of evidence that constitute more than sufficient probable cause, in our judgment." I nod to Travis, which was supposed to be his cue to take over the conversation.

Travis clears his throat and blankly stares back at me.

I motion to him, and he slides the folder across the table to me.

Harrison frowns. At this point, it should be the detective summarizing the evidence, not the prosecutor, but someone has to speak up.

"Your Honor, we have an eyewitness who reported seeing a vehicle that matches the description of one owned by, and registered to, Martin Weber. This vehicle was seen leaving the scene of the murder at a high rate of speed and almost striking a witness's vehicle. The witness, while not recalling the make, described the car as a new, two-door silver coupe with dark, tinted windows. That description matches Judge Weber's vehicle. In addition, the witness recalled three of the digits of the license plate. While the witness only recorded a partial tag, the part the witness did see and record matched a plate registered to a vehicle currently owned and operated by Judge Weber."

The muscles along Harrison's temples throb. He purses his lips and nods.

"The sheriff's forensic team was able to capture high-quality tire print impressions from the rear of the salon due to favorable ground conditions. The technicians were able to determine the make and size of the tires that created the tread marks. Their analysis also concluded that the tires that left the impressions recently had struck a sharp-edged metal object, such as a steel plate used during road work. The impact left several cuts and gouges in the tire tread on the vehicle's driver side." I flip to the next page.

Harrison adjusts his glasses and picks up the forensic report. After a minute, he says more to himself, "It's amazing what forensics can do nowadays. These tires look new, but forensics made a definitive match."

A silence descends on the room, which is so profound that it feels like I'm sitting at the bottom of the deep end of a pool. The pressure presses in from all sides.

Harrison sets the report down. "Do you have anything connecting Judge Weber to the homicide victim?"

My left hand instinctively shifts to the second folder I brought with me today—the one I haven't opened. It's my emergency folder, and I can't pull it out unless Harrison tries to block this request.

Inside the folder is a printout of the still shot taken from the officer's body cam. The date, time, and Martin Weber's name are clearly legible in Rachel's appointment book. I hold my breath, hoping Harrison doesn't make me play my trump card. If I show him the photograph, Harrison might ask why I'm submitting a still image of a deputy's body camera instead of the appointment book itself as evidence. That would force me to concede the evidence exists but not in our custody, not any longer at least. It would open the floodgates on conspiracies, evidence tampering, and spoliation of evidence. Those are not places I want to go right now.

I take a deep breath. "The forensic report is conclusive, Your Honor."

Harrison shakes his head. "The report shows Martin Weber's vehicle was there, Counselor, but that doesn't prove the judge himself was there. But do you have anything putting him in that car at the time your witness saw it?"

Travis opens his mouth.

I narrow my eyes and shoot him a discouraging glance. He had his chance to speak and developed laryngitis. He doesn't need to start talking now.

Travis coughs. "Sorry, Judge."

"No other tire prints were found in the back of the salon," I point out. "None. Not even from the decedent's vehicle. The victim's mother-in-law said she always parked out front so people would think the salon was popular. And the bloody shoe path led from the body out the back door."

Harrison stares at Travis and me and nods. "This is close, gentlemen. Close. I hope to heavens you aren't thinking of charging someone based on the paucity of this evidence, but, as you noted, this is not a trial, and the evidentiary threshold is low. So I am going to authorize this warrant. I will, however, add this word of caution; investigating a sitting judge brings challenges, some of which you might not realize right now, and perhaps even I don't realize yet. My job is secure. Yours are not. If you are wrong, this is a career-ending decision for you both. Are we clear?"

"Yes, Your Honor," I said, not fully registering the reality that he had just authorized the search of a colleague's phone.

As I get up to leave, Judge Harrison fixes me with a stare. "Colm, be extremely careful."

"I will, sir. Thank you."

In the legal system, a judge was king. And if I was wrong, this was treason of the highest order.

CHAPTER 39

BONES PARKED IN FRONT of the strip mall and headed to the last door on the right. A man with a razor blade stood inside removing Frank Hastings's name from the HASTINGS AND HARRIS LAW FIRM, PA sign.

Bones entered and crossed to the reception desk.

Charlotte Abbot set down her phone and smiled up at him. "Do you have an appointment?"

"No, ma'am." He flashed his badge. "I'm Detective Rick Denton and I have a few questions when you have a moment."

"Is this about Frank?"

Bones nodded.

"I'm still in shock. No one saw that coming."

"How long have you worked here?"

"Soon to be seven years."

"Always up front at reception, or did you help with any of the cases?"

"A little bit of everything—that's life at a small law firm. Answering the phone, typing, filing, making copies, holding clients' hands, blocking and tackling when the lawyers didn't want to meet with someone. I guess I did it all."

"How well did you know Frank?"

"About as well as you can get to know someone when you see each other five or six days a week for seven years."

"Was business okay? Was he under any extra stress or financial weight?"

"His practice was a little, shall we say, cyclical. He did a little bit of everything, but he probably wasn't the 'go-to' lawyer for anything. He was more of a jack-of-all-trades from wills to closings to divorce and criminal law."

"Did you keep the books? Would you have known if there were financial pressures?"

"I definitely did not keep the books, but I knew how things were based on his mood and whether he would have me call clients who were paying on installments and badger them to come in and pay."

"And around the time he went missing, how would you say things were?"

"I was doing a lot of calling, let's just say that."

"Do you know why Frank would have been at a cabin near the North Pacolet River?"

Charlotte picked the pen off her desk and shook her head as she stared at her computer screen.

"Did he have an appointment with a client?"

"There's nothing on the books."

"Can you double-check?"

Charlotte pivoted in her chair, wiggled her mouse, pressed a few keys, and shook her head. "Frank had no appointments listed on October twenty-first."

"Is there anything else I should know that I haven't asked you?"

"No. This isn't the first time things weren't right at the law firm. But we always managed to make it through."

"Thank you for your time."

Charlotte nodded.

Bones ambled back to his car thinking, *Now how would she know what day Frank died?* He hadn't said a word, and that information hadn't been released publicly or even to the family. Charlotte might bear a little further investigation.

◆

An hour later, Bones sat across from Dr. Ardell Sharp in the medical examiner's small office, reading Frank Hastings's autopsy report. These reports read differently now than they used to. When you're young, death is what happens to other people. Bones was about the same age as Frank, and he'd already lost friends to cancer and heart attacks. Autopsies used to be just another investigative tool. Now it's like the closing chapter in a novel.

"You're listing the manner of death as suicide?" Bones said.

"Of course I am. What else would it be?" Ardell slid his chair forward, placed his elbows on the desk, and proceeded to count off his reasons on his fingers. "The decedent tried unsuccessfully to hang himself. He was a very large man, weighing 311 pounds. The light-duty braided rope he used snapped, causing significant bruising around his neck."

"What about the bruising on his right wrist?"

"That could have been the result of his falling to the floor after the rope snapped. As I mentioned, Frank was a heavy man. Next, the skin on his right hand came back positive for gunshot residue. Third, there was stippling beneath the chin, and he left a suicide note. Have you interviewed Frank's brother?"

Bones nodded. "He confirmed the handwriting and signature were Frank's."

Ardell closed his copy of the report. "I'm surprised that you're surprised. We've been doing this together for decades. What has you questioning this one?"

Bones stood up. "I don't know. The closer I get to the end of my career, the more worried I am about getting things right, I suppose. This one is almost too neat. Plus, I keep looking for someone to tell me they saw this coming, that he was depressed or facing legal issues, something other than a dry spell in his practice."

"Detective, my options are pretty limited: accident, natural causes, suicide, homicide, or undetermined. It wasn't an accident or natural cause. It's definitely not undetermined, so that leaves homicide or suicide. I see no evidence he was killed by anyone else, so what are we left with? Suicide. It's all there—two attempts, residue, a note. Who knows why people take their own lives, Bones? I gave up trying to figure that one out. I know you are a homicide detective. You guys and gals see ghosts where I see science. Sorry to reduce your workload, but this is a suicide."

Bones nodded, but he wasn't quite ready to agree.

CHAPTER 40

I'M AT A BRISK jog as I pass through the lower parking lot of my old high school and head toward the track. This place is my refuge. There are so many happy memories from yesteryear, and this is where I come—religiously—once a week to work out the pain of the day, and the ones before, and the ones to come. It is a sanctuary in every sense of the word.

Back then, I ran this track more times than I can count. I preferred the short sprints, but unfortunately for me, the coach figured out I had a little endurance as well. So, it was the 800 meters, and before I knew it, he had me on the cross-country team.

Running was my religion back then, and on Thursday afternoons my convictions were rewarded—the cheerleaders would practice on the infield getting ready for Friday-night football or basketball when it was in season. We had to run no matter the cold, and those cheerleaders were so bundled up they looked like the Michelin Man as they fought off hypothermia.

That's when I saw her for the first time. The most beautiful girl I had ever seen in my life. Long, curly brown hair, blue eyes, and that smile. Her smile lit up the world. And dumb, slow me took about two weeks to figure out the smile was for me. That's when my life really began in earnest.

I still picture her every time I round the far turn closest to the school, like there's a rip in the fabric of time, and if I turn my head fast enough when I round that bend, she's still there.

Ally.

And God smiled on me the next semester and put me in two classes with her. Ally became the center of my universe—a place she occupied . . . well . . . still to this day. Every time I round that corner, there she is—smiling, happy, shy, gorgeous, all at the same time.

I'm nearing that corner now, so I break into a full sprint—like the old days trying to show off. I can picture her standing there. That's why I come here. Round and round I race, hoping that one more time our eyes will meet, and it will be like that first time—no distractions—just us. Things will be like they used to be.

My legs become a blur, and my lungs burn as I push myself even faster. She's standing there laughing and smiling, but it's as if she's distracted by someone else. She turns her head, looks away from me, toward someone, and her image is gone.

I slow to a stop midfield, close my eyes, and put my hands on my knees.

It never happens. I'm never fast enough.

A puff of dust leaps from the track a yard to my left.

The echo of a gunshot reaches me.

In the upper parking lot next to the school, a black sedan sits parked sideways with the driver's window open and a barrel sticking out.

Another shot rings and hits the ground a yard to my right.

Before I can move, the gunman fires four more times. Two on my left, two on my right, each barely a yard away, or so it seems.

I'm totally exposed and in the open. If he wants to kill me, there's nothing I can do. And for an instant, it seems symmetrical. This, in essence, is where life began for me, so why not let it end here, too?

I lift my chin and wait for the next shot.

The rifle barrel pulls back, and the window rises. The sedan speeds out of the parking lot and into the dusk.

Sirens sound in the distance.

I gulp in air and rub my eyes. From the close grouping of the bullet holes in the track, the sniper's intent wasn't to kill me. You can't be good enough to barely miss and not be good enough to actually hit me. But I'm only processing that now. Why didn't I try to run? Why did I stand there?

Mae would have a field day with that, but I don't need a psychiatrist to understand why. I stood there because I want to see Ally again.

CHAPTER 41

I N THE UPPER PARKING lot of the high school, I watch the deputy kick a small pile of broken glass, looking for whatever might lie beneath. The light from his flashlight gleams, sending rainbows across the tar.

Sirens sound, and the sheriff's personal cruiser barrels into the lot. Lloyd skids to a stop and gets out. "Colm, are you all right?" he calls over as the deputy runs to his side.

I nod.

"I'll be with you in one second," Lloyd says and proceeds to confer with the deputy.

After a few minutes, the sheriff strides over. "Evening, Colm. Tell me what happened."

"I was running, and six shots were fired at me from the top parking lot."

"Well, we didn't find any casings. They could have fallen back into the car. I put out a BOLO for a newer, four-door black sedan, possibly a Mercedes. You didn't happen to get a plate?"

"It was too far away."

"It's not much to work with, of course, but I am sure you know that." Lloyd shines his light on the ground. "Because of the tar we can't get prints. The broken glass is probably from bottles. Kids come here to drink and hang out. Have you been getting threats? Is anyone recently out of prison that you prosecuted? Anything the Department of Corrections picked up on phones or in cells about inmates who may be out for revenge?"

"I don't think you have the manpower to run down the list of people who have threatened me in the past, Sheriff, but there hasn't been anything lately."

"Can you think of anyone who would be shooting at you, Colm? Anyone at all—even if it's just a hunch?"

"Other than you? No, Sheriff." I look up and smile to make sure he knows I am not serious.

"Do you carry?"

"No. I have a .38 but I leave it in my nightstand . . ." My voice trails off. I only got the gun so Ally would feel safer.

"Well, I'm going to place a protective detail outside your house tonight."

I shake my head. "I don't think that's necessary. If that shooter wanted to kill me, he would have done it. He was too good to have missed."

Before Lloyd can respond, his radio crackles. "Sheriff? You're needed at Spring Florist. There's been a carjacking."

Lloyd reaches up and clicks the button. "Pete and Roy are nearby on patrol."

"I've already contacted them, sir. But I thought you'd want to know. The victim is Judge Martin Weber."

CHAPTER 42

I'M TAILING THE SHERIFF'S cruiser so closely people might think he's towing my car. As we race across town, I redial Bones, but it goes straight to voicemail again. I try Travis, but he doesn't answer either.

The next intersection is lit up like the Christmas tree in Rockefeller Center. There's an ambulance, three sheriffs' cruisers, two city police cars, and a fire truck, all with emergency lights blazing.

The Sheriff skids to a stop and so do I, narrowly avoiding his rear bumper.

"Truesdale, you almost hit me!" Lloyd yells and slams his door as he gets out.

I feign ignorance. "I thought you were escorting me, Sheriff. It felt good to speed, and for once, knowing I wasn't going to get pulled over."

Lloyd scowls. He doesn't always get my sense of humor. By that, I mean he never does.

EMTs are getting ready to load Martin into the back of an ambulance. Martin is protesting and waves the sheriff over. "Will you tell them that I don't need to go to the hospital?"

One of the EMTs stops tightening the straps and says, "I'm sorry, sir, but you were knocked unconscious. You need to be checked out."

"He's right, Judge. Let them do their jobs and tell me what happened if you can," Lloyd says.

"I stopped to pick up some flowers for Tiffany and . . ." Martin glances at the florist shop and shrugs. "I woke up on the ground with a screaming woman standing over me."

"A woman walking her dog found him lying in the parking lot," the EMT explains.

"She was screaming like I was dead. I rolled over, and someone had cut my trouser pockets open." Martin points to his slashed pants, which reveal the fabric of his pockets. "They got my phone, my wallet, and my watch." He holds up his left hand. "Thank God, they didn't take my wedding ring."

"Lie back down, sir," the EMT says as she helps Martin lie flat and cinches a strap across his chest.

"I'm gonna ride with the judge," the sheriff says.

"You're not following us to the hospital, Sheriff," Martin says, not quite understanding what Lloyd meant.

"I am literally going to ride in the back of the ambulance with you, Judge," Lloyd says as he walks beside the stretcher, helps lift it into the back of the ambulance, and begins to climb up with the EMTs.

"You don't have to do that, Lloyd," Martin says.

"I know, but I'm going to do it anyway. Weird things are happening today, and I'm going to make sure you get to the hospital and get checked out."

While I watch them load the stretcher into the ambulance, one of the EMTs swaps the gauze she pressed against the cut on Martin's elbow for a bandage. She pulls off her gloves, wrapping the bloody gauze in between, and places them in a plastic bag she tosses into the trash. Then she jogs to the driver's side of the ambulance.

I casually walk toward the trash can, keeping one eye on all the excitement. The ambulance doors close, and I inch ever closer to the trash can. We're going to need DNA from Martin, and now I don't have to get a warrant to take it. I smile as I remove the discarded plastic bag from the trash.

Travis emerges from the crowd and rushes over. He opens his mouth, and I lift my hand, cutting him off. "Let's talk over there." We cross the street and stop next to the Nu-Way liquor store.

"Of all the luck." Travis runs his hands through his hair. "Someone stole the judge's car, Colm. We can't catch a break in this case."

"Our next step after getting the phone data was going to be a warrant to search Weber's car. So, get with whomever you trust most in uniform patrol and let me know the second they locate it. Things are getting a little too coincidental. First, someone takes a shot at me and—"

"Wait. What? What are you talking about?"

I take ten minutes to bring Travis up to speed on the high school track shooting. By the time I'm done, he's pacing the sidewalk.

"Thank God they were a bad shot."

"Thank God they were a great shot. They easily could have got me. I was in an open field with nowhere to go. It was a message. I just don't know from whom or for what."

"What message does shooting at you send?"

"To back off. To look in another direction."

Travis's phone rings, and he answers it. He doesn't say much, but the longer the conversation goes on, the more melancholic his expression gets. "I understand," he says as he ends the call with all the conviction of someone reading a hostage note. "As if the day couldn't get any worse. Are you ready for a knockout blow? That was dispatch. A deputy found the car."

"Why is that bad?"

"Because it's at Jackson Park engulfed in flames. It was torched. The only thing we're catching is bad breaks."

I place both my hands against the back of my head. "These aren't breaks, Travis. Someone is covering their tracks."

"It's a complete loss. Even the tires melted."

"Good thing you took those photographs . . ." My voice trails off as I picture the close-ups of Martin's tires. "Hey, give me your phone. Open up the photos."

Travis hands me his phone as he moves beside me.

I scroll to the images of the tires. "Judge Harrison was surprised forensics made a match with Martin's tires because they looked new," I say.

"They're not." Travis points. "See how the tread is worn?"

"I know. But look at the rims, Travis. What do you see?"

"Nothing. They're squeaky clean. You could eat off them."

"Exactly. If you drive around South Carolina, your tires are going to have dust, dirt, and road spew all over them. These tires are immaculate—like showroom new. Martin had it cleaned professionally recently." I smile. "That means we still have a chance to get some evidence from inside that car."

CHAPTER 43

H AS ANYONE SEEN MY name tag?" Belle called out as she searched through the drawers in the kitchen next to the back door.

"It might be in the utility room, honey," her mother answered. "I took it off to wash your uniform last night. I hung it up to dry."

"You don't need to be handwashing clothes anymore, Momma. I can do that," Belle said, partially closing the door and putting on her uniform.

"You do more than enough, Belle. Besides, you fell asleep reading that book you were studying. I didn't have the heart to wake you."

"Thank you for doing that." Belle clipped the pin on the front, a couple of inches down from her collarbone. Most of the waitresses wore it lower. It seemed to work better for tips, especially with male customers, but she preferred people to look at her eyes.

"Is your brother up yet? He knows you need a ride. Why is he sleeping all the time? He should be out looking for work."

"I'll go wake Micah up, Momma. He's trying. Don't be so hard on him. He's sweet to give me a ride to work."

"Sweet? He does it so he can have the car the rest of the day doing Lord knows what."

"Be nice, Momma. Give him a little encouragement. I'll go get him up and then I really gotta go, so let me hug you both goodbye. I'll be home after my classes, probably close to eight, so don't wait on me to eat," she said.

"Come here so I can see the world's most beautiful waitress," her father said.

"You say that every day, Daddy."

"It's true every day. And the sweetest. And the kindest. Honestly, I don't know where you came from. Bend down here so I can hug you before you go." Her father reached up from the recliner. His eyes misted up. "And you do too much. Going to work early, then getting on the bus and heading clear across town for school. You should take the car. Ain't no telling what that boy is doing with it all day. All the people looking to hire and he can't find a job?"

Belle straightened up. "He's trying, Daddy. He really is. He's smart. He just needs to finish school to get a job that challenges him."

"It doesn't cost a thing to finish high school, or get a GED, or join the military. He won't do it. Mr. Gentry already said he could have my old job doing maintenance. There's nothing wrong with cutting grass, hauling off brush, and cleaning gutters. It's honest work, but Micah thinks it's beneath him. How can he lay in bed every day and not lift a finger? You're going to burn yourself out while he's sleeping himself to death."

"It's not forever. This is a rough patch. I'll be done with one more semester and get a job that pays more. We're fine for now. Just a little while longer."

"Fine for this month maybe, but Momma's insulin went up again. Everything is going up or getting up except your wages and my son." He shook his head and he huffed the way fathers do. "I told him not to quit school. And he's running with a group of fellow dropouts. I don't know what they do all day, but I bet it's gonna wind up getting them in trouble."

Belle's father, James, crossed his arms like he always did when he was finished talking about something.

"You better go get him up!" her mother called from the kitchen.

Belle glanced at her watch and hurried for the stairs. Taking them two at a time, she knocked on Micah's door but he didn't answer. "Morning, Micah," she said, opening it.

Micah's room was a mess. Clothes cluttered the floor and every flat surface. His TV was still on, muted.

Belle moved to the edge of the bed and shook his shoulder.

"I'm up. Get out of my room."

The alarm on his phone buzzed on his nightstand.

Belle silenced it and froze. A plastic bag filled with pills sat next to Micah's wallet.

Micah's hand shot out and swiped the bag. "I said, get out of my room."

"What is that, Micah?"

"Nothing. Get out, or you're going to be late."

Belle hurried out, unsure what to say or do but wanting to avoid more family confrontation. She decided to wait for the car ride to confront him, alone, without their parents around.

She descended the stairs and grabbed her book bag from next to the couch and set it near the door.

"You're going to hurt your back lugging all those books around," her father said. "But I'm so proud of you. You'll be the first, Belle! The first Atkins we know to get a college degree."

"I've got you—don't worry, I'll make the most of it."

"To God be all the glory!" Momma said, raising her hands and hurrying into the room with a brown bag. "I made you a little snack."

"Thanks, Momma. Don't forget to pray for me."

"We pray for you all day." Her mother kissed her cheek, handed Belle the bag, and hurried back into the kitchen. "I've got Gloria on hold."

"Maybe I can find a job where I can sit and work?" her father offered again. "There are jobs where you can put paint chips on a chain or put picnic items in a bag. It's minimum wage, but it's something. I can't watch my baby work herself to death while I sit here and do nothing. I feel worthless."

"Don't ever say that, Daddy. Never. God has a plan—even when we can't see it."

Micah walked into the den without uttering a word to anyone. Tall and athletic, he played four sports in high school and made good grades before quitting all of it. Apathy set in one summer and he said he was done with school and sports—and his self-worth seemed to quit as well. He scratched his head with both hands and rubbed his eyes. He grabbed the keys and muttered, "I'll be out in the car waiting, Belle." He opened and closed the front door behind him, never even looking at his father.

"How can one child be so good and one child be so . . ." Her father's voice trailed off.

"Don't say that, Daddy. Encourage him. Love him even when he doesn't love himself." Belle squeezed his arm and called out. "I love you, Momma. I'll see you this evening. Smile, Daddy." She paused at the door. "God is in control."

CHAPTER 44

ITURN INTO THE PARKING lot at The Junction a little quicker than I intended. My tires screech. I'm driving like a teenager, because my mind was wandering.

I'm rushing up to the entrance when I hear my name off to the right: "We don't close until nine tonight. There's no reason to drive like it's Darlington."

I see Belle has developed a sense of humor. "I don't know what I was doing. I guess I sort of zoned out for a second."

"It is a beautiful stretch of road."

"It's a little chilly out here. Wouldn't you rather take a break inside?"

"For sure, but I need the quiet to think. We got a letter acknowledging receipt of my parents' application, and they said to expect a hearing date soon. We have the right to have an attorney handle the case, but it's not required. We need to present medical or occupational evidence, I guess is the right word, of disability. So we are further along than we were, thanks to you."

"That was easy. Happy to help."

She takes a deep breath and stares at me. "Can I ask you a different question? For some reason, the closer I get to finishing school, the less certain I am that I made the right choice, if that makes any sense?"

"A lot of people wonder that when they get to where you are."

"I wanted to go to college because my parents did not have that chance. I know I want to help people when I graduate, but I majored in business and I am having a hard time seeing the end game, I guess. Do I go to work for a company and work my way up? Do I try to start a business and, if so, doing what? I guess I didn't think this day would come, when school ended and the real world began. I know that doesn't make any sense. I'm just rambling."

"Actually, it makes perfect sense. I majored in English and never wanted to teach, so my options were limited. That's why I went to law school—to extend or prolong the time within which I had to make any real decisions. It so happens I took some criminal law courses and found what I love."

"What is it exactly that you do?"

"I'm a prosecutor. It's all criminal cases, working with the police, working with victims, trying to solve a puzzle, and presenting that puzzle to twelve people in a courtroom. It's a mixture of public speaking and science and strategy. It never entered my mind to do this until I was exposed to it in law school, and now I cannot imagine ever having done anything else."

"I bet it took a long time to get there."

"You have plenty of time to have five careers if you want them, Belle. What are you, twenty-two?"

"Yes. I need to put my degree to good use and make a living and help my folks. They're struggling financially and sacrificed to put me on the brink of getting this degree."

"You can make a living and still follow your passions. You don't have to choose between the two. I would close the books for a minute and think. Think about what you love and what you're good at. And find a way to marry the two into what others call a career."

"I thought a business degree was what I was supposed to do, but my passion is helping others. That's what I love the thought of doing. I thought about teaching. But I don't know."

"The good news is you don't have to decide today. You just have to start thinking about it today. If you're serious about helping people, you should think about law school."

"Me? A lawyer?" Belle tipped back her head and laughed. "I wouldn't even know where to start. I don't know anything about the law or how to become a lawyer."

"But you do. You were out here working on disability forms the other day. Why not do that for others? Adoptions. Personal injury work. Trusts and wills. You could be a guardian for children. You could even prosecute people who hurt children. Prosecutors help people, too."

"Like you do," she added.

"The people I help are dead, for the most part. So, no, I don't get the feeling of satisfaction you might be looking for. Regardless, it's something to think about. Don't settle. Strive. That's my career advice. Strive."

"It seems like such a fanciful dream. I don't even know the process."

"But I do. It's pretty easy. You take the LSAT, see what your score is, combine it with your GPA, and see what schools you can get into. Let me ask you a personal question: How are your grades?"

"They're okay."

"And what does 'okay' mean?"

"I've made all A's so far, but this semester is hard. Why are you laughing?"

"Because a 4.0 isn't okay, it's amazing. So, the higher your GPA, the lower your LSAT score can be and still get you into law school. If it's something you want to pursue or have any interest in thinking about, let me know, and I'll drop some old LSAT prep material by the next time I come, and you can take some practice tests and see where you are."

"But I don't know anything about the law, Colm."

"That's why you go to law school, Belle. No one expects you to know it now. You wanna look over the material and see what you think?"

She nodded. "Deal!"

She smiled and the best and perhaps only good part of my day had arrived.

CHAPTER 45

TRAVIS STROLLED THROUGH THE entrance of the third car detail shop he'd visited that morning. The little bell chimed over the door, and a bored man glanced up from behind the counter. When he noticed Travis, he got off the stool he sat on and squared his shoulders. "Yeah, what?"

Each of Travis's previous visits this morning began the same way. For some reason, car detail shops seemed to attract, shall we say, a different kind of employee. And, like pawn shops, they could spot a cop a mile away.

"I'm not looking to jam up one of your workers," Travis said, trying to set the man at ease. "I'm looking for information about a car you may have cleaned in the past week."

"You got a warrant?" The man lifted his chin defiantly.

"I don't, but I'm happy to go get the broadest one I can get a judge to sign and look over every single aspect of this shop. I could always reach out to the IRS or the Department of Revenue to examine your books and see how you're handling tips. Or maybe the Probation Department might decide to ramp up its drug testing on some of your employees. Hard to say. But we can do it whichever way you prefer."

The man scowled but got the message and moved over to the computer. "Give me a second to log in."

"Take your time," Travis smiled.

While the man typed away at the keyboard, Travis stood at the counter looking around the store. A door with a large glass window looked out to the detail floor shop. Half a dozen men worked cleaning two cars. One of the cars was a Maserati and the other was an antique Corvette.

"What kind of car you looking for?" the man asked.

"A new silver Audi coupe. It had heavily tinted windows. The plate is W8N2GLF."

The man used one finger to type the information into the computer and pressed Enter. In the reflection of the mirror, Travis saw the screen go blank. "I got nothing here but let me check the slips in my office."

As the man walked to the office and pulled the door closed behind him, Travis eyed the computer. The man had blanked out the screen.

Travis set his elbow on the counter and slid it forward into a stack of brochures outlining the different cleaning options the detail shop offered. They slid off the counter and landed next to the keyboard.

"Oops," Travis said to no one in particular as he leaned over the counter. He quickly pressed the Alt and Tab keys.

A window appeared on the monitor asking for a password.

Travis shook his head, scooped up the brochures, and put them back on the counter. He began to pace. Travis walked over to the door and stared through the glass window into the detail shop. As the men cleaned the cars, they would throw their rags into four separate trash cans. The towels they were using were thick and didn't appear disposable.

As Travis wondered about what would be needed to get a warrant to search the trash here, he locked eyes with a man vacuuming the inside of the Maserati. The man was skinny and his neck and most of his face were covered in tattoos. He even had one across his forehead, but it was too far away for Travis to read it. Travis squinted as he tried.

The man dropped the vacuum and bolted out of the shop.

"Why do they always run?" Travis muttered and sprinted after the fleeing man.

"Chew? Where ya goin'?" someone shouted. "Yo, Chew?"

Travis raced out the open rear bay door. Behind the detail shop was a parking area and a large chain-link fence.

Chew scrambled over the fence like he'd done it a time or two before.

"Freeze!" Travis shouted as he ran forward, reflexively reaching for his shoulder microphone, which he no longer wore after being promoted to detective. Grabbing the metal of the fence, he scaled one side, pulled himself up, and dropped over the other side. His suit jacket caught on the metal, and his left sleeve ripped nearly in half.

Chew ran through the tall grass, headed toward an apartment complex in the distance. Travis dashed down the slope, slowly gaining on the fleeing man. At the bottom of the hill, Chew stumbled and pitched forward onto his stomach. Travis pushed himself faster, took three long strides, and pounced as Chew started to rise. Chew groaned as Travis's shoulder slammed into him, pinning Chew to the ground as he cuffed him.

"Don't even think of moving," Travis said.

Chew lay there gasping for breath and not saying a word.

"Do you have anything in your pockets I'm going to cut myself on?"

Chew shook his head and didn't look at Travis.

Travis carefully searched Chew's pockets. From the expression on Chew's face, there was something in there he didn't want the police to find. Most likely it was drugs, and the last thing Travis needed was to get stuck with a needle.

Travis pulled a wallet out of Chew's right pocket. In the left pocket, Travis's fingers closed around something metal but flexible. It felt like some type of chain. He pulled it out and held it up in the sunlight. The beautiful diamond tennis bracelet sparkled and gleamed.

CHAPTER 46

TRAVIS IS WAITING FOR me outside the Sheriff's Department's interrogation room door. He removes a see-through evidence bag from his pocket and proudly holds it up.

"You hit it out of the park." I hand him the stack of folders filled with papers that I'm carrying and take the bag in one hand while awkwardly working my phone with the other.

"It matches the photograph from the salon," Travis says. "Spot on."

I'm certain it does, but I still want to verify. I zoom in on the picture and there's no doubt—I'm holding Rachel's missing bracelet. The initial excitement dissipates when reality sinks in. I am holding what used to belong to a murdered young mother. "He had it on his person?" I ask.

Travis nods and hands me back the folders while taking the evidence bag. "I haven't said anything to him. I waited until you got here."

"Good work."

"I figured you'd want to lead the interview."

"No, you're going to be asking the questions, but I want you to take a different approach. Try to place him at the salon."

"What? You think Chew had something to do with Rachel's murder? I figured he found the bracelet cleaning the car."

That's exactly what I think, too, but I'm not sure Travis has the acting chops to pull off pitching the story I want him to sell. "It may be a long shot, but we need to rule Chew out. Then we work on how her bracelet came to be in his pocket. Eliminate him as a suspect while turning him into a witness. He'll be anxious to clear himself, but not too anxious to help us. Does that make sense?"

"It does. I'll do it. Do you want me to take lead?"

"Yes. But do me a favor: When I nod to you, take out the evidence bag and place it on the table. Not before, okay?"

Travis agrees, opens the door, and walks past Ronald "Chew" Ward, who is sitting on the side of a metal table fixed to the wall. Travis sits in the far chair on the opposite side, closest to the audio recorder. There are two cameras on the ceiling at either end, giving a clear view of the room.

I take the other free chair and slide it away from the side of the table, so nothing separates me from Chew. I set my stack of folders on the table.

Both Chew and Travis glance at the top one. In bold, black ink I've written: CASE FILE—RONALD WARD.

Chew swallows hard.

Travis begins.

"Why don't we start with where you were last week on Monday night."

"Monday? Last week?" Chew's face screws up, and he glances at me as if looking for the answer. "I don't know. What is this all about?"

"Take your time and think for a second, Ronald. Monday. Last week. Around dinnertime," Travis says.

Chew shrugs, but he can't keep his eyes off the folder with his name on it. The folder is as thick as a phone book and filled with paper. "I think I worked Monday, so I probably just went home."

"Was anyone there?"

"Me and my girlfriend split up. Why?" Chew scratches at his arm.

I glance at the sores he's hiding under his shirt. You don't need a medical degree to tell he's an addict. Even if he did remember something, it probably wasn't accurate.

"That's what I'm trying to figure out, Chew," Travis continues. "So, you were home. Is that the story you want to stick to?"

Chew nods. "Yeah. I mean, I think I might have been."

I place my left index finger down on the stack of folders with a dramatic thump. "So, if someone says that they saw you on Ender Road near the Cutz for All salon, they're lying?"

"Cutz for All?" Chew's voice rises as he repeats the name. He gasps. "Where that girl got killed? I had nothing to do with it."

I turn to Travis and nod.

Travis takes out the evidence bag with the bracelet inside and lays it on the table.

Chew starts shaking. "Hold on. I found that bracelet. I didn't take it. I found it."

I roll my eyes. "You're already in enough trouble, Ronald. Don't compound it by lying—"

"It's the truth. It was wedged down in the driver's seat of a car I was cleaning."

"That's not finding, that's stealing," Travis says. "That much we figured out, but what was the make of the car?"

"It was a silver Audi with tinted windows."

"If you found it last week, why was it in your pocket today?" I ask.

"I was taking it to show my cousin. I wanted to pawn it, but they'd give me less if it was busted, and my cousin, she used to work at a jewelry store."

The door to the interrogation room flies open. The sheriff stomped in, with a greasy-looking man in a high-priced suit on his heels. "Stop the interview. Mr. Ward's lawyer is here."

Chew's face pinches up. "I don't have no lawyer."

"Shut up, Ronald, and don't say another word." The guy in the suit slings out business cards like a dealer in Vegas. "You're my client, and this interview is finished."

"With all due respect, Sheriff—" Travis says.

"Save it, Travis," the sheriff snaps. "There's nothing I can do."

The lawyer, William Richner, asks, "Is my client under arrest?"

"He might be. We were discussing whether it was going to be for murder, larceny, or running from the police."

"Either charge him or he's coming with me," Richner says, while motioning for Chew to get up. "In the future, all questions regarding my client are to be addressed to me. I don't think I need to remind you of the Sixth Amendment, do I, Mr. Assistant District Attorney? Or maybe I do, seeing as how you've been gone a while now."

I don't take the bait. Instead, I say, "I'd love a review course on the Sixth Amendment, Mr. Richner, and you can throw in one on the Fifth, since it actually might be more pertinent. And then I'll return the favor by briefing you on the latest updates to the obstruction of justice and conspiracy statutes."

Travis looks to the Sheriff, but Lloyd is too busy escorting Chew into the hallway to notice. His lawyer follows and the door shuts behind them.

Travis jams the recorder off. "Now I have no idea what's going on." He glares at me. "First, you get me thinking that Chew may have had something to do with Rachel's murder. But that was a ruse to get him to admit where he found the bracelet."

"Yes, Travis. If we asked Chew about finding the bracelet in the car, he would have denied it and come up with some excuse for how it got into his pocket."

Travis opens the folder with Ronald's name on it and flips through the stack of blank pages. "What the hell? This whole thing was a bluff? Why not clue me in?"

"Because I wanted you to come off as genuine, and you did. Well done."

"And all for nothing!" Travis points at the door. "Chew lawyered up."

I place my hands behind my head and smile. "He did, but the cavalry got here a little too late."

CHAPTER 47

THE FOLLOWING MORNING, I sit down at my computer in my new basement office when there's a knock on my door, and Irene sticks her head in. "Are you ready for your update, sir?"

"Update on what?" I ask.

"Everything, sir."

I was sort of hoping to get a coffee before doing anything, but I'm still feeling some adrenaline from Travis locating the bracelet, so I wave her on inside.

Cradling her ever-present tablet, Irene stands next to the chair at attention and takes a deep breath.

"Are you going to sit down, Irene?"

"I'm used to standing while I give my report, sir."

"You're going to give me a crick in my neck, so please sit down. And please, call me Colm."

Irene sits and begins tapping away at her tablet. "I've forwarded you the report from your new investigator, Darrel Branson. I had—"

"Hold on a second. He said yes?" I knew Darrel a few years ago, so when I saw his name in the pool of applicants, it was a no-brainer to hire him.

"He was eager to start, and I have to say that he did a fantastic job analyzing the cell phone data you requested." She hands me a plastic-bound folder.

She waits as I read the attached summary. By the time I'm finished, my hand is nearly shaking with excitement. "This is perfect. And the summary is exactly what I'm looking for."

"Thank you." Irene smiles. When I raise a confused eyebrow, she explains. "Darrel prepared the report, and I thought it would be helpful for you to have a summary. I apologize."

"Oh, well, great job."

"I also coordinated these reports and the papers you gave him. There's a file for you, the DA, and two spares to give to whomever you deem fit." She hands me four folders.

I flip one open and whistle. "Where have you been hiding all of my career?"

"Does it meet your expectations?"

"No. You exceeded my expectations, Irene. This is the stuff of paralegals and longtime investigators. Great work. I better read up on this before my three o'clock with Cindy."

My email beeps at the same time as Irene's tablet. Her eyes widen. "I'm sorry, sir, but the DA wants to know if you can meet with her now."

I drum my fingers on my desk as I think. "Sometimes, it's not good to rush. Then again, if she's meeting with the mayor, it's probably about the judge, so I think I better arm her with the information she needs ahead of time. You've done more than I could ever ask for." I hold the folders up. "Unfortunately, the rest is up to me."

I head out of the office and to the stairs, taking them two at a time. At the top, I wait to catch my breath for a second before strolling out into the hallway and to Cindy's office.

"I thought you might be coming in to tell me you have a suspect in the Rachel Simone case. Please give me good news, Colm."

"I might have a viable suspect. But we are going to need to interview him and that's where it gets a little dicey."

Cindy looks at me out of the side of her eyes. "Having a viable suspect is a good thing, but you went and ruined it with the word *dicey*."

"Well, I will let you read it for yourself, and you tell me what word I should have used."

She opens the folder, reads a little, and rubs the end of her nose. She stares, blinking at the page, and slowly closes the report. "Judge Martin Weber. Are you serious?"

I nod. "I'm afraid I am."

"Judge Martin Weber," she repeats.

I nod again.

Cindy's eyes meet mine. "This would be a war. Please tell me the case is a slam dunk. Video. Confession. Nuns as eyewitnesses. Please?"

I take my time and lay out all the evidence we have on Martin like I'm running through a closing statement.

Cindy listens intently but doesn't interrupt or ask questions.

Once I've finished my summary, I add, "Plus we have Martin's cell phone data. While there are no calls from Martin's phone to Rachel Simone, his phone was at the salon on several different occasions for a number of hours. It was also there on the date and time of the murder."

Cindy rests her elbows on her desk and supports her chin on her thumbs. "The summary mentioned an incriminating text message from Martin's wife."

I flip to page nine to read the exact time and the exchange. "At 5:43 PM, Tiffany Weber texted Martin: UPSTAIRS WITH HEADACHE. DINNER IN FRIDGE. WANT ME TO COME DOWN AND HEAT UP? At 5:44, Martin responds: NO. IN OFFICE ON PHONE. DON'T DISTURB."

"I've missed the incriminating part," Cindy says.

"Martin wasn't home. He was at Rachel's salon."

Cindy nods. "I know, but if that was all you were looking for, Detective Hendrick would be in here instead of you. When is the other shoe going to drop?"

"I want to get a warrant to search Martin's house."

Cindy exhales loudly. "You can't be serious, Colm," she adds laying her head back on her large leather chair.

"He's destroying evidence, Cindy. We still may be able to get a forensic hit on his clothes or shoes. You would do it for Martin Smith or Martin Jones. We have to take this chance that evidence might still be there."

"No, we don't have to do anything, Colm. Not yet, at least. Not without speaking to him."

"It's better to question him after we do the search. Witnesses lie but evidence doesn't. If he knows we're looking at him, he's going to scrub his house like he scrubbed his car."

"You've told me what you have, Colm, but you haven't mentioned a word about what you don't have, which is a motive. And don't start with the whole 'the State never has to prove motive' thing. I know the law. But I also know juries. They are going to want to know why. Why would a judge do this and throw his career away, risk life in prison, to kill a hairdresser?"

"It's still just an assumption, Cindy, but I think Rachel and Martin were involved. One of Rachel's friends hinted at it, and there's something else that's important that I haven't shared yet."

Cindy's eyes harden.

"Look at page fourteen."

Cindy flips through the report and begins reading. Her fingers grip the binder harder and the plastic crumples. "You're saying that someone in law enforcement tampered with evidence? Why am I only hearing about this now? You should have come to me immediately with that so I could talk to Lloyd."

"Well, because that's the last person you should talk to."

"Is there anyone else you want to investigate? The mayor? The president? Me? Do you seriously want to investigate an elected sheriff and a sitting judge?"

"I wish we didn't have to, Cindy. I really do."

"When exactly do you plan on bringing the judge in for an interview?"

"If he wasn't a judge, when would you bring him in based on what we have?"

"Amanda?" Cindy calls out.

Amanda opens the door and says, "You have the meeting with the mayor in twenty."

"Cancel it."

"But it's with the mayor!"

"I know who it's with. Cancel it and hold my calls." Cindy looks at me. "I hope you know what you're doing, Colm."

I nod sympathetically and stand. "This is where the evidence is taking us, and this is what my gut tells me. You might want to call Judge Aaron Davis about the search warrant. I went to him for the cell phone warrant, so he's already been briefed on the case."

"Keep your eyes on your phone, Colm. And you can count on me being present for this interview."

I hurry out of Cindy's office and head back to mine. Along the way I call Travis.

"Colm? Did you get the green light?"

"I did. Go pick up Judge Weber. Be respectful. But this is nonnegotiable. He needs to come in and be interviewed. We can't make him talk, but we can make him come. I'll be waiting for you at the Sheriff's Department."

CHAPTER 48

LECTRIC. THAT IS THE only word to describe what being inside this interrogation room feels like. Sure, I have had important interviews with career offenders, psychopaths, and sociopaths who don't know the difference between a lie and the truth, but never a judge involved in such a gruesome crime.

Sitting beside Travis, I glance up at the camera, then over at my newly promoted detective. Do I ever miss Bones right now. I can't tell if Travis is contemplating saving his job by running out of the room, or steeling himself for the most contentious interview of his short career.

We've poked a bear, and that bear is either guilty of murder or will have a long memory about what we put him through.

The door opens. A deputy holds it, and Judge Weber strides inside.

I advised Travis not to stand, and neither do I. Typically, you might want to play to a suspect's ego, and that would not be hard with Judge Weber, but let's see if we can use his self-importance against him.

"Thank you for coming in. Since we are interviewing you in your unofficial capacity and not as a judge, we will refer to you as Mr. Weber or Martin, whichever you prefer, if that's okay with you."

I doubt Judge Weber liked the demotion to merely being treated like every other person would, but he acquiesces with a nod.

I hold my hand out toward the metal chair across from me. "Please, have a seat."

Travis begins. "You have the right to remain silent. Anything you say can be used against you in a court of law. You have the right to speak to an attorney and to have an attorney present during any questioning. If you cannot afford an attorney, one will be provided for you at government expense. Do you understand these rights?"

Martin bristles. "Of course I do, son. I've given testimony on their import at the State House. I've taught a class on those rights." He sets his elbow on the table and levels two fingers at Travis's face. "And I graduated at the top of my class at Emory Law School. I don't need a lawyer. I am one and was before either of you two were even a glimmer in your parents' eyes."

While he is lecturing us on his familiarity with Miranda and its progeny, I notice his Emory Law School ring. He wears the large gold ring on the ring finger of his right hand, and the diamonds surrounding the school's logo gleam.

"We appreciate your time," I say, trotting out the good cop play. "Detective Hendrick would never have called you in unless we thought you had valuable information."

Travis clears his throat and picks up his pen.

While he opens his notebook, I text Cindy:

WE NEED AN ADDITION TO THE WARRANT. MARTIN'S RING.

"Before we begin," Martin interrupts, "I need to make something crystal clear, up front. I am deeply ashamed of what happened between Rachel and me. We had a brief romantic relationship beginning three months ago. It eventually became intimate, for which I am embarrassed and ashamed and remorseful. I let myself down and succumbed to weakness, but having an affair is not murder, nor is it a crime. I realized, albeit too late, how very much I am in love with my wife, and accordingly, I broke off the relationship with Rachel. It ended amicably."

Travis is taking notes furiously. I want to remind him it's being recorded, but he's so focused on the notepad, I don't think he'd notice my setting off a flare.

"Rachel still cut my hair," Martin continues. "It was awkward, but people make mistakes and again, I'm not proud of my indiscretion, but I wanted to lay the truth on the table from the beginning."

I take a deep breath. The judge is playing chess, and his opening move was a smart one. Admit to what was already known, but couch it as some revealing confession and, most important, admit to what is wrong but not criminal. Martin figured if this statement was ever introduced in any court proceeding, he would equip his attorney with a defense without ever having to take the stand himself. By admitting to the affair, his attorney could argue how honest and forthright he was, when, in reality, he scrubbed his car, torched it, covered all his tracks, and obstructed the investigation.

Travis shifts in his chair and crosses his arms. "So, you admit going to the Cutz for All salon on Ender Road?"

"Many times, Detective. In fact, I was there the day Rachel was killed. She reached out to me, so I stopped by. It was a cordial conversation, but I also made it clear once again that our relationship was over for good."

"How did she take that?" Travis asks.

"As well as can be expected, I guess."

"What time was that when you went by last, Mr. Weber?" Travis asks.

"Close to three o'clock in the afternoon. After that, I returned home and remained there throughout the night. My wife and son were there, and they can certainly attest to that."

Travis turns the page in his notebook and frowns. He flips forward a page and then back two. His lips move, but no sound comes out as he reads from his notes.

Martin glances at his watch. "If there's nothing more, gentlemen, I do need to return to court and get some bond orders out before I leave town. I'm taking my wife on a trip to Paris. This trip was planned and paid for a month ago, and I would hate for you to have a question for me while I was gone, so please, ask everything now."

Travis is furiously jotting notes. He flips back a few more pages in his notebook and begins reading again.

"Detective?" The judge sighs. "I really do need to get to court, unless you have further questions—"

"If you were at home when Rachel was murdered, why did your cell phone ping out at the salon at precisely the time the medical examiner says she was killed?" Travis blurts out.

I could kill Travis with my bare hands at this point. He just threw our whole plan of questioning out the window. He laid too many cards on the table. In fact, he showed our entire hand.

The judge's face pales. He sits more upright; his once self-assured expression now turns deadly serious. "No. That's not . . ." He touches his right hand against his temple and winces. "I'm sorry. As you know, I was the victim of a violent crime days ago. I suffered a concussion, and I feel unwell. I apologize, but any further questions will have to wait. I am not physically able to go forward. I'll need to cancel court, too. My apologies. My doctor warned I might have post-concussion symptoms."

Travis looks at me helplessly.

"Would you like us to arrange a ride home for you?" I ask.

"No." Martin stands. "That won't be necessary. Thank you for understanding." He marches to the door and out to the hallway.

The door closes with a bang.

Travis drops his pen on the table. "I shouldn't have said that. I panicked. I screwed up."

"Yeah, you could say that, Travis. This isn't show-and-tell. This is where we keep our information close and try to get his." I glance up at the camera, wondering how mad Cindy is right now. I take a deep breath. "Let's hope Cindy got the search warrant because that interview was worthless, and we won't get another crack at him."

CHAPTER 49

LATER THAT AFTERNOON, AS Cindy, Travis, and I make our way up the front walkway of Judge Martin Weber's home, I glance over my shoulder at the six deputies following us.

Before we're halfway to the house, the front door rips open and Judge Weber stands there, cell phone to his ear with his eyes blazing. He's wearing jeans, a blue T-shirt, and sneakers, hardly the majestic look of a judge sitting atop a bench. "Really, Cindy? You really feel this is necessary? I've done everything you asked me to do. I would have given you consent to search if you asked."

Tiffany comes to his side and moves behind him. Her eyes round with unasked questions.

"We have a warrant to search your home, Judge." Cindy hands him the papers.

"I'm calling my attorney."

I don't know if it's because he's yelling at Cindy or if I'm sick of hearing him, but I say, "I thought you said earlier you couldn't find a better lawyer than yourself?"

Cindy gives me a sideways glance, then says to Martin, "We'll make sure this is done as quickly as it can be without jeopardizing thoroughness. Why don't you and everyone in your family gather in the living room while we conduct the search?"

Martin crumples the warrant in his hands.

"What is this all about?" Tiffany asks.

Martin grabs her by the elbow. "I'll explain it inside."

"Is Lucas home?" Cindy asks as everyone follows her in.

Tiffany shakes her head. "No, he's out with friends. Has someone threatened Martin?"

"I think it's probably best if your husband explains," Cindy says.

Tiffany's hand touches her chest, her lip trembles, and she hurries over to her husband. Martin pushes her away and shouts into the phone, "I don't care who he's with! Go get him and get him now! Tell him this is Judge Martin Weber and it's an emergency."

Travis explains again to the deputies what evidence they're looking for, where they can and cannot search, and how to take photographs and document everything as it lies before bagging or testing anything. Then he, Cindy, and I head upstairs.

Martin's home is grand, like a successful judge's home should be. Each object seems to have been selected solely to demonstrate, to either others or himself, his wealth, power, and influence. From photos of him traveling the globe to those where he is posing with the rich and power- ful statewide, the simple act of climbing the stairs is like reading his vast résumé and a who's who of luminaries, past and present.

We head for the master bedroom. An enormous king-size bed is in the center, but only one side appears to have been slept in while the other half has magazines and books strewn over it.

"Aren't we going to look in here?" Travis asks as I head for the walk-in closet.

"I want to get the shoes he was wearing," I say.

There are a dozen men's shoes all neatly slid onto a rack. I stare at a pair of Doc Martens as I pull on my gloves. I crouch down and Cindy and Travis crowd around me, gazing over my shoulders.

Travis shines his flashlight on the shoes.

I point out the dozen small, dried dots across the top of the right shoe. "We'll field-test those drops to see if blood is present and then send them to the lab for a full DNA profile, but it sure looks like blood to the naked eye."

Muffled shouting echoes up from downstairs. It's loud and continuous.

Travis races out of the room, followed by Cindy and me. Their voices carry up the stairs and down the hallway.

"You're a pig, Martin. How could you do this to us? After all I poured into this marriage and sacrificed for your career? A hairdresser?" Tiffany screams.

"Now is not the time, Tiffany. I made a mistake!"

"A mistake is calling someone by the wrong name or putting on the wrong-colored socks. A monthslong affair is not a mistake—it's a series of lies!"

I run into the living room and stop.

Tiffany sobs, tears streaming down her face as a deputy places her arms behind her back and handcuffs her.

Martin stands beside the fireplace, his hand pressing against his nose. "Stop that," he says to the deputy. "Release her at once."

"What are you doing, Jill?" Travis asks the deputy, looking as confused as everyone else.

"She hit him in the face," Jill says. "It's on my bodycam. She walked over to him and struck him in the face, which resulted in bodily injury."

"It was a slap," Martin says. "It gave me a scratch on my nose. It isn't really even bleeding, and I'm not pressing charges against my wife."

Cindy exhales. "Martin, you know better than that. It's not up to you whether to press charges or not. It's an act of interpersonal violence committed in front of a deputy, and it's on video. I told you we were going to handle this by the book, just like we would anyone else, and anyone else would be arrested for interpersonal violence. What happens after today is up to a court and a jury, but we cannot act as if she did not commit a battery."

Tiffany sobs. "What? No! It's his fault. This is all his fault. This is the fourth time he's done this to me. All I did was slap him. I didn't mean—"

"Stop talking, Tiffany. This will all go away, I promise."

"To hell with you and your promises, Martin." Tiffany sobs.

"I'm going to sue the whole lot of you," Martin bellows so loudly, the windows shake. "By the time I finish with you two"—he jabs a finger at me and then Cindy—"no one in the state will hire you."

"Good thing I'm elected, Martin," Cindy says.

Running footsteps echo from the hallway. A deputy sprints in, holding up a clear, plastic evidence bag. Inside the bag is a cell phone. He hands the bag to Travis and says, "This was hidden on top of the liquor cabinet in the office."

"I demand to see that warrant!" Martin shouts. "It doesn't include climbing on ladders looking on top of shelves and cabinets. You have greatly exceeded the limits of your authority today, and there will be a reckoning. That I can assure you."

Travis takes the phone, and as he does, his finger touches the side button. The screen flashes and comes to life. He looks at the screen and slowly shakes his head. He stands there blinking with his mouth hanging open. He holds the phone up for Cindy and me to see.

The last message the phone received is displaying on the locked screen. It's from Rachel, and it reads:

DON'T COME. LEAVE ME ALONE!

The message came in at 5:14 p.m., the day she was murdered.

I stare coldly at the judge. "Detective Hendrick, please place Martin Weber under arrest for the murder of Rachel Simone."

CHAPTER 50

INEVER LIKED IT GROWING up when people sort of claimed a certain pew at church as "their pew" or "their booth" at a restaurant, and yet here I have become that person, sitting in what has sort of become "my booth" at The Junction.

There's something about coming here that centers me. When all you see all day, every day, is malice and hatred, you begin to believe it is all that exists. You get the proportions in life out of sorts.

Nothing like a diner menu to recalibrate life.

This place—the drive to and from town—it's sort of my hour of peace. Last night was a tough one. I had trouble sleeping, which isn't new, but the cause was. I was staring at the ceiling running the list of evidence through my mind. Is this all there is? Is it enough?

We need the DNA results from all our evidence collected and Cindy requested an expedited review, but the state lab moves at its own pace.

I grab my leather, saddle-like briefcase, leave cash for the bill, and head for the door. I descend the steps as Belle exits the side door of the diner. She was working in a different section of the restaurant today, so our paths had not yet crossed. She calls my name and waves as I head over to say hello.

"You look tired, Colm," Belle says. "Is everything okay?"

"It's nothing. Just work. I'm fine, thank you for asking. I brought something with me." I open my briefcase and take out four thick books. "These are old LSAT practice tests. There's also a study guide and, once you go through these guides, we can talk about an online review..." My voice trails off as I notice the two men parked in the van next to my car. The man in the passenger seat is holding something in his hands. It catches the sun and gleams before he lowers it behind the dashboard.

Belle turns to look at what distracted me.

The driver, a short man with shaggy hair, gets out of the car and runs directly toward us.

"Belle, get behind me." Whatever these two men have on their minds doesn't involve her. "That's far enough, boys. Whatever you're looking for, you're not gonna find here, so head on."

They aren't armed unless you consider two cell phones and a video recorder to be weapons, but still, this isn't the time or place for whatever they want to discuss.

"This is Jeff Fisher and Paul Harris coming to you on scene," Jeff says into his phone. "Mr. Truesdale, it is true you're planning on charging Judge Martin Weber with murder?" the shorter man asks, as the taller one aims a handheld camera in my face. "Did Judge Martin Weber kill the hairdresser, Rachel Simone?"

I turn to Belle and say, "Take these books inside and head on back to work."

"Is there a connection between Rachel Simone's murder and someone shooting at you the other night, Mr. Truesdale?" Jeff says.

Belle gasps and drops the books. They land on the grass with a thud.

"Head on in."

She nods. Her eyes look like saucers. "Should I call the police?"

"No, I'll handle this, Belle."

After she gathers the fallen books and heads back to the diner, I turn toward the two internet sleuths and let them have it. "Let's get one thing straight from jump city. If her image, or her description, or anything about this young woman appears anywhere, I will hunt you down and make your life one living hell. Do you understand? You can write whatever you want about me. But if I see so much as a word about her, you will have an enemy for the rest of your miserable lives, and I don't think that's in either of your best interests. Are we clear?"

"Did the assistant district attorney just threaten us on video?"

"No. I made you a promise. And I'll keep it. She's off-limits."

"We'll keep her out of it, but you have to give us something."

"Yeah," the other one pipes up. "A picture of the grieving young prosecutor talking to an attractive waitress would get us lots of clicks."

"Maybe, but you wouldn't be out on the street to enjoy it. Either she's omitted from your story or I'm taking your equipment and having you arrested for interfering with an investigation. For all you know, she's a witness and you just intimidated her."

"Okay, okay. But give us something."

"Turn off your recording devices and we can have an off-the-record conversation."

"We have a First Amendment right—"

"You think I care? You show up and scare the hell out of someone, when all you had to do was wait for me to get to the courthouse. This is as good as it's going to get for you two. You get your clicks. You get your scoop. No attribution. Or the cops seize all of your equipment as evidence of obstruction and intimidation. You'll have to come up to the Sheriff's Department to claim it, but that's going to take a long time. They have a huge backlog. Of course, by then, our forensic team will have gone over it, and who knows what they will find. Maybe some naughty pictures or videos? If you want to play it out that way, we can."

"All right, we'll delete it."

"Good. I'll watch while you do it."

After waiting for them to delete the video and making sure they removed it from the deleted videos and photos section and shut them off, I relaxed a little.

"Off the record, without attribution. In fact, you can't even say it was from a prosecutorial source, a search warrant was executed at the home of Judge Martin Weber. The investigation remains active."

"And you being shot at is connected with the murdered hairdresser?"

"I don't know. Nothing has been ruled in or out yet." I nod curtly and begin to walk away.

Jeff shouts after me. "One last question. Is it true Rachel Simone was allegedly involved in drugs and prostitution?"

I spin around on a dime. "What did you just ask? Is it not enough that someone took her life? You want to take her name, too? She has a son."

Jeff stares into the camera and makes a slashing motion in front of his neck. He looks back at me. "I did say allegedly."

"Try to hide behind that and see where it gets you. Her family will be garnishing your wages until you die at Trembling Hills nursing home." I dared them.

I sprint to my car, slam the door, and pull out of the parking lot, my spinning tires flinging gravel everywhere. I am so busy being mad, I forgot to go back inside the diner. In the rearview mirror, I see Belle standing in the doorway of the diner, watching me speed away.

I'm still furious when I reach the courthouse, only to find three news vans, all with their satellite arms raised. This has truly become a media circus. I should have seen it coming, but I was too busy trying to do my job.

I drive around the back and park. The rear entrance looks clear, so I get out and walk with my head down. My foot hits the bottom step and it's like I step on a mine.

The rear doors of the building burst open and a crowd of reporters and cameramen stream out, surrounding me. They thrust microphones in my face, shout questions, and press in from all sides.

"No comment. You can talk to the district attorney. We neither confirm nor deny anything." I keep repeating it as I try to fight against the tide.

The crowd parts as three deputies push through and form a protective circle around me. They lower their shoulders, and we make our way inside the building.

As the doors bang shut behind us, Cindy walks forward. She already looks exhausted. "Things have hit the fan, Colm. Everyone from the sheriff, the mayor, and the governor have been calling."

"Maybe we're doing something right then."

"You're going under the microscope, Colm—like you have never been before. Watch every word you say and every move you make, because a thousand people out there are rooting for you to make a mistake."

CHAPTER 51

I'M SITTING AT MY desk, still trying to calm down from my run-in with the reporters, as I finish off my second cup of coffee. Pushing my keyboard aside, I write down the list of evidence we've compiled against Martin and listed it in the order of how probative a jury might view it.

Even the difference between typing away on a computer and the tactile function of holding a pen and writing in longhand proves the point of our justice system: How you do something has as much significance as the final outcome. The process is as important as the result. There is something cathartic about holding a pen and a legal pad and creating— something I don't get by using my desktop to type. So, I write in longhand at moments like this when I need creativity and I need to believe what I am writing.

Irene knocks on my door and stands there with a blank stare like she just watched a scene from a horror movie. I know the look. It's like blinking SOS with your eyes.

"Tiffany Weber would like to see you."

Of all the things I thought might come out of her mouth, that sentence was not on the list. But prosecutors are taught to never appear surprised—even when they are. So, I sit up straight, Irene moves aside, and Tiffany enters.

Tiffany moves to the chair without looking me in the eye. "Thank you for seeing me, Mr. Truesdale."

"Certainly. Now, Mrs. Weber, technically you have pending charges in the office and, while I am not handling the case myself, I am duty bound to warn you that if you say something about that matter, I will likely have to pass it on to whoever is handling your case."

Tiffany's lip trembles and she sniffles, "I'm not here to discuss that. I'm here to talk about something else."

I don't have any tissues to offer her. Irene knocks and reenters, saving the day with a bottle of water and a little minipack of tissues. She silently places them on my desk, closer to Tiffany Weber, and slips back out of the room.

Tiffany takes two tissues and dabs at her eyes. "My rings. Y'all took them," Tiffany says. "They said they're evidence of the assault. Do you have any idea how humiliating this is for me? It's one thing to have a husband who cheats and gets arrested for killing his lover. That's bad enough, but all of those rings didn't come from him. One was from my late parents when I graduated college. One belonged to my mother. I'm asking you to find the humanity to let me have some or all of my jewelry back."

"I can get them back for you if you like, or I can try to, I should say. Technically, they are in evidence at the Sheriff's Department, but I'm happy to make a call if you want me to."

She stares at me with hopelessness, which I've seen many times, including in my own mirror. "Part of me wants them all back. I've never taken my wedding ring off, not even for surgery. But then again, why bother? What's the use? It's over. Therapists, counselors, retreats . . . I can't do it again. I just can't. But talking about my marriage is not the reason I am here."

I'm careful not to cross my arms and instead lean in. It's a technique to make people more at ease.

"As much as I hate that man right now," Tiffany continues, "I know Martin didn't hurt that girl. He isn't capable of something like that. He killed our marriage, but he couldn't, he wouldn't, hurt another person."

I bite the inside of my cheek where I always do when I want to say something but realize the futility. I've heard those words so many times from wives or girlfriends trying to get charges dropped on a boyfriend or husband. And more than a few times it was the last thing I ever heard from them. Maybe they were successful at pleading for their men and got a bond lowered, or even got charges dropped by refusing to cooperate and testify, and then it turned out that man who "could never hurt me" wound up doing much more than that.

"You don't believe me?" she asks.

"I can't discuss the case, but my experience has taught me that people are capable of just about anything, given a certain set of circumstances."

"Perhaps you're right, and it would be out of character, but then again, so were lots of other things he did. This will end his career. It's already ended our marriage, but this will kill Lucas. That's why I'm here." She reaches into her purse, removes a single piece of folded paper, and slides it over to me.

I open it. There are three sets of numbers, each with six digits.

"Those are the pins Martin uses. He uses those for everything. If the code is only four digits, drop the last two."

"Why are you giving this to me?"

"I saw that phone you found in his office. I assume he used it to communicate with the girl. He's done it before. They send pictures of themselves back and forth. Sexting, I think they call it." Tiffany stares at her hands. "Unlock the phone, and I'm certain that you'll see my husband is a cheat, but he's not a killer."

"Have you seen what's on the phone?"

"No. Not that one. But this isn't his first affair. So, I know how he operates. He gets caught, swears it's over, destroys his phone, and things are okay for a little while."

"When you first came in, you said that you didn't believe Martin hurt that girl. But now you're giving me his password?"

"To prove you wrong, Mr. Truesdale. He's no killer. I'm sure the texts will prove that."

I remain poker-faced and nod. She doesn't know that I have the texts between her and Martin. She was home—he wasn't.

"Understood, ma'am." That's all I say, hoping she might keep going with her demonstrably false exculpatory statement. Those things are better than confessions.

Tiffany shrugs. "There's nothing to add. Martin came home from work. I made him dinner. We ate together. We watched some TV and went to bed. So, you see, Mr. Truesdale, there isn't any way my husband could have hurt that girl." She stands, holding her purse with both hands. "And thank you for offering to get my rings back. The marriage is over, but I would like them. I know it sounds silly, but you must know what I mean."

"I appreciate you stopping by and letting me know this, Mrs. Weber."

Tiffany smiles. "Good. Thank you. I don't know if you're aware of this, but my husband believes there's no better prosecutor out there than you."

"Thank you for saying that."

Tiffany leaves my office, and I stare down at the pin codes.

She wants to save him. She thinks she did him a favor.

I pick up the paper with the pin codes off my desk.

We shall see whether she handed me a bullet or a blank.

CHAPTER 52

THE CURRENCY OF GOVERNMENT work is office space, and right now I am broke, having been kicked out of my old office and banished to the basement. But I still needed a motivated team, which means we needed to meet and divvy up assignments. I commandeered an old conference room across from my office and moved the broken furniture and closed case files into a storage room as Irene transformed it into a new command center. She positioned a whiteboard at the end of the room. In the center is a rectangular table with half a dozen chairs. New notebooks, pens, a glass, and a coffee cup sit before each seat. A water pitcher; a coffee carafe; plastic creamer cups; assortments of sugar, tissues, and some wrapped mints are in the middle. Most of these were her ideas, but I have taken a liking to this notion of military formality and uniformity. I could use a little more structure in my own life. Our inner office team is nearly complete now. Two in-house investigators to liaise with Travis, a paralegal to help me organize our evidence for trial, a victim advocate for Rachel's family and friends to know when court dates are set, and Irene who does the work of three people.

Irene has listed all the evidence in each member's notebook.

I read it over and take a deep breath, then turn to my newly assembled team of investigators. "I think we are going to do this one a little differently."

I pick up the remote off the table and turn on the large TV mounted to the wall. It flickers and displays the first slide in my presentation.

"Let's begin with the witnesses or potential witnesses. Pull all criminal histories, convictions, and non-convictions. For the convictions, get certified copies. For arrests, get the incident reports and anything else you can find. The best cross-examinations take place weeks or months before trial. Preparation wins cases, not Perry Mason or Mat-lock moments."

I click to the following screen.

"In the next column are the exhibits we either intend to introduce or expect the defense will introduce. Below each exhibit is the chain of custody and how we plan on getting that piece of evidence into the trial."

"Not to interrupt, Colm, but what if there is a dispute on an item of evidence?" Stevie Ray, one of my new guys, asks.

"Column four is the most important column of all," I say. "That's where all of our questions, issues, problems, and challenges go. Column four will be our lives for the next weeks and perhaps months."

I stop and wait until all eyes are on me. "I hate surprises, boys and girls. It's our job to think like a defense attorney thinks, to think like a judge thinks, to think like a juror will think, and anticipate. We need to look around corners and see the ghosts before they see us. We must be creative and never be caught flat-footed. There will be setbacks; there are in every trial. But now is when we begin to plan for those setbacks, not late one afternoon in the middle of trial. 'Chance favors the pre-pared mind.' That is my favorite quote, and it comes from the guy who enabled you to drink milk without dying, so you owe Louis Pasteur a lot. He's famous. I am not, so my quote is simple: 'I hate surprises.' So, if everyone understands how I do things and why, let's get started with the easiest part, which is the list of witnesses."

Someone knocks on the conference room door.

"Uh, oh," Steve chuckles. "I hope it's not a surprise."

Laughter ripples through the room.

Darrel Branson enters. "Good to be back, sir." A medium-built man with close-cropped salt-and-pepper hair smiles as he strides over to me.

I shake his outstretched hand. "I thought you were going to start later in the week?"

"I was supposed to, but when Irene said we were getting together to take stock of where we are, I had to come. You know me, Colm. I have a fear of missing out." He adds a wink.

Next to Bones, Darrel was the brightest investigator I ever worked with. He understood what so many law enforcement folks did not, which is that the arrest is the beginning, not the end. Nothing matters if you can't get a conviction, and the distance between probable cause and beyond a reasonable doubt is a long car ride.

"Take a seat. We just started."

"A guy can't resist coffee and PowerPoint." Darrel chuckles as he pours himself a cup and sits down.

I move to the front of the room and launch into an overview of what many of them already know. I add the caveat that there is a difference between what we think, what we believe, what we know, and what we can prove. We have to get from knowing it to proving it.

"Rachel Simone was a twenty-six-year-old single mother who began a relationship with Judge Martin Weber at least two months ago, maybe longer. We'll know more once the computer techs process Martin's burner phone."

"What about Rachel's phone?" Darrel asks. "I didn't see mention of it in the report."

"We haven't located it. It was either taken, or missed and destroyed in the fire. Hopefully, we have a workaround through Martin's burner phone."

I switch to the next screen, and a map appears on the TV.

"We have analyzed some of the data from the defendant's personal cell phone. It places him at the scene twice on the day of the murder. He stopped by the salon at three fifteen p.m. and again at five thirty-four p.m."

Darrel clears his throat. "You're still looking for critical feedback in the meetings, aren't you?"

"I'd much rather hear it from you than a judge or jury."

"The data places the phone at the scene, not necessarily the judge."

"That's true. But in addition to the cell phone location, we recovered a set of Doc Martens shoes from the judge's house that forensics has matched to the bloody prints found at the scene."

Steve laughs. "Now that's ironic. Judge Martin wears Doc Martens?"

"Forensics also discovered blood spatter on the shoes. We sent the shoes and Martin's class ring off to see what can be taken from the items and is fit for testing."

"Why the ring?" Darrel flips through the report. "I thought the killer wore gloves."

"He did. But the ring finger ripped open. I think it was because of the school ring Martin wears."

"That's smart. Real smart. Speaking of those gloves, what were the DNA results for them and the tissues they found near the back door?"

"The report from the lab just came in. Irene's printing out copies now. We also have recovered a tennis bracelet from Martin's car."

"I might put that under your potential problem column. Column four, is that right?" Darrel says.

"That's correct. What have you found out?"

"I ran a criminal history on the worker who found it. Ronald's record isn't the best."

"No, but nuns don't work at detail shops. I can explain that to the jury."

The door opens, and Irene walks in. I expected her to be carrying a stack of reports but there's only one in her hand.

"Was there a problem with the copier?" I ask.

She shakes her head. "I was reading the report before I copied it. It's not what we were hoping for, sir. They found Rachel Simone's blood on the discarded latex gloves, but there was no DNA inside the gloves."

I take the report from her and begin to read. "The DNA match for Rachel's blood is conclusive, but the results from inside the gloves are consistent with hand sanitizer."

"That's not a shock," Darrel says. "The judge would be familiar with the fact that DNA is left behind when you put on gloves. He probably wiped his hands down with sanitizer to hide his DNA before he put the gloves on."

Irene nods but then starts shaking her head. "That's not the bad part. It's the tissues."

"Do you mean the tissues found near the backdoor?" I ask.

"Yes, sir, those," Irene says.

My eyes grow wide as I read the results aloud. "Cindy sent a sample of Martin's DNA that I recovered from his carjacking. The DNA on the tissue is only a partial match."

"How is that possible?" Darrel asks.

"Because it is familial DNA. Martin has a son named Lucas," I say.

Steve clears his throat. "That's definitely going into column four."

Yep, and the bigger column four gets, the worse our case is.

CHAPTER 53

I CLIMB THE STEPS TWO at a time, racing toward Cindy's office. She's putting together a press release on the arrest of Judge Martin Weber, and I need to head her off—at least for now. I dash out of the stairwell, sprint down the hallway, and hurry through the waiting room, giving a quick wave to Amanda but not waiting for her response. I shove Cindy's door open while yelling, "Don't send anything to press yet!" And I wait for her reaction, hoping I am not too late.

Cindy is sitting in front of her computer, her fingers hovering above the keyboard. "This better be good. I am getting inundated by the media, and we have to put something out, even if it's a nothing burger."

I grab the back of one of the chairs in front of her desk and try to catch my breath, managing to say, "We may have a problem."

It is Cindy's singularly least favorite saying.

"I don't have a workaround yet, because I came to see you first. Please tell me you haven't sent the press release yet."

Cindy slowly reaches for her mouse like she's dismantling a bomb. "No, but my finger was on the trigger."

"There's been a development with the DNA. It is not only partially exculpatory, but it may point to third-party guilt. I have to figure out how to deal with it."

Cindy clicks the mouse and grabs the arms of her chair, and I can see the tornado coming. "Well, this is a fine time to figure out the suspect might be factually innocent."

"Technically, we don't make arrests, the cops do, and . . ."

"Don't even start with that, Colm. What is this evidentiary issue and what is your solution?"

"There were tissues found at the crime scene that had blood on them.

We, of course, believed the blood would have been either Rachel's or the judge's. Those tissues were discarded or dropped or otherwise left near the back door where we believe the killer exited her salon. But the DNA didn't come back to either Rachel or the judge. It was close to the profile from the judge but not a match. More like the judge's son, Lucas, not Martin."

Cindy closes her eyes. "Why didn't you wait until those results came back? He isn't a clear and present danger to the community. Why not wait?"

"Because we couldn't wait, Cindy. The judge already had the car detailed, then he set fire to it. He was—"

"We can't prove he torched his car, can we? Have you charged him with arson? Have you charged him with insurance fraud? Have you charged him with obstruction of justice, Colm? The answer is no to all of those questions because you can't prove any of it. Hunches don't win cases, evidence does."

Cindy was looking more and more exasperated with me, but she wasn't done.

"So let me make sure I have this right: Less than forty-eight hours after we authorize the arrest of a sitting judge, you're telling me there's a pretty good possibility the judge actually had nothing to do with the murder?"

"We don't know that yet. We still have his shoes, which are being processed for blood spatter right now, and we can prove his car was in the back parking lot and his cell phone was in the area."

"Correct me if I'm wrong. That would mean you have a decent case against his shoes, his tires, his car, and his cell phone, but nothing placing him there. In fact, there is a witness who alibis him as, in fact, not being there. Is that about right? What do you have that you can actually put in front of a jury that places the judge himself at the crime scene at the time, or even near the time, of the murder?"

"Nothing, I guess," I admit. "But we can't rule out the possibility that both Martin and Lucas were involved. The fact that the son was present does not mean the judge was not."

"So, what is your plan, Colm? Arrest the whole family and let the jury sort it out?"

"Darrel is pulling background reports on the son as we speak. Travis will pick him up and bring him in for questioning."

"Do you have any idea how bad this makes us look? Martin Weber wasn't a flight risk."

"He was going to Paris. France won't extradite in a capital eligible murder case. But there is one piece of good news," I offer. "Tiffany Weber came to my office this morning. She provided the pin code to the burner phone we recovered from the judge's home office. It's a veritable treasure trove of texts, photos, and videos proving an affair."

"What about murder? Murder and adultery are not the same, Colm."

"Correct. But it is evidence of a motive."

"Well, it might be, except the victim of the adultery also swears her husband was home with her that night."

"That's true, she did. But his cell phone pinged at the salon."

"You could fly a 747 through the holes in this case, Colm. Not only is there evidence of his actual, factual innocence, there is evidence pointing to a third party not named Judge Weber!" Cindy slams her hand down on the arm of the chair. "This is the worst-case scenario. And for the life of me, I don't understand why you didn't wait."

"Or he may have destroyed more evidence, Cindy. I get it. It looks bad right now. But give me a chance to clean this up."

"You better clean it up fast. In the meantime, there will be a complete press blackout. No one is to speak to anyone on or off the record. You need to get with Detective Hendrick and sort this out ASAP." Cindy takes a deep breath and lays her head back in her seat. The pause seems eternal, and I can see the wheels spinning. "This case has gone to hell. You won't like this, but I want you to bring Dillon Bickler on to assist you."

"If I'm going to straighten this out quickly, bringing Dillon on will only slow me down. Give me one day. That's all I ask."

"I'm not making any promises I can't keep, Colm."

"Then I appreciate you trying." I stand and get out of her office as fast as I can.

When I reach the hallway, I pull my phone out of my pocket and call Travis. The quickest way to get answers is to figure out how Lucas's blood ended up in the salon. And the only person who can tell us that is Lucas.

CHAPTER 54

SITTING BESIDE TRAVIS IN the interrogation room, I study Lucas Weber. Or try to. He's eighteen years old and looks more like a boy than a man. The line between adolescence and adulthood is uneven. The contrast is evident in his social media presence. In his posted photos, he's flexing, flashing gang signs, dressing like a wannabe rapper, and even mimicking the shooting of an assault weapon at some perceived, imaginary foe.

Now that he's sitting in front of real cops and prosecutors, he's a meek teenager. Perhaps he's both a menace and a mouse.

"How did you know Rachel Simone?" Travis asks.

"She cut my hair," Lucas says, blinking back tears. "My father didn't hurt her. He wouldn't. And my mom's wrong. He wasn't having an affair with Rachel."

"Hold up there, Lucas." Travis sets one elbow on the table. "Let's not confuse what we want with what we know. How do you *know* your father wasn't seeing Rachel?"

"Because he's way older than she is. She was young enough to be his daughter. There's no way. No way." Lucas has a look of genuine disgust that his father could be with someone closer to his age than his mom's. "Plus, Rachel wasn't like that. She would never do that to another woman, to a wife. She was focused on her business and Henry, her son."

"When was the last time you saw her?" Travis continues.

Lucas runs his hands through his short hair and sets them on the table. "The morning that ah, it, uh, happened. She cut my hair."

Travis nods and flips the page in his notebook.

My focus shifts to Lucas's hands. "Can you let us see your hands with your palms up, Lucas?" I ask.

Puzzled, Lucas still complies. "Sure, why?" He angles his palms toward the ceiling.

There's a fresh cut inside the fingers of his right hand.

"That looks like it hurt," I say. "What happened?"

"I cut it working on a truck."

That's a little too vague for me so I press him. "What kind of truck, and where, and what exactly were you working on?"

"I'm changing out the head gasket on my F-150."

"Changing out a head gasket? That's a big job."

"It's not too bad. I like doing it. My grandfather was into trucks. I've been working on them ever since I can remember."

"Still," I continue. "That's going to take a lot of time. How long have you been fixing the head gasket?"

"A few weeks. I'm almost done."

I lean forward. "So, your truck hasn't been operational recently. How did you get around?"

Travis sets his notebook down.

"Borrowing my dad's car for the most part."

"The Audi?"

"Yep. That's his car."

"Do you take it when you want to, or have you two worked out a schedule as to who gets it when?"

Lucas looked at me like I'd lost my mind. "I mean, it's his car, so I'm kinda at the mercy of when he needs it or doesn't."

"Since you mentioned borrowing his things from time to time, and it looks like you and your dad are about the same size, do you ever share clothes? Does he borrow your jersey or do you borrow his suits?"

"No, he doesn't wear anything of mine but sometimes I do 'borrow' his things," Lucas smiles, adding some air quotes to make sure we get the drift. "He doesn't like that, though, so if you can avoid telling him, it might save me a lecture."

"Just clothes, or have you ever borrowed his shoes, too?"

Lucas nods. "We're the same size—exactly now. But I wouldn't say 'borrow.' He doesn't know I wear them from time to time. But I don't have any real dress shoes, so I do wear his, but only after he's left for work."

I lean forward, placing my elbows on my knees so I'm closer to Lucas and eyeball-to-eyeball with him. "You and Rachel must have been close. You even remember her son's name, Henry, right?"

Lucas nods.

"You're eighteen and Rachel was only twenty-six. She was nice and obviously attractive. I see how you might be interested in her. But I'm curious. How did you know she wasn't dating? That's kind of personal chitchat for a haircut?"

Lucas swallows. "Well, to be honest, she seemed to like being around me. I made her laugh a lot. I sort of took that to mean ... I mean ... that's part of why I went to see her at the salon the morning, you know, she umm, passed away."

"What do you mean, part of why you went by?"

"To ask her if she wanted to maybe go do something after work."

He sits up while he's talking, getting more and more animated, like he's trying to convince us and himself.

"She said she didn't have time for any kind of relationship right then because of her business and Henry. But she wasn't mean about it."

"Let's switch gears for a second, Lucas." Travis starts laying the printout from Lucas's social media account on the table. "Tell us; what is this, Lucas?" Travis asks, jabbing his finger on an Instagram post of Lucas posing with two curved knives in his hand. "You wrote, and I quote, 'If you mess with me, you'll get the point. If you mess with us, you'll get the handle.'"

Lucas shrugs and opens his hands upward: "What do you want me to say? I was talking trash."

"To whom and about what? You're holding two knives in one hand and flipping the world off with your other one. Who were you talking to?"

Lucas shakes his head. "Just some jerks carrying signs about my dad at the courthouse. They sort of threatened him. I don't know what it was all about, but I was letting folks know not to mess with my father, you know? I wasn't serious."

I use my left hand under the table out of Lucas's view to motion Travis to back down a little, but he can't resist thrusting his finger into Lucas's face and pointing at a scab on his chin.

"Where did that cut on your face come from?"

"Shaving."

"Shaving?" Travis laughs. "With what, a chain saw? When did that happen?"

"The morning I was going over to ask her out. I guess I was nervous."

"What a load of garbage, Lucas." Travis rolls his eyes.

"Detective," I interject before Travis completely destroys any remaining rapport with the suspect, "we've all nicked ourselves shaving while we were thinking of something else. Let's hear him out."

Travis ignores me and continues to press. "You got all dolled up, went to the salon to ask Rachel out. She said no! You got angry because she turned you down. She scratched your face trying to save her life while you stabbed her over and over and over again!"

By this point I am ready to arrest Travis for committing a criminally inept examination, but as I reach for Travis's arm, Lucas stands, doubles up, and vomits all over the interrogation table.

CHAPTER 55

BONES SAT AT HIS kitchen table eating a microwaved meat loaf. He took another piece of bread out of the bag and used it to mop up the gravy as he pored over the report of Frank Hastings's death.

Two of the bullets recovered from the scene were worthless forensically. One deformed when it struck the TV and the other obliterated as it passed through Frank's skull. But the third bullet, the one fired into the wall, matched the .38 revolver found at the scene.

But why fire three shots?

Bones stuffed the last of the meat loaf in his mouth and leaned back in the chair. He closed his eyes and pictured the crime scene. Frank, despondent, grabbed the rope. It was light duty and only rated for two hundred pounds. Colm said Frank wasn't the brightest guy, but why would he use a rope that was on the edge of supporting his weight to kill himself? Maybe he wasn't smart enough to know the tensile strength of the rope?

Saving the file, Bones threw the food container in the trash and headed outside to the garage. After digging around, he found a length of rope. He grabbed a stepladder, tied off one end, and made a loop at the other end. Sticking his foot into the loop, he stepped off the ladder.

The rope snapped and Bones landed on his back on the cement. He swore and groaned as he rolled onto his side. "Of course it was going to break, you idiot. What the hell did you think would happen? Why do you insist on proving what you already know?" he muttered.

He didn't expect his feet to swing forward. He thought he'd fall straight down.

"That explains the bruising on Frank's arm," he said as he rubbed his sore wrist.

He stood, dusted himself off, and picked the rope off the floor. His eyes widened.

"Bingo."

He hurried back to the house and pulled up the crime scene photos. Switching over to the picture of the rope, he smiled. The rope Frank used didn't break at the knot, it broke in the middle.

Bones sat back in his chair. Maybe Ardell wasn't right after all.

CHAPTER 56

"CINDY WILL BE BACK in a second," Amanda says, looking everywhere except at me. I've seen her act this way before. It's like a meteorologist telling you it's going to rain the afternoon of your wedding. People don't like delivering bad news, and people like Amanda don't like being in the middle of the storm. The clouds have been gathering. That much I can tell from my brief interactions with Cindy over the past couple of days. But Amanda is forecasting more than rain. Her eyes tell me it's a hurricane. "Cindy asked if you could wait in her office."

"Certainly." I don't like surprises or being unprepared, so I contemplate trying to pry some information from Amanda about what precisely is on Cindy's mind. I opt to leave her out of it.

Cindy's office is quiet with the door shut, like a crypt. Mine is a little less ornate and a lot noisier. The pipes rattle, and the footsteps from the hallway above echo through the holes under and over the doors. You can even hear squirrels, or at least I hope they're squirrels, running around above the cheap tile ceiling.

Cindy's door opens and she marches in, followed by Dillon Bickler. Cindy's face is expressionless as she crosses behind her desk, but Dillon gives me a sympathetic smile, which I hate, as he takes the seat next to mine.

"We watched the interview with Lucas Weber," Cindy begins. "What are your thoughts, Colm?"

"Lucas didn't do it."

Dillon does a double-take and stares at Cindy in disbelief. "I'm at a loss, buddy. You're the one who proved Lucas was there. Are you listening to yourself?"

"It's obvious Lucas cared about Rachel—"

"Which is why he did it." Dillon sits on the edge of his seat. "I believe

Lucas liked the girl, too, but she rejected him. When Lucas finds out Rachel is sleeping with his own father, he loses it. He snaps. It's manslaughter. Voluntary manslaughter: killing in the sudden heat of passion with sufficient legal provocation."

"I know the law, Dillon. I've actually tried homicide cases, which is something you can't say. What I don't get is your version of the facts. Lucas doesn't believe the judge is sleeping with Rachel. I just got through talking with him. He's a naïve kid, with a crush on an older woman."

Dillon looks at Cindy. "It's not a complicated case. They both did it. Both had motives. Both had the opportunity. Both have reasons to protect each other. They acted in concert with each other."

I shake my head furiously. "There's only one set of bloody footprints, Cindy."

"Of course there is one set, Colm," Dillon adds. "Martin waited in the car. Think it through. Martin is furious with Rachel because she dumped him. They both feel betrayed and drive to the salon. Martin even tells her that he's coming over. Lucas loves his dad, and he hates this girl now. Lucas goes inside wearing his daddy's shoes and slice, slice, slice, the deed is done."

"Cindy, you can't possibly be buying that," I say. "He couldn't win a high school mock trial competition with that argument."

"Right now, I don't know what to think. More twists and turns than a pretzel. But I do know this: There are lots of eyes on us right now and we have to stop getting things wrong and start getting at least something right."

"It's not that complicated, actually," Dillon assures her. "And this is what I propose we do to move it forward. We offer one of them a deal and prosecute the other. I would start by offering the kid. He's barely an adult in our system. He would have certain mitigators going in his favor at sentencing anyway: youth, no record, coercion, under the influence of an older person. We could flip Lucas on his father, or we could flip the judge. He's older. Even the minimum sentence for murder is really a life sentence for him. Maybe he loves his son, maybe he doesn't. But regardless, he loves himself more. This way, Cindy, you can claim victory all the way around."

"You want to cut a deal with the person who actually did the killing, Dillon? Working your way down the totem pole? Using a parent against a child? Is that your best jury argument?"

"Stop it, both of you." Cindy holds up her hand and looks at me. There's genuine sorrow in her eyes. "Colm, we're going to give a new quarterback a chance. I'm switching you out for Dillon. If he wants you to stay on and help or second chair him, well, that's his call. I'm sorry, Colm. I gave you a chance, but it isn't working out. You can blame me for letting you come back too soon."

I nod and stand up, suppressing the full panoply of emotions from embarrassment to anger. It's no use trying to change her mind. I know her well enough to realize her decision is final. She would have been better off stabbing me. I do give her credit, though—at least she stabbed me in the front and not the back. In the front and straight through the heart.

I cross the floor, open the door, and close it behind me.

Amanda glances up but immediately looks away. She knows. She knew all along.

Out in the hallway, I hang my head in disbelief. Cindy was not only taking the case away from me, but she was also taking my reason to keep moving. Work was all I had left. She knew that and yet she took it. That's what hurts the most.

Footsteps sound behind me.

Dillon jogs up and stops. "Hey, Colm. I want to say I'm sorry. But after everything that you've been through, maybe this is a good thing." He pulls out a card and hands it to me. "Can you make sure your secretary sends me all the case info? And make sure to let her know I needed it yesterday. Thanks, buddy."

I watch Dillon hurry back to Cindy's office. That may have been worse than what Cindy did. It's one thing to be replaced. It's another thing to be pitied. I don't need his pity. I need to go home and spend the evening with my one true friend, Jack, last name Daniels. We have a lot to talk about.

CHAPTER 57

BONES WAITED IN DR. Ardell Sharp's office staring at the skeleton in the corner. The door behind him opened and a frazzled Dr. Sharp hurried in. "My apologies, Detective."

Bones stood and held out his hand, but Ardell marched around his desk and flopped into his chair without shaking it.

"I don't know how I missed it. Of course, hindsight is twenty-twenty, but I'm going to . . ." Ardell wiped his hand down his face and shook his head. "I apologize. This could have a ripple effect, you understand? I testify professionally. This mistake could carry a very negative impact on law enforcement and the DA. Most of my testimony is for you guys, as you well know."

"It's not a mistake. You've reexamined your initial findings before finalizing them."

Ardell smiled and he nodded. "Yes, that is correct. What we discussed was a preliminary finding subject to final review, which I have not yet done."

"What did you find?"

"My assistant is writing it up now, but we found bruising both on Frank's neck and on his right wrist consistent with digital manipulation. In other words, caused by hands with very large fingers. And from the layering, the bruising from the hands happened prior to the bruises from the rope."

Bones crossed his arms. "I sent the rope to forensics. They found, and will testify, that the rope was cut partially through before it broke. In other words, it had help breaking."

"I'm changing my conclusion. Frank Hastings's cause of death will be listed as a homicide."

CHAPTER 58

THE BRAKES HISSED AS the bus pulled alongside the curb and stopped.

"Thank you, sir." Belle waved and smiled at the driver and descended the steps. "I hope you have a wonderful evening. Who knows, I might see you again on the ride back home."

"You too, miss." The driver smiled. "Thanks for listening to me ramble on."

She stopped on the curb and looked up at him. "You're welcome! I know you and your brother will patch things up. Don't be afraid to make the first move, even if you think he should. Like you said, your mom would be smiling down on you if you did."

"I'll be looping back in an hour if you need a ride." He waved and shut the door.

Belle walked along as the bus pulled out and headed down the street. She counted the houses as she walked in a neighborhood she'd never been in before. The homes were so nice and the lawns so well-manicured. She stopped when she saw the number on the front of Colm's house come into view. His was a two-story house set back from the road a little more than the neighbors. It was as pretty as a postcard. The front door was red with a brass pineapple knocker.

A wave of doubt crashed over Belle. What was she thinking coming here? He wouldn't want to have a waitress he barely knew showing up on his doorstep. She had good reasons after what happened this morning, and she was worried about him.

Why do I feel guilty checking on someone? He checks on me at work. What's wrong with reciprocating? There's nothing wrong with checking on a friend. I feel like we're friends. Maybe he doesn't.

She wasn't going to run away because this felt uncomfortable.

I'll knock and if he answers, say, "I was worried after this morning," and then be gone again.

She kept rehearsing what she'd say if he opened the door and was preparing what she would write if no one was home. She began hoping for the latter. But she straightened her back, gathered as much confidence as she could muster, marched up the steps, and rang the doorbell.

The seconds ticked by.

The front door opened. Colm was dressed in a T-shirt, jeans, and socks. He stood at the entrance to his home staring blankly at her. It was definitely him, but it wasn't a Colm she had ever seen before. No light. No humor. He didn't even smile.

"Hello, Colm," Belle awkwardly waved. "I'm so sorry for stopping by unexpectedly. I know you must be busy with work and everything and I won't stay but one second."

Colm glanced up and down the street and asked, "How did you get here?"

"I took the bus. There's a stop a few blocks down."

"How did you know where I live?"

Belle blushed as she felt the heat rush to her cheeks. "I, umm . . . well . . . your address was on the old LSAT books and study guides you let me borrow. I was worried after this morning and, you know, with those men saying someone shot at you. Then you took off. I'm glad you are all right." Belle turned to walk back down the front steps.

"I'm doing fine, Belle. It's kind of you to check."

"Are you sure everything is okay? Did something else happen?"

"Oh, no, everything is fine. Just a really hectic day at work, that's all. If I had known you were coming by, I would have . . . I would have . . . well, I would have been more prepared to be a better host."

Most of the people in Belle's family didn't drink alcohol, but she could tell Colm had been drinking. "Is there anything I can do to help?"

Colm tried to manage a laugh and said, "You'd need to be the district attorney for that to happen, and I don't think you would enjoy running for that office."

"Tell me what happened. I probably can't help but you've listened to me before and I'm happy to do the same for you."

"There's nothing that can be done. My boss took me off a case today, and that case meant a lot to me. But it's nothing I can't recover from. You're very kind to check." He rubbed the back of his neck and glanced at the driveway. "Can I help you get home? I probably shouldn't be driving right now, as you can tell. I can call Bones or someone to give you a ride. Actually, I have an extra car. You're welcome to borrow it if that would help."

"I am so sorry that happened to you. I don't know anything about what you do, but if you want to talk about it, I'll listen."

Colm took a deep breath and ran his hand over his mouth. He glanced into the house, then back at her, and asked, "Where are my manners? I'm so sorry. Come in, please. It's a mess. Can I get you some water or we might have a Coke hidden away somewhere?"

Belle followed him inside. The house was lovely. The floors were a deep, natural wood, and the walls were light gray. A beautiful, quaint home in a tree-lined neighborhood.

"I'd love a glass of water and if I could use your restroom, the bus ride was a little longer than I anticipated."

"Oh gosh, yes. Of course. Down the hallway on the right." Colm pointed and he walked toward the kitchen. "I'll get that water for you."

Belle walked down the hallway and glanced at the photographs lining the walls on both sides. Photo after photo, Colm smiling in a way she had rarely seen. But he wasn't alone. He stood with his arm around one of the most beautiful people Belle had ever seen. They were laughing in one picture like they had heard the funniest joke ever told. *That's not a sister,* she thought. The look emanating from their eyes was different. This woman was tall and athletic, with the most radiant smile. Belle felt like a peasant dressed in a waitress uniform gazing at a queen.

Who is she?

That question was answered by the next photograph. Colm, in a tuxedo, embracing the same woman, but this time wearing a gorgeous white wedding gown.

She felt humiliated, shocked, and completely out of place. She hurried for the bathroom, reached for the door, turned the handle, and pushed it open, but it wasn't a bathroom.

A pink fan with painted balloons hung from the ceiling. Cartoon animals circled the walls. Soft, fluffy pink carpeting led to a crib in the corner. The crib had the moon and stars attached to one side of the railing hanging over where the baby would sleep.

Belle covered her mouth and backed out, closed the door, and retreated down the hallway.

"We can talk in the kitchen or the living room if you're more comfortable there," Colm said. "Again, I apologize. The house is a wreck."

"I'm so sorry. I can't stay," Belle hurried toward the front door.

"What? Why? You just got here."

"I only came to check on you. I just remembered I was late for something back home. I do need to go." Belle yanked the door open and fled down the steps.

Tears clouded Belle's vision as she ran as fast as she could toward the bus stop. It would be an hour before the bus would come back around but she didn't care. She needed to get away from that house, those pictures, the crib, and him. Shame began to course through her soul, but why? She had done nothing wrong.

"Why didn't he tell me?" she wondered as she ran. "What a fool I am."

CHAPTER 59

I STAND THERE IN STUNNED silence, watching Belle run down the sidewalk and out of sight. What happened? She went from walking to the bathroom to sprinting down the street.

What am I missing?

I step back inside and close the door. I can't blame her for leaving, I don't suppose. Even I don't want to be around me right now.

I head through the house and back to my cell, which doubles as an office. But this time I have nothing to work on. I sit down in my chair and close my eyes as my grim reality sets in. Everyone I truly loved is gone. The only thing I had left, my calling, is slipping through my hands.

Life dealt me a worthless hand of cards and work was all that kept me at the table. And I ran out of chips. Not just ran out, but ran out in the most humiliating way imaginable, replaced by a two-bit brown-noser who wasn't even very good at property crime cases. Now, he's the go-to homicide prosecutor. The "artist" has been replaced by a blind monkey with a paintbrush.

I pour a tall glass of whiskey. No sense keeping up pretenses now. I wander the house in a daze and head down the hallway.

I raise my glass in mock toast to myself. "Well done, Colm! When you fail, you fail in spectacular fashion for the whole world to see."

The sooner I get drunk, the sooner my failure will be complete.

I've studied defendants and jurors and judges and cops all my professional career. And for the life of me, I cannot figure out what happened in the course of two minutes from the front door to the bathroom in my own home.

I head back through the living room and into the hallway. I haven't used the hall bathroom in a while. Was there . . .

The nursery door is slightly ajar.

Seeing a glimpse of the pink carpet rips me to shreds. I retreat to my office and sit down in the one place I feel somewhat at home. Tonight, my glass won't stay full or empty for long.

The sun begins to set, and the doorbell rings again. Why is my doorbell ringing so much, tonight of all nights?

I stand and stagger into my desk, sending papers scattering to the floor. I head out to the living room, unsteady on my feet.

"I'm sorry," I say, yanking the door open.

Bones stands on the top step and waves his hand in front of his face. "For breathing on me. You should be. How much have you had to drink?"

"Not enough yet."

"Grab your jacket and I'll take you to get something to eat."

"I don't want to eat."

"Compromise," Bones grins. "I'll get a pizza delivered."

I shake my head and grab onto the doorknob to steady myself. "Not tonight. I'm, ah, working on something."

"I can see you are working, Colm. But I think the job is about finished. What the hell are you drunk at dusk for?"

"I'm sorry. I just don't want any company tonight."

Bones holds up his hands. "I know what tonight is. I was your best man, remember? You may not want company, but you need it. Sometimes talking about it helps."

"Talking doesn't change a thing. It's another lie we tell ourselves. Really, truly, Bones. I love you like a brother, but if you ever had any compassion for me at all, let me be alone, please. I am begging you."

I see a look of hurt on my best friend's face that I have seen only twice before. He nods without uttering a word and leaves.

I stumble back to my office and stare in dismay at my desk. The bottle is empty. I head to the kitchen and open every cabinet, but there's nothing to drink there.

Mercifully, I remember a case of beer stashed in the garage, a holdover from long since passed cookouts with friends. I'm sure the beer is old and stale, but I don't care. Holding on to the wall like a sailor walking the deck in a storm, I manage to get to the garage. I close one eye and search the shelf in vain, but the world is spinning.

I stumble back into the car parked in the garage and my hand feels the handle. I don't plan on going anywhere. I can't go anywhere. I'm not even sure I can make it back inside. My goal is to simply not fall down, so I open the car door and flop onto the seat.

People used to talk about hitting rock bottom. I would listen politely but, in truth, we all have different bottoms. For some it's divorce, the loss of a parent, or financial straits. For others there's a different bottom. I have finally concluded there is no bottom for me. I lost the only two people I will ever love with every fiber of my being. And now I have lost the only thing that made life worth living. This isn't bottom. It's a free fall.

I'm tired of feeling like this. I'm tired of feeling anything. The loves of my life are gone. My professional identity is gone. Mainly my desire to keep trying is gone.

I pull the car door closed. I fumble through my pockets searching for my keys. I lean back in my seat, start the ignition, and close my eyes.

There's a difference between wanting to die and being tired of living.

Right now—I'm tired.

CHAPTER 60

JD STARED AT THE camera feed of Colm's house playing on the computer monitor. "Something's wrong."

Knox leaned down and stared at the screen. "I don't see anything."

"That's my point. Where is Colm? He hasn't gone out and he hasn't come back to the den."

"Maybe he passed out. He was drinking a lot—even by his standards."

JD grabbed the van keys off the table. "This feels different. Get your delivery uniform on. We're going over there."

Fifteen minutes later, Knox drove slowly past Colm's house. "The garage is closed, and his car is still here."

"Pull over down the road a little and stop," JD said.

"Where?"

JD glared. "Wherever a delivery van would normally park, Knox."

Knox stopped at the end of Colm's driveway.

JD powered down the window and listened. "Shut the van off."

Knox shook his head, but his beefy fingers twisted the key in the ignition.

"Do you hear that?" JD said.

"Not really. What am I supposed to be hearing?"

"It's a car engine running on the other side of the garage door."

"Why would Colm start the car? It's not that cold outside. That's a pretty stupid thing to do."

"Not if you're trying to kill yourself, it isn't."

JD grabbed the fake delivery box, hurried up the driveway, and looked through the small glass panes at the top of the garage door.

Colm sat in the driver's seat; his head slumped against his chest.

Suicide king, here we are, JD thought, relishing this moment.

And then the moment passed, and JD grabbed the garage handle and yanked up.

Not yet. Not like this.

The roll-up door clanked and rattled as it rose, releasing the deadly fumes. Running around the car, JD opened the driver's door.

Colm sat unmoving. He wheezed, and his eyes flickered but didn't open.

JD shut the car off, grabbed the keys, and hurried back to the van.

Knox pulled back onto the road, and they sped away. "Why did you do that? You should have let him die."

"Let him take the easy way out? The only thing worse than failing enough to kill yourself is failing at killing yourself. He's suffering, but not enough. Not like I want him to."

They rode in silence for a few minutes. The silhouettes of the trees streaked by. The night chill swept through the partially open van windows.

"How did you know Colm was trying to kill himself?" Knox asked as he turned onto the main road.

JD shrugged and stared into the night. It didn't take a genius to figure out what Colm was going to do. He hit rock bottom. Broken people do stupid things when they think there's no other way out. Besides, that was the same exit to life JD opted to take. Except no one came to JD's rescue—the car ran out of gas.

CHAPTER 61

I OPEN MY EYES AND close them immediately to avoid throwing up. I'm sitting upright but I'm not in my recliner. I feel fabric and metal. I peek and the room spins like vertigo. I'm in the driver's seat of Ally's car in the garage.

Alcohol, anger, and self-pity didn't mix well last night. That much I can remember.

The longer I sit there, the images become sharper, but so do the memories. Something else happened, but precisely what?

I stumble out of the car and to the kitchen. It looks like someone ransacked the place. Did I do that? I make it to the bathroom and eventually into the shower. I brush my teeth twice, but I still can't quite get the taste out of my mouth. Last night slowly comes into focus as I get dressed. I stare in the mirror and don't recognize the person I see.

The doorbell rings.

Maybe they'll go away.

The bell rings again.

I stop halfway down the stairs and gather myself.

Keys jingle. The doorknob turns, and my front door swings silently open.

That's impossible. Only Ally and I have keys to the house.

I stop on the stairwell to see who this intruder is.

Mae strolls through the front door. "I got worried when you didn't return any of my calls."

My hand shakes on the railing and my knees buckle, so I sit. "Believe it or not, Mae, I feel worse than I look. I wish you didn't have to see me like this."

"Trust me when I say I've seen worse," Mae says as she walks in and sits down on the stairs, too.

"I don't know, Mae. It's pretty bad and really humiliating. I think the weight of everything came crashing down last night. I don't have total recall, but I think I tried to hurt myself."

"What do you mean by 'hurt yourself'? Drank too much? You've been doing that for months."

"I think it might be even worse than that." I stare down at the floor. "I think I gave up."

Mae looks at me with tears welling in her eyes. "I'm glad you didn't do whatever it is you think you almost did. But you can't go on like this. As your psychiatrist, I won't allow it. As your family, what you did, or almost did, is the most selfish thing you can do to the people who love you. You of all people should know that."

At this point tears are streaming down both of our faces.

"Colm, you're serving a sentence for a crime you didn't commit. I'm going to help you escape this prison. It will take time, toil, tears, and maybe even some anger, but we are starting today."

"I should have seen it coming. I made a career out of reading other people, and I was good at it. And then I miss the most important signs for Ally. I failed the person who needed me the most at the time when she needed me the most. That's what I can't get over, Mae."

"I feel the same way, but feeling it doesn't make it true. This whole thing was an unbearable tragedy, an unforeseeable, now seemingly unbearable chain of events, which we somehow must bear. You're not going to live like this, and I'm not going to let you. You can pack your things, or I will do it for you. But I am not leaving without you. And if you think you can stop me from dragging you to my car, you're wrong. I'll call Bones."

I hang my head. "I don't know how to break this cycle. I can't sleep. When I drift off, I hear Ally screaming after she found Jaci in her crib. And I run to the nursery but it's too late. Always too late."

I take a long, ragged breath.

"The two people I loved the most are gone. They aren't coming back.

I don't know if there is a next life, but I am tired of this one. Either way, I win. Either there is the nothingness, or there is the reunification Ally believed in. I'm okay with either now, you know? Anything other than being stuck in the middle between what was and what might be. I can't stay there."

Mae nods. "Yes, I do know. But I also know neither would want you like this. You have a gift they don't have. What you call 'stuck in the middle,' they call 'life.' I know you hate hearing this, but we are going to stay stuck in the middle a bit longer, Colm. At least until you see that the middle is all you will ever have control over."

I stare down at my hands and rub the place I used to wear my wedding ring.

"Ally would have wanted you to stay on this side." Mae smiles. "The side you do believe in."

I open my mouth, but there's nothing to say. She's probably right.

"Ally always said that was your tell to know she'd won the argument."

"What was?"

"You bite the inside of your cheek and stop talking." Mae interlocks her hands behind her head, tilts it to the ceiling, and laughs.

After a moment she stops, but it echoes off the walls.

"It's been a long time since anyone laughed in this house," I say.

"She would have hated that, too. She loved to laugh, Colm. You made her laugh. You made us all laugh. Here's the deal, Mr. District Attorney. Either you come with me, or I call Bones and he carries you out. Which is it going be?"

I take a deep breath and nod.

Mae stands. "Let's get some stuff together for you. There's a place where we can work our way through this."

She holds out her hand and I take it.

CHAPTER 62

BONES SAT IN HIS car, parked alongside the diner. He was used to hunkering down for long stretches on stakeouts, but this was different. He wasn't waiting on a bad guy. He was waiting on a good girl. He'd been there for nearly an hour waiting for Belle to go on her break.

The side door to the diner finally opened, and Belle walked over to the picnic table carrying a book in her hands.

Bones flicked his cigarette out of the window and exited the vehicle. His door creaked loudly as he swung it shut, and Belle stared in his direction.

He had no idea what he would say even as he approached the table. "Hi, Belle."

"Good morning," Belle smiled, but it was quick. "Are you meeting Colm?"

Bones shook his head. "No, ma'am, I am not. But that's kind of why I'm here. I'm overstepping the lines a little, but I have a tendency of doing that from time to time. I wanted to try to explain something and bring you a message, if I can. Do you mind if I sit down?"

"I don't, but no one owes me an explanation. There isn't much to say." Belle put her hands in her lap and focused on them.

The picnic table rocked as Bones straddled the bench. "Actually, I think there might be. This is where you may have to forgive my bias. I've known Colm a long time. He's more like family than a friend or coworker. We've been through a lot together personally and professionally. Anyway, he called last night, and we had a long talk. Your name came up, which is why I'm here. He mentioned you stopped by his home and then left kind of abruptly. He wanted to apologize for the way he was with the drinking and everything. He's in a little better spot right now."

"No apology necessary. We all have bad nights. Tell him not to worry one bit. I just would have liked to have known everything before I went. I misread him, I guess."

"How?" Bones asked.

"I didn't know he has a family."

"Had, Belle. Not has."

Belle gazed at him with confusion and shock. "What are you saying?"

"I'm saying his wife and daughter are gone. That's what I'm saying."

"Why didn't he say something?"

"He doesn't even talk about them to me."

Belle grabbed Bones's hand. "Can you please tell him how sorry I am? I had no idea. I can't imagine the grief he's carrying."

"No, I'm not going to tell him any of that."

Belle winced and leaned away.

"You are. He needs your voice in his life. So, whatever you have to say, you should say it yourself. Tell him whatever you think might help him."

"I will. I promise I will. When do you think he'll be back this way?"

"Not for a little while, but when he's back, treat him like you always have. No pity. No patronizing. Just be you."

CHAPTER 63

IT'S ONLY BEEN FIVE days, but Mae was right, I needed to change. Dramatically change. Reborn, in a sense. I stare at my hands like I haven't seen them in a long time.

I'm sitting on an examination table waiting for the phlebotomist. I need people or a purpose. I do have some people who care about me, but I miss the sense of professional purpose that has kept me going. I can't fix the Rachel Simone case. That one is gone. It's in Dillon's hands now. He's going to charge Lucas, I know it.

I know in my gut Dillon is wrong, but instincts don't win cases. Facts and evidence do. Dillon will say Martin Weber drove his son to the salon and Lucas killed Rachel. Lucas struck the fatal blow, and Martin was an unwitting accomplice. Lucas will either plead to manslaughter or stand trial for murder. His father will be offered accessory after the fact. Martin will take the deal, and Lucas will take the fall.

The door swings open. "Good morning," Sandy says as she carefully lays glass tubes from the front of her nursing uniform on the metal cart she rolled in with her. "How are you feeling?"

"Much better, thank you."

She wraps a large blue, elastic-like tourniquet around my arm. "I'm sorry to keep you waiting. When it comes to waiting, I'm like a pediatrician. I have little patience! Get it? Patients—patience?" She laughs, but as she sticks the needle into my vein, her ring cuts her latex glove. "Oh, snap!" She pulls back, and a stream of blood streaks across her arm and onto the floor. "I'm so sorry. What a mess! That almost never happens. Don't worry. I won't let you bleed to death. You aren't a hemophiliac, are you?" She chuckles.

I shake my head, only half-hearing what she said. My heart begins to pound a little quicker in my chest, and that familiar glow of adrenaline clicks on. I bound off the table and race out to the nurse's station. "I need to use your phone."

The confused nurse stares at me but doesn't move or say anything.

"Please, it's an emergency."

She hands me the receiver.

"Thanks." I reach over the counter and dial. "Irene, it's me, Colm. Yes, I'm fine. I need a huge favor. Grab a pen."

CHAPTER 64

I'M PACING ALONG THE fence at the far end of the hospital, which runs alongside a two-lane road. The eight-foot-tall fence surrounding the grounds has narrow gaps between the mesh, an outward-angled top, and a slick, smooth surface to prevent climbing.

I smile when I see the old Charger speeding down the road toward me.

Bones parks on the shoulder and hurries over, carrying a coil of rope. "Hey, Buddy. Is there a reason I'm not going to the front door?"

"I'll explain in the car. Toss the rope over the fence."

Bones hesitates. "I thought you came here to get some help."

"I got it. Throw me the rope."

"I don't like this, Colm. You haven't been discharged."

"You can bring me back—but right now I need you to trust me."

Bones shrugs, holds on to one end, and heaves the other.

Hand over hand, I climb to the top.

Behind me, someone shouts.

I scramble over and drop to the ground.

Bones's eyes widen. "Run!"

We sprint for the car as a half dozen orderlies rush forward, yelling.

Bones jams the gas pedal to the floor and the Charger rockets down the road. "Did I just break you out of a mental health facility?"

"Yes and no." I power down the window to feel the wind on my face.

"Now is not the time for lawyer doublespeak. Do you have any idea what Mae will do to me?"

"I'll explain it to Mae. I was a voluntary patient, so legally I should've been able to leave, but the nurse on duty insisted that I had to request to be released in writing, then that has to be reviewed and approved by the on-call doctor, but I can't wait. The preliminary hearing is in two hours."

"What hearing?"

"The Rachel Simone case."

"You're off that case."

"Technically, off. But I'm reassigning myself. Irene got the new DNA results back from the lab. Dillon won't take my calls and Cindy won't listen. She insists I talk to Dillon first. I have to try to stop him from making a huge mistake."

"So, I did break you out of a mental health facility."

I laugh. "Look at it this way, buddy. You got me a day pass. We have to run by my house to get a suit and then get to the courthouse—ASAP."

Bones grinned and flicked on the sirens and lights.

CHAPTER 65

WHILE BONES PARKS THE car, I run up the courthouse steps, taking them three at a time. I hurry through security and make it to courtroom twelve before the prelim begins.

Not surprisingly, the gallery is filled with spectators who whisper away as I hurry down the aisle and over to Dillon.

"Dillon, I've been trying to call you. You need to ask for a delay," I say, trying to catch my breath.

"Listen, Colm, this isn't your case anymore, and to put it bluntly, I don't need your help."

"I have a new forensics report that came back that you have to look at."

"I will—later. It's a simple probable cause hearing, nothing more. Besides, I know what you're trying to do. You want me to ask for a delay so I look unprepared." He motions to the jam-packed room. "The media is here. I'm not missing my chance, so don't try to ruin this or steal the moment."

"This isn't about you and me, Dillon. This is about Rachel Simone. Ask for a continuance or, at the very least, read the report." I hold a copy out for him.

"I couldn't care less about another report right now. The rules of evidence don't apply in a prelim. As you should know, we can use hearsay, so I'm not sweating it. If you don't like it, take it up with Cindy." He points to the back of the courtroom. "She just came in with the Mayor and the Sheriff. Not your show anymore, Colm."

If looks could kill, Cindy would be on trial for homicide. She fixes me with a stare but, positioned between the Mayor and his entourage, she's stuck in the middle of the row. The Sheriff walks to the front to speak to a court security officer.

The door to the back chambers opens. The bailiff cries, "Hear ye, hear ye, the Honorable Judge Nancy Mayweather is presiding."

Judge Mayweather is no friend of lawyers, despite the fact that she used to be one. But she is as sharp as they come. Mean, but sharp. Dillon just found himself in a lion's den covered in lamb's wool.

Everyone rises, including the gallery seated behind me.

Judge Mayweather was a former public defender who somehow managed to get elected to the trial bench. She is tough on everyone, but especially on prosecutors, which makes sense, seeing as how tough they were on her for years when she was a public defender. She knows the rules of evidence backward and forward. She suffers no fools.

I sit in the gallery on the bench behind the prosecutor's table. I'm only three feet away from where I'm used to sitting, but it feels like a different planet. I wonder whether I can actually watch someone else handle one of my old murder cases. It's a little like watching someone else raise your children.

"Next on the docket is *State v. Martin and Lucas Weber*," the bailiff says.

"Dillon Bickler for the State, Your Honor."

A man in his mid-fifties with a suit that easily costs what I make in a month, rises and says, "Paul P. Davis III for Judge Weber, Your Honor."

"Stephanie Key Lighting for the defendant Lucas Weber, Your Honor."

Stephanie is a crackerjack attorney, no doubt, but she isn't as experienced as Paul, nor does she have the judicial ties he has. She's plenty good, but Paul Davis is next-level expensive and a few tiers above what the Webers can afford on a judge's salary. Paying for Paul and Stephanie both? Clearly someone else is paying the Webers' legal expenses. I doubt if Martin will disclose that on his annual judicial financial statement.

The whole Weber family is present, with the dutiful Tiffany Weber sitting right behind her husband and son. Other members of the community, and their friends, flood that side of the courtroom. That might make a difference in a jury trial, but there is no jury in a preliminary hearing. It's just a judge, and she will not be moved by a room full of family and friends. And of course, cameras line the back wall of this relatively small courtroom. Rows and rows are taken by members of the print media. Even the two knuckleheads who confronted me at The Junction are here.

The judge lifts her gaze as silence falls over the courtroom. "Before we begin, let me remind everyone present. This is not a petit trial. This is not a grand jury proceeding. This is a preliminary hearing solely to determine whether there is sufficient probable cause to support the arrests of Martin Weber and Lucas Weber. They have been charged with murder and conspiracy to commit murder."

Lucas turns in his chair and casts a terrified glance back to his mother.

She gives him a reassuring nod and motions for him to pay attention to the judge.

"And let me make myself perfectly clear at the outset. If I hear so much as one word from anyone, other than counsel or a witness, I will hold that person in contempt of court. I am not a magistrate judge. I am a criminal court trial judge. I have the same powers down here in this courtroom that I have upstairs in my own. While the nature of the proceeding is different, the nature of my powers is not. I will not tolerate any outbursts or shows of emotions. If you cannot control yourself, now is the time to leave."

"May it please the court, Your Honor, Defendant Martin Weber makes a motion to be severed, and for his hearing to be separate and apart from the co-defendant Lucas Weber. Concomitantly, we ask for a continuance," Martin's attorney, Paul, says.

"Your motion for a continuance is denied, but I will hear from the State on your motion to sever. What says the State, Mr. Bickler?"

"Well, Your Honor, if we could get started, I will show that these two defendants acted in concert and conspired to kill Rachel Simone. Severance is not proper. They should be tried together. The hand of one is the hand of all under *State v. . . . ,*" Dillon says.

"I know the law, Mr. Bickler. But I'm going to need a little more than what you think is proper. I make that decision. You cannot disadvantage one defendant by trying him or her with another defendant who might have exculpatory evidence. It would be a due process violation to deny one defendant his or her full defense simply because you have chosen to charge them together. Charging them is your decision, and indicting them is your decision, but trying them, protecting their constitutional rights, and considering whether probable cause exists are my decisions, so you best address the specific question of whether one or both defendants would be denied a full defense by being tried jointly."

I want to shout at Dillon that he should argue for separate juries, one for Martin and one for Lucas, but Dillon misses his chance. He clearly didn't see that coming, and his lack of preparedness is on full display.

"I will take the motion for severance under advisement, Mr. Davis," the judge says. "That is not something which must be decided today. There is no jury present and we all know, or should know," she says, casting a condescending look at Dillon, "that hearsay is admissible in a probable cause hearing but, while the rules of evidence may be out the window in a preliminary hearing, the Constitution is not. So, for the time being, I will not severe them for purposes of this hearing, but you can reserve your motion for whoever is assigned to preside over the trial. Call your first witness, Mr. Bickler."

"Thank you, Your Honor. The State calls Detective Travis Hendrick," Dillon says.

I would never have called Travis first. Travis knows too much, not too little. I want to scream, "Dillon, this isn't the actual trial. Call someone who doesn't know anything firsthand. Hearsay is all you need to survive this hearing." But I don't want to be held in contempt of court, and this isn't my case anymore.

Travis walks with his head high as he's sworn in.

"Detective Hendrick, can you summarize your evidence against Martin Weber first, and then Lucas Weber?" Dillon begins.

"Yes, Mr. Bickler. We interviewed Martin Weber, and he denied any involvement in the murder of Rachel Simone. But his car was present at the murder scene, they were in a sexual relationship, and drops of her blood were found on his shoes when we executed a search warrant at his home. Now Mr. Weber claims his son wore his shoes, his son borrowed his car, and that he, Martin, was nowhere near the scene of the murder at the time of the murder. He also states his son frequently borrowed his car, borrowed his clothes, and borrowed his shoes."

A murmur runs through the courtroom.

"We then interviewed Lucas Weber because his DNA was found at the crime scene on bloody tissues." Travis continues, "Lucas's DNA profile matched the DNA profile from those bloody tissues found at the murder scene. Lucas claims he went there earlier in the day to ask Ms. Simone out and claims he then went home and never left again. He does have cuts on his hand, which he claims were from repairing a car, but they could have been from the knife used to kill the victim."

"Hold on a second." Judge Mayweather pins Dillon with a stare. "Counselor, your evidence against Martin Weber is his son's testimony, combined with some scant circumstantial evidence that his vehicle was there. And your evidence against Lucas Weber is that his blood was found on a tissue, but can you actually place him at the scene? Is your position that Lucas hired his father to commit this murder and was not present, or is it your position that both were present at the murder scene?"

"Well, Your Honor, we're working under a theory that they both went there together."

"And what evidence do you have to support that theory?"

"It's our working theory of the case, Your Honor. But we do have Lucas Weber implicating his father and Martin Weber implicating his son."

"That's well and good, Mr. District Attorney, but how do you plan on introducing the evidence Lucas Weber has on his father, since Lucas is a defendant? You can't call him as a witness. He has a Fifth Amendment right not to testify. You can't introduce his statement, a statement cannot be cross-examined, so you have a Bruton problem."

Dillon looks lost, in large part because he is lost.

I sit there feeling like I'm watching a first-year law student stutter his way through criminal procedure. A Bruton problem means the co-defendants can't implicate each other without creating a conflict between the co-defendant's right against self-incrimination and the defendant's right to cross-examine witnesses. So, Lucas can't be called to testify against Martin because it would incriminate himself, and vice versa. And you can't introduce the written or oral statements because statements can't be cross-examined. Furthermore, Martin may want Lucas as an exculpatory witness, but Lucas would be unavailable because he, too, is charged with murder. A joint trial with separate juries is what Dillon should be arguing for.

"And how will you prosecute Lucas Weber when the main witness implicating him is his father, who, too, is a defendant and cannot be compelled to testify? How are you going to prove your case, Mr. Bickler? You have not only charged both of your star witnesses, but you may have also charged key defense witnesses who cannot be compelled to testify. Do you have any witnesses who can actually testify in a real trial without violating the Constitution?"

Dillon opens and closes his mouth but doesn't say anything.

This has become a train wreck.

"I am highly inclined to either dismiss these warrants for lack of probable cause because your evidence is fundamentally tainted or, at a minimum, order you to try them separately, Mr. Bickler."

I can't take this anymore, so I do the single dumbest thing I have ever done in my legal career. I stand and walk toward the prosecution table. "Your Honor, may it please the court, Colm Truesdale for the State, appearing alongside Mr. Bickler. The State calls Lucas Weber to the stand."

"Your Honor, I object," Stephanie says.

"You don't need to object, Counselor. Either Mr. Truesdale has lost his mind, or he thinks this is some kind of game. It is axiomatic that you cannot call a defendant to give testimony against himself, Mr. Truesdale," the judge says, her voice rising with each syllable.

"You're correct, of course, Your Honor, unless the State immunizes him, which we are doing, right now. We're dropping all charges against Lucas Weber."

Everyone in the courtroom starts talking at once. I glance over my shoulder. Cindy is on her feet and marching forward. She stares at me like . . . well, like you would stare at someone who just escaped from a mental institution.

At this point Dillon's astonishment has worn off, but his anger has switched on. He leans over to me and whispers through clenched teeth, "What are you doing to my case, Colm?"

"Trying to salvage it, Dillon."

"Have you lost your mind?" Cindy whispers as she reaches my side.

I meet her hard stare with a cold, calm resolve. "No, ma'am. This is the only way. I need you to trust me."

Judge Mayweather is so shocked, she doesn't say a word to quiet the gallery for what seems like a full minute. She picks up her gavel and brings it down three times.

Dillon shakes his head and says to Cindy, "You're not seriously going to listen to him, are you?"

Cindy doesn't take her eyes off mine. The muscles in her jaw clench. "If you're wrong, you're done. I'll drive the bus over you myself."

The judge bangs her gavel again. "Did I hear you correctly, Mr. District Attorney?"

"You did, Your Honor. Full use immunity from prosecution for Lucas Weber. He is not in any legal jeopardy and, therefore, has no right to remain silent."

Dillon glares at me. "Congratulations. You just committed career suicide."

I ignore him. I don't care if I lose my job. I'm not going to watch the person who killed Rachel Simone go free because Dillon couldn't be bothered to read reports and take some advice.

Judge Mayweather motions to Lucas. "The witness has been granted immunity from prosecution. You may take the stand, Lucas Weber."

"Do I have to, Judge?" Lucas asks.

"Yes, you have been granted immunity. You are no longer in legal jeopardy and so yes, you can be compelled to testify. I'm not sure Mr. Truesdale knows what he is doing, but it's already done. You're no longer a defendant in this murder case."

Martin grabs the arm of Paul's chair and sticks his finger in Paul's face. I can't hear what Martin is saying, but he's clearly not happy. Paul sits there, looking shell-shocked at what just happened.

In his defense, no one saw this coming.

Lucas takes the stand. It takes me a couple of minutes to explain to him that he's in no legal jeopardy.

"On the morning of October twenty-second, did you borrow your father's car?"

"Yes, sir."

"And where did you go?"

"I drove to 151 Ender Road—the Cutz for All salon."

"Had you been there before?"

"Yes sir, many times."

"And why did you go on the morning of October twenty-second?"

"I object." Paul stands. "My client never gave consent to the witness to drive the car."

"Overruled. This is criminal court, not a conversation around the dinner table, Counselor. Your client can take that up when he gets home—if he gets home."

"Can you repeat the question, sir?" Lucas asks.

"There is nothing to be nervous about, Lucas. Just tell the truth and don't worry about who it helps or hurts. Stick to the truth. Why did you go to Cutz for All on the morning of October twenty-second?"

"I went to get my hair cut."

"Is that the only reason?" I ask.

"Do I have to say this?" he asks, covering the microphone.

"Yes. It's important, Lucas."

"I asked Rachel Simone if she would like to go to dinner."

Some laughter seeps through the courtroom as Judge Mayweather pounds the desk with her gavel.

"Let's back up a moment, Lucas. You said you were going to the salon to ask Rachel out. So, before you grabbed the car keys off the counter, what did you do?"

"I showered and got dressed."

"Did you shave?"

"Objection, Your Honor. What is the relevance of this?" Paul objects.

"Mr. Truesdale, you have a short leash and it's about up."

"This is going somewhere, Your Honor, and I could get there quicker if I could lead the witness, but I am trying to do this the right way by asking direct questions."

"I will give you a little leeway on leading, even though it's direct examination. But just a little."

"You shaved, did you not, Lucas?"

"Yes, sir."

"Did you cut yourself while you were shaving, Lucas?"

"Yes, sir. I had a hard time getting it to stop bleeding."

"How did you try to get it to stop bleeding?"

"I got some tissues and tried to press on the cut, but I nicked myself pretty good, and it kept bleeding. So I went to my dad's bathroom to get a styptic pencil."

"Objection, Your Honor." Paul stands and raises his voice. "What is the relevance of any of this?"

Before the judge can rule, I walk away from the prosecution table and toward the bench, raising a forensic report. "Your Honor, I'd like to present State's Exhibit Number One, marked for identification purposes.

This report contains the results of the chemical analysis of tissues found near the rear exit door of 151 Ender Road. These tissues were found the night of Rachel's murder."

"Let me see the report, and do you have a copy for the defense?"

"Of course, Your Honor." I wink at Paul when I hand it to him.

He doesn't wink back.

After a few minutes, Judge Mayweather sets the report down. "Okay, I have read the report, Counselor. You may proceed."

"The report states that, in addition to the conclusive match of Lucas Weber's DNA, specifically blood, there were also trace amounts of alum commonly found in a styptic pencil, and trace elements of butylated hydroxytoluene, butylated hydroxyanisole, triethanolamine, stearic acid, potassium hydroxide, glycerin, palmitic acid, and sulfates. In other words—shaving cream. Additionally, the tissues in question did not match any of the tissues used at the salon."

Judge Mayweather steeples her fingers together. "I see your point. The tissues that implicate Mr. Lucas Weber had evidence of blood, shaving cream, and a styptic pencil."

"May I resume my questioning of the witness?"

"You may."

"What did you do with the tissues after you used them to stem the blood from your shaving cut?"

"I threw them in my father's bathroom trash can."

I walk forward and look Lucas in the eye. "Lucas, you have been granted full immunity. The answer to my next question, by law, cannot implicate you, no matter how you answer. Was Rachel Simone alive when you left her salon?"

"Yes, sir."

"Did you return to the salon at any point thereafter?"

"No, sir."

"Did you have anything to do with the murder of Rachel Simone?"

"No, sir," he says with tears welling in his eyes.

"Do you know who did kill Rachel Simone?"

"No, sir." Lucas's lips tremble.

Martin and Paul confer for a moment. Martin glances back at Tiffany, and she nods.

My stomach tightens because I know what's coming.

"No questions, Your Honor." Paul smiles. "We do, however, reserve the right to recall the witness for the purposes of this probable cause hearing, since it is now only pertaining to Martin Weber."

"Do you have any other witnesses, Mr. District Attorney?"

"I may, Your Honor, but I am happy to allow the defense to call a witness out of order if they wish to do so. They seem anxious to present a rebuttal witness."

Paul Davis takes the bait and swallows the hook. "Your Honor, the defense calls Tiffany Weber."

I cross back to the prosecutor's table and sit down.

Dillon whispers, "What are you doing, Colm? You didn't present enough evidence on Martin Weber."

"Watch and learn, Dillon."

CHAPTER 66

DO YOU UNDERSTAND, MRS. Weber, that you and your husband both have a spousal privilege against testifying?" the judge asks.

"I do, Your Honor."

"And do you wish to waive that privilege?"

"I do, Your Honor," Tiffany says.

"And Mr. Martin Weber, you also have a privilege, which you could invoke, to prevent your spouse from testifying as it relates to any marital communications. Do you understand that?"

"Of course I do. I am a judge. And yes, we're calling her as a witness, so we are in fact waiving that privilege."

"Very well. Come around, Mrs. Weber."

Tiffany Weber is sworn in and takes a seat on the witness stand. She clutches a cloth tissue as Paul approaches the box.

"Mrs. Weber, you swore in a previous statement given to law enforcement, marked as Defense Exhibit One for the court, that you, your husband, and your son, were all home at four o'clock p.m. on October twenty-second."

"Yes. We were all home," Tiffany says with a thick Southern accent.

"Did anyone ever leave the house?"

"No, sir, they did not."

"So, at the time the state alleges Ms. Simone was murdered, you, your husband, and your son were all home, and no one left, is that correct?"

"Yes sir, it is correct."

"And what is your degree of certainty on that, Mrs. Weber?"

"I am one hundred percent certain."

"Your witness, Mr. District Attorney."

I cross to the small table in front of the large TV and pick up the remote. "Your Honor, marked for identification purposes is the security video taken from Hill Brothers Self Storage Center on the night of October twenty-second. This would be State's Exhibit Number Seven. Permission to play the video?"

"Any objection from the defense?"

"Nothing from Mr. Weber, Your Honor."

"You may present your evidence, Mr. Truesdale."

The TV flickers to life and I press Play.

"The camera is motion-activated, and the range that sets it off is limited to a car passing by the gate closest to the edge of the road. At five thirty-four p.m., a silver sedan triggers the camera as it exits the road and drives behind the salon. Do you recognize that car, Mrs. Weber?"

Mrs. Weber glances at Martin, then shakes her head. "No. The video is very grainy."

"At five forty-three p.m., you'll notice the headlights behind the trailer blink back on, and at five fifty p.m. the car is still there."

"Objection, Your Honor. Speculative," Paul says. "The prosecution has no way of knowing the same car is still parked behind the salon. You can't see it."

"The State enters into evidence the forensics report regarding the tire impressions located in the rear of the salon as State's Exhibit Number Twelve. The report clearly indicated that only one set of tire tracks were visible."

"Overruled. Continue."

"Did you notice that the headlights blinked, Mrs. Weber? They didn't snap on. They flashed. That doesn't happen when you start a car. That only happens when you use a remote key fob to unlock it. So, if someone was waiting in the car, they wouldn't need to have unlocked it remotely, would they?"

Mrs. Weber shrugged. "I'm not sure. It's not my car."

"The car was parked behind the salon for sixteen minutes. It took the murderer only seven minutes to exit the car, kill Rachel, and return. What were they doing for the other nine minutes?"

"Objection. Speculative."

"Sustained."

"You still claim that you, Martin, and Lucas were home at five thirty-four p.m. on the night of October twenty-second?"

"Yes, sir. All night."

I pick up a report off the prosecutor's table and pretend to read from it as I cross to the witness box. "Your Honor, marked for identification purposes are the cell phone records from Martin Weber's phone. This would be State's Exhibit Number Two, and Tiffany Weber's phone records would be State's Exhibit Number Three."

The judge nods, Paul remains silent, and I continue.

"On the night in question, you texted your husband at five forty-three p.m. asking if he would like you to heat up his dinner that was in the refrigerator, correct?"

"Yes. I was in my room and he was in his office."

"He replied at five forty-four p.m." I read from the text: "NO. IN OFFICE ON PHONE. DON'T DISTURB."

"That's correct."

"Did that anger you?"

"Well, it was a little rude, I thought."

"And you texted him back."

Tiffany looks at the judge. "I was upset and used language I normally do not use."

"Oh, don't worry, Mrs. Weber, you aren't on trial for using impolite language. When you text, do you use speech to text?"

"With my accent?" Tiffany places a demure hand on her chest. "Not on your life."

Laughter trickles through the room.

"Those are lovely fingernails, Mrs. Weber. I would imagine it's difficult to type with such long nails."

"Objection! Speculative. Argumentative, Your Honor," Paul says.

"Get to the point, Truesdale."

"Let's discuss your reply to your husband's text message. Your response was six individual messages containing four hundred and twenty-one words."

"I was angry."

"It appears so. Now, I hold in my left hand the location data for your cell phone, Mrs. Weber. It reveals that your phone was at your home on the night of October twenty-second."

"That's right, Mr. Prosecutor," she says.

"But the report regarding your husband's cell phone"—I shake the papers clutched in my hand—"This report shows *his* phone was actually at 151 Ender Road that night."

Tiffany's chin quivers. She holds the tissues to her mouth and sobs. "I'm so sorry, Martin."

"Shut up, Tiffany!" Martin rises out of his chair.

The judge bangs her gavel. "Counsel, control your client."

Paul grabs hold of Martin's arm and pulls him back down.

"I can't do it. I'm sorry, I can't." Tiffany sobs. "Martin left that night. My son heard him go, and I did, too. I'm so sorry, Martin."

"I object, Your Honor," I say.

"Excuse me?" The judge's eyebrows travel in opposite directions.

"I'm objecting for the defense, seeing as how he's preoccupied arguing with his own client and not listening to the testimony."

People laugh and I motion for them to quiet down, surprised they do.

"The witness doesn't know when or if the defendant, Martin Weber, left the house," I continue, "because Tiffany Weber wasn't at home."

"What on earth are you talking about, sir? I most certainly was home. I'm offended," Tiffany says.

"You may be offended, but you were not at home. You left your cell phone at your house. I'll give you that. But you took your husband's phone and drove his car to 151 Ender Road."

Tiffany stares at Paul, waiting for him to protest.

Paul looks at me and stays seated in stunned silence.

"That's ridiculous," Tiffany says. "I was home. You have the cell phone records."

"Your phone was home, but to paraphrase Shakespeare, 'The lady doth text too much, I think.' All of the data from your cell phone is recorded to the millisecond. Your response of four hundred and twenty-one words in six individual text messages happened so quickly, it would be impossible for a human to speak or type that fast."

Judge Mayweather's eyes widen.

"The only way those messages could have been created is if they were created by a computer and sent as an auto-reply. Which is why I requested a warrant to search your phone, Mrs. Weber, for an SMS auto responder, which I'm sure we'll find."

Tiffany glares at the defense table for some help.

Paul crosses his arms. She's on her own now.

Tiffany stares daggers at me. "Well, Mr. Prosecutor, if that's all you have, you've got nothing."

I smile. "You would be right, Mrs. Weber. But the good news for me is that's not all that I have. We discovered a set of discarded gloves in the trash can near the beauty salon. Your Honor, the State introduces State's Exhibit Number Four."

I open the sealed evidence bag and lift out a plastic bag containing one of the gloves. "The ring finger was sliced open, and because we didn't realize it was actually you wearing your husband's shoes, we thought it was Martin's class ring that cut the glove open. But it wasn't."

Silence falls over the courtroom.

"You made three big mistakes, Mrs. Weber. One, when you took the bloody tissues out of your bathroom trash can to plant at the salon, you assumed Martin cut himself, not your son. Two, you waited behind the salon until you saw the air-conditioning truck coming. For eight minutes, you sat there and then pulled in front of them because you wanted them to witness your husband's car. And they did see it. Kudos to you for that. It was smart."

"And what's the third?" Tiffany stares coldly at me.

"The third wasn't so smart. You slapped your husband and scratched his face while your home was being searched. Remember the day we executed the search warrant, and you assaulted your husband?"

"I just found out he had an affair!"

I shake my head. "Actually, you already knew." I return to the prosecutor's table and hold up another evidence bag. "This phone was discovered in Martin Weber's office on top of his liquor cabinet. You said that you have never seen this phone before or knew what was on it."

"I've never seen that phone!"

"Then why are your fingerprints on it?"

"How am I supposed to know? It's my house. Maybe I touched it when I was cleaning up?"

"That's possible. But it fails to explain why on October third, at ten twenty-five a.m., someone viewed over a dozen videos contained on this phone. I don't know if you are aware of this, Mrs. Weber, but your phone keeps track of what time files are accessed. And those files were accessed on October third at ten twenty-five a.m. At that time, this phone was at your home. Your phone was at your home, and your husband, Martin Weber, was in court in front of over a dozen witnesses."

"That's right!" Martin says. "I was presiding over probation violations—"

Judge Mayweather banged her gavel. "Silence the defendant, Counselor."

"After watching these videos, you, taking along your phone, drove to 151 Elder Road and stopped outside the Cutz for All salon. We have both the location data from your phone and security video evidence."

Tiffany sits up straighter. "Yes. I found my husband's phone and I accessed it. I watched videos of him and that vile woman. . . . And, yes, I drove over there to confront her, but I didn't. I couldn't. I wanted to, but I couldn't. So, if you have security footage showing me there, I'm certain it will show that I never went inside the salon."

"You're right, you didn't go into the salon on October third, but that's when you started to plot your revenge against both Rachel and Martin. That's why you gave me the pin codes to access his phone. You provided Martin's motive, means, and opportunity. You planned everything very well, except when you killed Rachel. Even though you were smart enough to wear two sets of gloves to hide your DNA, your big diamond ring tore a hole in both of those gloves."

"You can't prove that. I'm not on trial. He is."

"Not yet you aren't." I reach into the inside pocket of my suit jacket and remove a plastic evidence bag and a lab report. I hold the see-through bag high, showing off the diamond ring inside. "You recognize your ring, don't you, Mrs. Weber? You even came to my office trying to get it back. You said that while you were still mad at Martin, you didn't like not wearing your wedding ring. You said people would notice and say things."

"You said you would give it back."

"Well, the reason I couldn't give it back then was because it was being held as evidence in your assault case, and I'm glad it was. It occurred to me recently, when I was getting my own blood drawn, how messy murder is. Especially stabbing someone nineteen times. And then I realized it was your ring that broke through the gloves, not Martin's. So I took the liberty of sending your rings to the state lab for DNA testing. You'll never guess what they found. Rachel Simone's DNA, in the form of blood, trapped between the center diamond and the gallery of your engagement ring. The only way that blood got there was if the ring was actually on the killer's hand. And since you never even took it off when you had surgery, that ring was on your hand when you stabbed Rachel to death."

Tiffany has a look of equal parts pride and resignation on her face as she says, "For twenty-nine years, I wore that hunk of coal on my hand and stayed faithful to that philandering, pathetic excuse of a man." Tiffany glares at Martin, her eyes burning with hate. "Do you know I worked three jobs to help put him through law school? I gave him a son and the best years of my life while I made excuse after excuse for all of his affairs. Everything he wanted, I gave him. I exercised because he said he wished I was more toned. He even told me to cut my hair. He said a woman my age doesn't wear it long, so I cut it."

Martin shifts nervously in his chair.

Tiffany's eyes are cold, and her voice is hard. "Nineteen inches I cut off because he said it was time I embraced the hands of time and not fight against it." Tiffany's hand strokes the side of her pixie cut. "I cut it all off—for him, and it still wasn't enough."

I walk slowly forward until I'm standing in front of Tiffany. "You spent a lifetime helping him. You were there for Martin's goals. There for Martin's needs. You were a dutiful wife who did everything he asked. But after you cut nineteen inches off your hair, what does he do? He shacks up with another woman."

"Not just another woman, Counselor—a young, blond gold digger with long hair. He's the one who committed murder, Mr. Truesdale. Martin murdered my life. My career. My goals. All of it was sacrificed for him." She thrust her arm out, pointing at Martin.

Everyone in the gallery is talking at once.

The judge bangs her gavel.

"He took the best years of my life and then when he was tired of me, he traded me in for some younger woman. I read the texts he sent her. After all I did, he promised her that he was going to leave me. He'd cast me aside for some hairdresser!"

"And you couldn't allow that, now, could you? So rather than kill the person who actually did steal the best years of your life, you decided to take the life of an innocent woman who didn't even know your husband was married. Did you know that, Mrs. Weber? Did you know Rachel broke it off because she refused to violate the sanctity of your marriage, and her reward for that was you stabbing her nineteen times? Nineteen times you pulled that knife back and stuck it into a woman you knew nothing about. One stab for every inch of hair he told you to cut off."

Tiffany Weber turns to the judge. "I invoke my Fifth Amendment right." She exits the witness stand and walks over to me until we're standing inches apart. She calmly stares at me as she leans in and whispers, "Well played, Counselor. But I haven't played all of my cards. And when you get me in front of a jury of my peers, they're going to see me as a woman left with only one choice."

"No, they won't. They'll see you as a defendant who killed the wrong person and then tried to frame the person you had the real malice for." I motion for the deputies. "Please arrest Tiffany Weber for the murder of Rachel Simone."

CHAPTER 67

MARTIN WEBER DRIED HIS hands as he exited the bathroom and crossed back to his seat at the hotel bar. After the trial, he got in his car and headed east. He made it as far as you can get—Garden City Beach.

He stared down at his half-finished martini still sitting on the bar and he could almost hear Tiffany nagging him about leaving his drink unattended. But what was he going to do, take it into the bathroom with him? He picked up the little plastic stick and fished for the olive.

The bartender set a Manhattan down on the bar.

Confused, Martin bristled. "I didn't order that."

A slender, feminine hand came into his peripheral view. "I did, for you," a tall, long-legged blonde in a thigh-high green dress said, touching him on the shoulder.

"Do I know you?"

"Not yet, you don't. But I hate to drink alone and figured you might, too. Don't worry one bit. I'll put it down as a business expense. Don't go getting all old-fashioned on me. Women can buy drinks too, you know."

Martin slid the new drink back to her and sipped his own. "Thanks, but no thanks."

"I'm Crystal. Are you local or traveling?"

"Not interested is what I am."

"Married?"

"Not anymore." He raised his glass and said, "The things we do for hate."

Crystal's laughter trailed off. "I'm sorry. I thought you were kidding. You're serious, aren't you?"

Martin nods. "Yeah, unfortunately. Long story."

"I've got time and no place to be if you feel like talking. I'm a good listener."

Martin tore the edges of his drink napkin. "You wouldn't believe me if I told you."

"Try me," she said, touching his shoulder.

Martin glanced down at her hand, his eyes traveling along her arm to her body. She was out of his league and he knew it. He'd made that mistake before, and it nearly cost him his freedom. "Have you ever heard the expression 'Fool me once'?"

She nods.

Martin finished his drink. "You're a little too good to be true. Have a nice night."

Crystal rolled her eyes. "Your loss."

Martin slid off the stool and headed through the bar and back into the hotel. By the time he reached the elevator, the few drinks he'd had were hitting him hard. A man in a baseball cap got to the elevator before him and pressed the button.

Martin leaned against the wall and waited.

The doors dinged and opened.

The man brushed by Martin and got into the elevator, but at least he held the door.

"Fifteen," Martin said as he stumbled to the back.

The elevator rumbled and Martin grabbed the banister. His eyelids were so heavy. He couldn't keep them open. Martin's chin tipped forward, and he jerked his head back up. He had a lot to drink but this felt different than simply being drunk.

His mouth tasted funny.

Something else was wrong. The elevator was going down.

"I said fifteen."

The doors dinged and slid open, revealing the dimly lit hotel basement.

The man in the baseball hat raised his head and stared at Martin.

Martin gasped.

"Good evening, Your Honor." Jean Boucher smiled, his one blue eye gleamed brightly, while his gray eye remained the color of death.

CHAPTER 68

BONES MARCHED THROUGH THE door of Harris Law, and Charlotte's eyes widened.

"Hello, Detective." She nervously glanced out at the parking lot. "Good to see you again. Can I help you?"

"You sure can. You can start by telling me the truth. That cabin where Frank's body was found was a rental, except no one rented it. The owner says that it was broken into. I'm trying to figure out why Frank drove all the way to the North Pacolet River, broke into some random cabin, and shot himself in the head. He passed a thousand places to kill himself along the way."

Charlotte sat up straighter. "I wish I knew that, too, Detective. All I can tell you is there were no appointments listed in the book for Frank on October twenty-first."

"Yeah. You keep saying that, and it sounds as strange as it did the first time you said it. Normally, someone would say Frank didn't have any appointments. But you specifically say 'listed in the book.' Is that some kind of doublespeak that gets you off the hook if it comes out you lied about knowing about an appointment that wasn't on the books?"

"I am offended, Detective. Extremely offended at the mere suggestion that I would be withholding information on a matter involving someone I cared very much about."

"I am worried about what you are withholding, ma'am. That much is true. I am equally concerned about what you do know. I never told you what day he died. We haven't even told his family. So how did you know to look on October twenty-first?"

Charlotte crossed her arms. "Listen, I'm just a receptionist. A receptionist with a family. I do not want to get involved in this."

"It's too late for that. You are involved. The question is how and why. Why did Frank go out to that cabin? Who was he meeting?"

Charlotte set her elbow on the desk and rubbed her eyes with her thumb and index finger. "A lawyer. Frank was filing a complaint with the Disciplinary Board about a lawyer and the guy called the office. He was furious. He said he wanted to talk Frank out of filing the complaint, that it would kill his career, and they needed to work something out. But I wasn't supposed to know that."

"And how did you know it?"

"I don't want to say. Maybe I should get myself a lawyer to protect myself?"

"Maybe you need one. Maybe I should take you in, book you for obstruction, and let you sit in jail until you find a lawyer? I'm sure your kids can walk home from school."

"How can you even suggest such a thing?"

"You haven't seen anything yet. So, start talking or else we will see how good your kids are with their sense of direction. I'll ask you one more time before I take you in for impeding an investigation. Does this lawyer have a name?"

"Can you keep me out of it?"

"I'll do my best, but I can't make any promises."

"That's not good enough."

"It's as good as it's gonna get."

Charlotte took a deep breath. "Colm Truesdale. His name was Colm Truesdale."

CHAPTER 69

THIS IS THE BEST I have felt in . . . well, in such a long time. The grief is still there. It will always be there, I guess. But the guilt is slowly giving way to the realization that the life I was living was no way to honor the people I loved or the ones who loved me back.

I'm sitting on a wooden bench and sort of feel like you would being in an old church, but this one is outdoors and beside a diner. The preacher isn't some old white guy rambling on about some story I've heard a thousand times. Rather she's a young woman of color who just lives out what others talk about.

"My parents are over the moon!" Belle says as her shoulders squeeze together. "Their disability was approved. I can never thank you enough for your help with that."

"You really did it all. I just pointed out a couple of small, little things."

"Well, we both know better than that. They either would have been declined, or it would have taken so long to process their application. One of these days, you'll have to tell me—and them—how you pulled that off!" Belle says.

"I wish it was a good story with lots of twists and turns, but it was pretty easy. I called a friend. That's what friends do." I smile. "Tell me about you. What's the latest?"

Her eyes widen with excitement. "I tried the sample LSAT. There's a lot of room for improvement, but I did better than I thought I would have."

"I'm not surprised. You're smart. You can do whatever you set your mind to. If you need a tutor for any of the sections, or have any questions, all you have to do is ask."

Belle grins. "Okay. I'm asking! Do you mind helping me?"

"Not at all. I'd love that."

We sit there soaking up the sun. Her break ends in six minutes.

A slight breeze, a cloudless sky, the company of a friend—things are slowly getting better.

CHAPTER 70

J D SAT IN THE corner booth of The Junction watching the happy little couple seated at the picnic table. They were finishing up their conversation. The waitress needed to get back to work, and Colm needed to go to the courthouse to, no doubt, bask in the glow of his victory.

Picking up a knife and moving it underneath the table, JD opened a new deck of playing cards. Colm seems to have triumphed over his guilt and grief. The golden boy had risen from the ashes. Worse yet, he seemed happy. We can't have that.

"Maybe I should have let him die," JD muttered, tearing the King of Hearts in half.

Suicide King. So close.

Flipping through the deck, JD removed the Queen of Hearts and took out a pen. After a minute, the drawing of a noose fashioned from a men's necktie emerged around the Queen's throat.

You'll never be able to stop what's coming next.

The waitress crossed over to the table.

"Good morning. Are you ready to order?"

JD read her name tag. "Belle. What a great name."

Belle blushed. "Thank you. What's your name?"

"Jane. But my friends call me JD."

ACKNOWLEDGMENTS

Thank you to Fox News and our CEO, Suzanne Scott, who has taken so many chances on me, including allowing me to write this book. Also, a special thanks to Lauren Petterson, Jennings Grant, OM, and everyone else who helped make this dream of writing a crime book come true. Thank you, Dana Perino, for being a constant source of encouragement in all facets of life. Thank you to Christopher Greyson for being such an incredible, talented, and patient partner.

Thank you to all the women and men in law enforcement, prosecution, and the judiciary who made those two decades so professionally rewarding. And a special thanks to the victims of crime and their families and friends who provided a glimpse of light in the otherwise dark world created by crime. To paraphrase Rust Coyle from True Detective: the light does win—it just takes a while to realize that.

ABOUT THE AUTHORS

TREY GOWDY is a former state and federal prosecutor who handled thousands of criminal cases and took nearly one hundred cases to jury verdict. He prosecuted scores of murder cases, including seven death penalty trials. He served in Congress for eight years, chairing two committees and leaving in 2019 to return to South Carolina. He hosts the weekend primetime show *Sunday Night in America* on FOX News Channel and *The Trey Gowdy Podcast* on FOX News Audio. He and his wife, Terri, have two children—both lawyers—and have had four dogs: Judge, Jury, Bailiff, and Justice.

CHRISTOPHER GREYSON is an award-winning, *Wall Street Journal* bestselling author of mystery, action, and thriller novels. Recognized as one of the top 100 Kindle authors of all time, his acclaimed works have sold over 3.5 million e-books, print copies, and audiobooks. An accomplished speaker, actor, and prolific storyteller, he has written more than twenty novels, ranging from pulse-pounding thrillers to sweet, cozy mysteries.